Death on the River Thames

A JOHN RAWLINGS MURDER MYSTERY

DEATH

ON THE

River Thames

Deryn Lake

LUME BOOKS

LUME BOOKS

Published in 2021 by Lume Books

Copyright © Deryn Lake 2021

The right of Deryn Lake to be identified as the author of this work
has been asserted by them in accordance with the Copyright, Design
and Patents Act, 1988.

ISBN 978-1-83901-459-8

Typeset using Atomik ePublisher from Easypress Technologies

www.lumebooks.co.uk

This book is dedicated to Miss Elizabeth Shah, the kindest, the best and the most beautiful surgeon who has saved my life twice. Her sweetness and good humour put patients at their ease and her skill is beyond doubt. She deserves all the praise one can possibly give her – and a Damehood. Also my dear Sally Lampitt whose compassion, patience and help are beyond compare. I am lucky to know you both.

Chapter One

One fine April morning when the world was alive with splashing showers followed by sudden sunshine, John Rawlings, Apothecary, large breakfast consumed and morning paper read, stepped out of his front door and sniffed the air. Before him, alive with fishing boats, wheeling gulls and raucous shouts, was the River Thames, flowing along without complaint as it had done since time began. Behind him was a small row of elegant houses with bright front doors and large gracious windows which overlooked the waterway. Smiling to himself and wielding his cane with a certain pride, John sauntered into the day.

There were several people walking the towpath that morning, nodding their heads slightly as they passed one another. John raised his tricorne politely for the ladies, fractionally bowed to the gentlemen, and swirled his stick as he made his way. He had been living in this delightful riverside spot for a year now, having returned from the colonies of America, witnessing the Boston Tea Party, then sailing home the following March, sensing that there was going to be almighty trouble—and how right he had been. England was now at war with the settlers and there was blood and dissent and misery on both sides of the

Atlantic. But on the Apothecary the sun was shining. His business in producing carbonated water had thrived in his absence and his home in Nassau Street had frequently been full of his employees. Therefore, John had decided that it was high time he bought a country place for himself and his family, and his daughter and sons had shouted their delight when they had seen the glorious location.

"Oh, please buy it Papa," Rose had exclaimed, looking at him with all the charm of Emilia, his wife, whose death had almost ruined his life and who the girl closely resembled. Meanwhile, his twin boys had gazed with awe at Oliver's Island, the tree-filled eyot in the middle of the river, imagining parties and music and fun-filled days on its banks. So it had been settled and they had moved in twelve months ago.

His neighbours had been polite and kind but lacking that wayward streak that was so vital a part of his own character. But all that had changed a month ago when—oh joy of joys—a ragamuffin of a fellow had moved in right next door. Johan Zoffany the painter, complete with his boisterous entourage, had taken up residence. And now, even as he thought of him, John heard that heavily accented voice ring out.

"John, my friend, what a morning. How are you?"

And there he was, standing on his doorstep, his light blue eyes—set slightly on the squint—narrowing as he stared up at the fitful sun. The Apothecary, delighted to chat to him as always, retraced his steps.

"My dear sir, how very nice to see you. How are you?"

Zoffany ran his hand over his receding hairline, pushing his brown wig back slightly. "I have had better days, my friend. Alas."

"Why's that? Anything I can help you with? I am a qualified apothecary, you know."

"I had heard a rumour that you were. I am currently suffering from a stiffness in the hands which is a poor condition for a painter."

"Indeed it is. I shall go to London tomorrow and bring you back a liniment made from jessamine flowers. That will loosen your tendons if you rub it in twice a day."

"Thank you, my friend. Stand with me a moment and admire the scenery. I am escaping from a house of women."

Obligingly the Apothecary stood beside him and together the two men admired the general pleasantness all about them. A young apprentice was coming towards them, tall, fair of face and whistling a tuneful air. Passing them were a group of well-dressed women, laughing and gossiping in the sunshine, several small children playing around the adults. The light over the river was crystal clear, the water throwing back its glittering reflection, thousands of diamond droplets falling from the oars of the fisherfolk. It was unbelievably blissful and just for a second the Apothecary closed his eyes, feeling that he was a step closer to heaven. And then there was a child's voice screaming, someone exclaiming "Oh great God!" and the rush of air as a person moved swiftly into action.

John jolted back to full consciousness and gazed with horror at what he saw. A child's head appeared briefly above the waters of the Thames before it disappeared beneath the surface. The young apprentice, jacket thrown upon the ground, was diving in as John thought of doing the same. Zoffany had started to run forward even while the group of women moved nonchalantly onward down the path.

A second later the apprentice appeared, thrusting himself up out of the water, raising his arms high, in his grip the limp body of the youngster. John sprang into motion, bending low to receive the little bundle of inert flesh in his grasp. The he swung the poor child by the heels so that the swallowed water came pouring out before he laid her flat on her back and started to pump her chest as his old master had taught him to do many years ago. The girl gave a gurgling gasp and out of her mouth bubbled some more water, then she opened her eyes and looked round her dazedly.

John spoke. "Don't worry, sweetheart, you fell in the river but this kind gentleman pulled you out."

He turned to glance at the apprentice who was looking extremely dashing, soaked to the skin, hair sleeked back like a wet pelt, eyes bright with searching underwater.

"Carry her into my house," Zoffany was saying. "Poor child, poor little liebchen."

They hurried inside and John went straight to the kitchen, stepping through a flurry of maids, to search for some lavender. Finding it, he swiftly powdered down the flowers and added it to boiling water to give the little girl a calming drink. In the parlour he found her, crying her eyes out, being tended by a woman who—or so John believed—was the painter's second wife, though one could never be quite sure with Zoffany. The child looked up as John came in and he found himself being regarded by a pair of bluebag eyes fringed by wet black lashes.

"Are you feeling better?" he asked.

"Somebody pushed me in," she answered miserably.

"Really? Are you sure you didn't just fall?" he answered, setting the cup down.

"Yes, someone did. I know. I felt it."

"But possibly you were wandering by the river and accidentally tripped." John said—and deep within him he knew that old stir of excitement that meant something new and interesting was about to happen.

"No, truly. I was walking along and next thing I was thrust into the water." The bluebag eyes filled with sudden tears.

John handed the child the glass. "Tell me what happened. From the beginning."

She got off the lap and the woman who had been cuddling her rose to her feet and silently left the room. John took a chair and helped the little girl up into another beside his.

"First of all allow me to introduce myself. I am John Rawlings of Nassau Street, Soho, and Strand-on-the-Green, Chiswick. How do you do?"

"And I am Lucinda. I'm four."

"So who pushed you in? Did you see them?"

"No. I had stopped walking and was bending down to look at a stone and then I felt a hand push me."

The Apothecary nodded. "Who was it?"

Over the rim of the cup, out of which the child was drinking, the blue eyes met his. She shook her head.

"I know it was one of the people I was with."

John nodded gravely. "How very interesting." Distantly he heard a rapid knocking on the front door and he raised a finger to his lips. "You must keep it a secret for now. Don't tell anyone, Lucinda. You must pretend that you tripped and fell. It's important."

"Why?"

"Just because it is. I can't explain now."

He got to his feet as a large woman flew into the room, knocking a small stool flying. "Oh Jesus is merciful," she shrieked loudly. "Lucinda sweetest, you are alive and well." She snatched the child to her formidable bosom, bellowing loudly, "Who is her saviour? I must reward him."

The apprentice, who stood in Zoffany's hallway drying his hair with a towel, looked round, interested. Zoffany, on the other hand was absorbing the child's details with his eyes, a trick that only a painter could have. John, an old hand at summing people up, betrayed absolutely no information whatsoever. Disappointed by the lack of response, the woman asked, "Who is the master here?"

Zoffany stepped forward. "I own this house if that is what you are asking, madam."

She opened her mouth to answer but before she could do so another woman entered the room. There was a crystal moment as she swept a deep curtsey before Zoffany and then nobody so much as breathed. The newcomer was truly beautiful—flawless in fact. Her lovely face only equalled by her superb figure. The painter put out a long-fingered hand to raise her up, smiling like the artist he was, gazing at a voluptuous dish of cream. John, observing, wondered if there could be a flaw in the diamond.

"My dear sir," she said, her voice as thrilling as her looks, "I believe one of my party was nearly drowned and was only saved by a gallant young man who is presently with you. May I ask who it is?"

"You may ask, my lady," Zoffany answered, his voice full of exciting Germanic undercurrents, "and I will tell you. It is the young apprentice who stands before you."

The gorgeous stranger looked at the youth with the very slightest curve of her lips. "Then it is to you that I must offer my profound thanks, sir. I am grateful from the bottom of my heart."

The young man spoke up with alacrity. "Thank you, madam. Please let me introduce myself. My name is Nathaniel Hall and I am nearing the end of my apprenticeship to Mr. Mawson."

"Do you mean he who runs the brewery?"

"I do, madam. He is a great something grandson of the founder."

"A good position indeed. And how much longer do you have to serve?"

"I shall apply to be made Free shortly. In about nine months' time."

She made another delightful curtsey. "Then let it be hoped that our paths will cross again." She turned to the child at last. "Come along, my sweet. Say thank you to the kind gentlemen. They saved your life."

Lucinda gave them a small sad smile. "Thank you very much indeed."

The large woman picked her up and swept her out of the house; the beauty curtsied again and made a stylish exit. There was a momentary silence broken by Nathaniel who gave a deep whistle as he straightened from his bow, then hastily apologised.

"Sorry, gentlemen. I forgot where I was for a moment."

"No need for that, young man. We all felt the same—at least I did," John answered cheerfully.

Zoffany said nothing, merely rolling his gleaming eyes spectacularly.

"I wonder who the child belonged to," John added as an afterthought.

Once again the painter looked blank and the apprentice lad was halfway out of the front door so, as nobody replied to the question, it remained hanging in the air—unanswered.

Two nights later Johan Zoffany gave an evening party. By now the reputation of the talented artist had grown enormously. His patrons were leading actors of the day and it was said that he was a particular favourite of the queen herself, with whom he spoke German in a soft and gentle voice. So much so, in fact, that Johan had been commissioned to paint her with her two eldest sons, to say nothing of likenesses of George III. But there were no members of the royal family present on this intimate occasion. Instead, dressed in the sharpest fashions, the height of the latest hairstyles reaching three feet in some instances, the lady guests wafted their way amongst the crowd, aware of the sensation they were creating. John, surveying all with a slightly cynical eye, was glad that his mistress of many years standing—the actress Coralie Clive—had bowed to fashion only slightly and had her hair swept up and woven with fresh flowers.

As she entered the room her vivid green eyes searched for John, found him, and crinkled at the corners for now, at long last, they had a relationship that suited them both perfectly. The call of the theatre had been too much for Coralie to resist and with the help of her older sister—the celebrated actress Kitty Clive, now a very old lady and retired to a villa in Twickenham—she had managed to make a return to the stage. Meanwhile the money acquired from John's side-line of producing carbonated water had prompted him to buy his lovely country house away from town but too far, alas, from the London theatres. So, despite the fact that they loved one another, they had made the decision to live apart, which had worked out well for both of them. John, to this day still, was haunted by the memory of his dead mistress, the incomparable Elizabeth, the dark lady of his midnight dreams. While Coralie was too great a star ever to love a man to the exclusion of everything else. Now, though, both of them were filled with delight at the sight of the other.

"My dear, you're here. I was wondering if you would make it."

"I was determined to come. I wasn't in the third act and I got permission to miss the curtain call."

"I'm delighted you did. How did you get here?"

"I took a coach as far as Kew Bridge and then hired a small boat."

"That is the only snag about living in this glorious spot—water. Sometimes at high tide the river comes into the basement."

"It would not be…"

"Yes, I know. Hopeless for you to dwell here because of the theatres."

"But John, my dearest, it is such fun when I do visit. The picnics we take to that sweet little island, the peace and quiet of the gentle unfolding of the river. I love it here, sweetheart. You know I do."

"Just as I love the stink of London. The piles of dung and excrement left in the streets to rot, the dead babies, dogs, cats, abandoned. The innocent children—forsaken, forlorn, and hopeless—deposited outside the Foundling Hospital. The footpads and robbers, the highwaymen

8

who pillage your coach when one dares to set forth. A wonderful place indeed."

"Come now, sir, you were brought up there and had the time of your life. Don't argue, you told me so yourself."

"That was because I had a wonderful father."

"You are beginning to make excuses. Are you trying to tell me that you are no longer content with our arrangement?"

John could see the glint in his mistress's eye and realised that to pursue the topic would be foolish indeed. Instead he said, "My sweetheart, I love our way of living and would change nothing about it. We were both being very childish in even discussing it. Give me a kiss to show that you still love this decrepit old fool who is being so grumpy and miserable."

She grinned, a brilliant rainbow of a smile. "Indeed, I do love you." And she plonked a kiss on his proffered cheek.

There was a stir in the doorway as another entrant arrived. John stared as the perfect creature who had accompanied the unfortunate drowning child stood perfectly still, listening to small cries of wonderment and the bellow of a deaf old man, "Lord love me, I could bed her down had I any ability left."

There was a small ripple of laughter and the Beauty allowed herself a fleeting smile before unfreezing from her pose and stepping into the company. Zoffany was upon her in an instant, taking her by the arm in the most familiar manner and steering her forward to meet his friends. She passed right by John, who bowed elegantly, she however gave no sign of recognition and merely inclined her head.

"How rude," he whispered under his breath.

Coralie caught the remark. "Why? Do you know her?"

"She was here the other day. With a small girl who had accidentally fallen into the river. At least I presume it was accidental…" He stopped talking for a moment as he realised what he was inferring. Coralie raised an arched brow but did not interrupt. "Anyway, she now chooses to forget that we have ever met."

"Oh, la! And you find yourself in a regular twit because a beautiful woman fails to recognise you."

John smiled wryly. Truth to tell, Coralie knew him so well that she could recognise all his little conceits and vanities. Nevertheless, he responded with spirit.

"And la to you madam. I suggest that you go and greet your host and be quick about it lest he will think you grown too grand to acknowledge him."

And with that he took her by the elbow and propelled her in the direction of the painter who, having introduced his beauteous guest to a horde of bowing admirers, was at that precise moment standing alone and smiling at the goodly crowd that paraded before him.

"My dear Johan," said Coralie, "a pleasure to be in your company once more."

They were off, heads together and laughing like long-lost friends. John again found himself alone. Inwardly he sighed. The days of his wonderful sky-blue youth were over and done for sure. He was forty-nine years old and had a grown-up daughter and twin boys catching up fast. Yet, or so it seemed to him, time had flashed by and all these events had come in months, not great long yawning years. In his day he had loved several women, some more wisely than others. Yet above all of them one in particular still came to haunt his jumbled dreams. Elizabeth, of the tumbling black hair and eyes deep as the fathomless ocean, often came to taunt his sleepless nights. He would never be free of her. With a sigh, John shrugged back his shoulders and faced reality. He had wonderful children, good friends, a sound and prospering business. He could think of thousands who would willingly exchange places with him. Smiling crookedly, he went to join the other guests.

It was obvious that he would be one of the last to leave. Madame Clive, on this occasion, had refused his offer of a bed for the night and the loving cuddles that involved, and was staying with an old and dear friend nearby. Thus, he and Zoffany remained when all the glasses had been removed and the servants had blown out the extra candles, ending the evening with a fine glass of port. The Apothecary broke the comfortable silence.

"I thought that beautiful woman behaved most oddly tonight."

Zoffany's eyes looked at him with a definite squint in the shadowy light. "To whom do you refer, my friend? There were many beauties present tonight."

"But only one who outshone the others."

"That is a very ungallant remark if I may say so."

John chuckled. "Nonetheless I think you know who I am talking about."

"You mean the woman we met the other day. The one who was chaperoning that wretched child who fell in?"

"Who else?"

"But she wasn't here. You are mistaken, sir."

John stared, his glass half-way to his lips. "Yes, she was. I saw her arrive. And you came forward to greet her."

"I tell you she was not present."

"Johan, are you losing your reason. I saw her plainly. I bowed but she sailed straight past me."

Zoffany chuckled, a low musical rumble. "But why are you so perplexed? Surely the answer is obvious."

"Not to me it isn't."

"You appear totally mystified, my friend. Come. I have something to show you."

Lit only by the candles that they carried with them, the two men climbed the winding and shadowy staircase that led to the top of the house and here Zoffany threw open a door leading to what would normally have been the room where the female servants slept. But it had been transformed. Running the length of the building, a wall had been knocked down and extra windows put in to produce a studio. It was in this place that Zoffany created the masterpieces that were going to please generations after he had long since turned to dust.

"God's life!" breathed John, totally impressed. "So this is where you work."

"Mostly, yes. Of course I also paint in other people's homes. D'you know that when I first came to London I decorated the interior of clock faces. I am rather proud of that."

But John did not answer. From canvas after canvas, propped against the wall, leaning one upon another, half hidden in the shadows, silent faces looked out at him. Wrinkled old men, bony-visaged beauties, corpulent businessmen, stared at him in the quiet and splendour of that amazing studio. Behind him he could hear Zoffany lifting something but could not bring himself to turn his head and gaze away from the colour and brilliance of the German artist's workmanship.

"You're a genius," he muttered. Zoffany either could not or did not want to reply. Eventually, though, John turned around and saw that a particular painting had been pulled out and placed on the easel. He approached and examined it. It was of her, the beautiful creature who had smiled at him so charmingly on the first occasion they had met, and tonight had cut him dead. She was sitting at her dressing table, staring into the glass at her gorgeous reflection, which stared back at her quizzically.

"You *do* know her," John protested.

Johan chuckled. "Look again my friend. Look carefully."

John did so, raising his quizzing glass, peering at the picture as if his very life depended on it. And then, suddenly, he saw it. The painting was not of one woman but of *two*. The mirror was not a mirror at all but plain glass through which the subject was looking at what could only be her twin sister.

"There are two of them," he said, his tone accusing.

"Of course," Johan answered. "The woman with that unfortunate little girl was the Duchess of Derwent, whose husband is that hulking brute, the Duke of Derwent. Tonight my party was graced by the presence of the Lady Lovell, her identical twin sister, who you have yet the pleasure of meeting. A trick I believe they play on people from time to time."

"Well, I'll be damned."

"I'm sorry, my friend, I saw you looking askance and I couldn't resist it."

"I'll forgive you if you let me spend another few minutes here."

"Provided that you touch nothing I will give you precisely ten."

And so it was that John Rawlings wandered around that Aladdin's cave and gazed almost with fear at the carnival of characters who leapt out of the canvas and paraded before him. Faces, colours, all of them recounting their own original story.

Why was it, he wondered, that some people are born with a gift so vivid, so original, and so real, that they could transform the lives of those who afterwards beheld or heard what they had bequeathed. What was it that singled some out while others simply were born and died without leaving a trace behind them for generations, as yet unborn, to delight in?

Chapter Two

The Theatre Royal was packed to overflowing. Servants had gone ahead to occupy their master's seats and could be seen snoozing in the boxes set upon the stage itself and in various other parts of the house. Upon their employer's arrival they would bolt up to the Gallery to join their fellows and those members of the public too poor to pay more than the measly sum of a shilling to see fine plays and outstanding actors. This was the noisiest and least controllable part of the theatre. Yet above this, to the left and right, rose an even higher tier. This viewing space was known as the Slips and was patronised by those who queued outside and entered by a further staircase leading off the main one. The Slips had a hard wooden bench on which to sit and were partitioned off for those who wanted privacy—as did many who sinfully sat there.

This night John Rawlings was accompanied by his daughter, Rose. She was like the flower after which she had been named—growing more radiant as she developed. Her wonderfully rich red hair, her shining eyes, her delicate complexion, all made heads turn when she entered the theatre. Old lechers leered, young bucks gazed, enjoying the knowledge of their potency, while middle-aged men, green with envy, felt the anxious need to buy strengthening pills. John, worldly-wise as he was—had not quite realised the effect she would have, offered her his arm as they made their way into a box situated in the row just above the Pit.

There were five rows of boxes above this notorious seating space. In the front part of the Pit—almost on top of the orchestra—sat the hoi polloi of society: clerks, critics and clodhoppers, together with ladies of the night on the look-out for custom. This particular area was dreaded by the actors because of the constant buzz of conversation which came from those who frequented its comfortless backless benches and green baize covering. Joining this den of iniquity but separated from it by a walkway were the Stalls proper, in which sat people from the professional classes. The Pit cost three shillings, the seats behind, four. Just above them were a few boxes on a level with the stage. It was into one of these that John escorted his daughter.

On the tier above were the Best Boxes where sat the aristocracy, the heads of state and the wealthy. The fee for this was five shillings per seat. Above them were three more tiers each declining in cost. At the top was the Gallery where sat the servants and working class, the cost a humble shilling. But above the Gods—the nickname for the Gallery since time immemorial—reared something more sinister and even cheaper. Built on the side and occupied by those who did not suffer from vertigo were the notorious Slips. These cost a few humble pence, their view of the stage minute, their anonymity assured, and were the worst seats in the house. John felt slightly queasy even at looking up at them but a quick glance at Rose reassured him that his daughter was completely taken up with viewing the stage. Her yearning to tread the boards herself had not gone away and she was now of an age when to do so might be the answer to her recent bouts of quiet restlessness. John decided there and then to speak to Coralie quite seriously about the matter.

The play began. *The School for Scandal* by Richard Brinsley Sheridan had been joyfully received since its premier three years ago. Since then, with slight modifications, it had appeared regularly in the repertoire. Tonight the part of Lady Sneerwell was being played by Coralie Clive, much to the delight of John and Rose. The role of Lady Teazle was being taken by the gorgeous Miss Chester and that of her husband by the likeable John Henderson, visiting from Bath. A very small child, surely little more than two years of age but nonetheless a member of the cast, caught John's eye for his brilliant gestures and movements. Glancing at the theatre programme which he had bought in the street outside John saw the name was Master Grimaldi.

The show proceeded amidst gales of laughter, the audience literally rocking about in their chairs. On the benches of the Pit students and critics clutched one another as they fell around, one chap laughing so much that he ended up on the floor. The humour was high, the acting first rate, and John was just drying his eyes when a movement up in the Slips had him suddenly gazing upwards. Slowly but surely a figure was descending from them, not quickly as in a terrible fall but with horrible precision. It was that of a woman, her ankles secured one to the other, bound to a rope which was hanging in mid-air above the stalls below. Inverted as she was her clothes had descended into a bell-like shape, completely covering her face and extended arms, which thrashed somewhat feebly as the poor creature was being lowered. The rest of her was completely naked leaving nothing to the imagination.

She was stoutly built, of some middle years, or so John guessed. Her skin was very pallid in contrast with her stays which were a dark brown in shade. Her most privy part was clearly visible and her breasts, which were inclined to be pendulous, were now pushing up towards her chin. Of her face nothing could be seen at all. Sensing movement overhead the entire audience began to peer upwards and there was a murmured gasp as they saw the figure hanging, all her hidden secrets thrust before the world. The patrons of the Pit began to point and exclaim, and the movement of heads as every eye glanced to the Slips was quickly picked up by the actors who struggled gamely to keep the show going.

John, after a moment of sheer gaping, collected himself. Murmuring an excuse to Rose he left the box and hurled round to the theatre's secondary staircase which led to the Gallery and Slips. He had never been the fastest runner and now as he panted up its dark and unlovely steps he felt all of his middle-aged years. But eventually he passed the entrance to the Gallery, where he noticed that the gathered mass had risen to its feet and were all staring at the unfortunate woman with some rather unseemly comments ringing in the air. A few more steps and he was in the Slips, his head reeling momentarily as he glanced below at the theatre so far away. A slumped figure of a soldier who had been on duty controlling the Slips's occupants was groaning on the floor. Briefly checking that the man was still breathing, John hastened on. A small crowd had gathered round and he pushed his way through saying, "I am an apothecary, let me pass," in rather a dramatic manner. He was in the theatre after all.

It was obvious that the wretched woman had attended the play alone for there was a cloak and fan tossed carelessly onto the spare seat. Lying on the floor was a lonely pair of gloves. But it was to the thick piece of rope from which the victim was suspended that John's attention was drawn. It was attached to one of the pillars supporting the theatre's dome which rose up within easy access to the left of the space in which she had sat alone. Beckoning to the burliest man in the small crowd which had gathered behind him he hauled at it, helped by the stranger who was much stronger than he was. There was a mighty cheer from the whole of the audience as the poor creature slowly rose aloft. She finally drew level with the Slip box and the strong man pulled her in while John administered smelling salts—he always carried a bottle just in case—after adjusting her clothing about her and thus restoring her middle-aged modesty. But she did not respond, having slipped into unconsciousness. It was at that moment that Rose, somewhat dishevelled and very pink in the cheeks, appeared.

"Is she dead?" she asked, gazing at the poor wretch, eyes wide.

"Not quite," John answered tersely. "But she could have been if left long enough. Rose, she must have ice and towels to wrap round her head. I think I should take her to hospital."

"I'll help you carry her out, Apothecary," offered the strong man. "Make way there."

Most of the audience were retaking their seats and the way down the stairs was relatively clear. John could tell by the distant sound of laughter that the play was continuing and that the actors were giving it their all, diverting the attention of the crowd away from the near catastrophe that had recently taken place.

Outside several hackney coaches were drawn up in preparation for the end of the performance and John and the strong man—who had introduced himself as Jem Clements, shoemaker—carried the poor woman into one. Rose, meanwhile, with great presence of mind, was directing the driver to take them at fast pace to St. Thomas's, one of the oldest and mightiest of London's hospitals. It had been founded as part of the infirmary of St. Mary Overy Priory early in the twelfth century and renamed as St. Thomas Spital when Thomas `a Becket had been made a saint in 1173.

John had never been more relieved than to hand his poor patient over, knowing that now she would be properly revived. He also had the forethought to leave his full name and address with the medical staff. He then invited Jem Clements back to Nassau Street for a reviving drink, richly deserved by the pair of them, to say nothing of Rose who had hovered usefully throughout.

Much of the house in which John Rawlings had been raised from early childhood had now been turned over to the people administering the sparkling water business, but a great deal of it remained as it once had been. As far as John was concerned Sir Gabriel Kent's ghost was still there. He could picture him, smiling a welcome as the somewhat ill-assorted trio made their way towards the front door. But here Jem hesitated.

"What's the matter?" asked John.

The answer was simple but direct. "I am only a shoemaker, sir. I usually go in by the tradesmen's entrance."

"But tonight you are my guest. You did a great service for that poor wretched woman. Please enter."

As the trio made their way inside John could have sworn that Sir Gabriel Kent crossed in front of them, gliding into the library silently, without turning his head. So he *is* still here, he thought. Meanwhile, Rose, relishing her role as hostess, was ordering the servants regarding the refreshments, and John, ushering Jem, made his way into the library. Sitting in his father's old chair John studied his visitor, who only sat down when requested to do so.

He was younger than the Apothecary had first thought. Obviously still in his twenties. A crop of jet-black hair was tied back with a scarlet bow—probably worn on occasions reckoned to be important, John considered—and these were enhanced by the crystal depths of Jem's sparkling eyes. They were very attractive, as was the man himself. John immediately decided to order a new pair of boots. As Rose entered the room Jem struggled to stand and the whole six feet of his magnificent frame was revealed in his shabby best clothes.

"Jem, this is my daughter, Rose Rawlings."

The shoemaker bowed magnificently and John thought that put in a well-tailored coat and with a few elocution lessons he could almost pass as someone of *bon ton*. Not that that mattered a jot, he hastily informed his mental process. Rose was quite clearly struck by the beauty of the man because she dipped her best curtsey and smiled up at him in what John could only think of as a very warm manner.

"Do sit down again, Jem. Ah, here come the drinks," the Apothecary put in, amused that his daughter was a regular little flirt.

An hour later the shoemaker, somewhat the worse for wear, rose once more and said that he really must go as he had to open his shop in the early morning.

"Where is it situated?" asked Rose, a trifle too carelessly.

"In Paternoster Row, Miss Rawlings. It was owned by my grandfather to whom I was apprenticed. He brought me up as both my parents had died."

"So you are a cordwainer?" John asked.

"Yes, sir, I am. I was made Free of the Company by Patrimony last year."

John looked at Jem afresh. Not just some poor labourer but a Freeman of one of the oldest companies in the city of London. The Worshipful Company of Cordwainers had been formed in 1272 and the apprentices had to work long and hard. John had been made free of the Worshipful Society of Apothecaries—founded four hundred years after the venerable Cordwainers—by Redemption, which meant that neither his father not his grandfather had been an apothecary—not that he knew who they were, of course. But Jem's direct ancestor had meant that he had been made free by Patrimony because shoemaking was his family heritage. An honour indeed.

"Why were you sitting in the Slips?" Rose asked innocently.

"I wasn't actually. But I heard that poor woman give a shriek and ran up to help her."

"How brave."

Jem assumed an air of nonchalance. "Think nothing of it, Miss Rawlings."

John, who had rapidly been reassessing the young man, rose to his feet.

"It really has been a pleasure to meet you, Jem. I do hope that you will call again. On second thoughts, I will call on you soon. I need a new pair of boots—and, of course, some pretty shoes for my daughter."

"Pretty footwear for a pretty lady," Jem answered—and John realised with quite a shock that his daughter was growing up before his eyes.

Chapter Three

When he had bought the house in Strand-on-the-Green John Rawlings had planned to spend a certain amount of time there, whilst still using his old home at number Two Nassau Street when the need to visit London arose. He had also planned to spend three days a week back at his wonderful shop in Shug Lane, Piccadilly. And this morning, still being in London following the terrible adventure at the Theatre Royal, Drury Lane, he walked the old familiar route, looking at life and feeling that incredible rush of excitement that the beautiful, smelly, adventurous town always brought about in him.

His shop window gleamed with an assortment of exciting things to purchase though, obviously, nothing of a more delicate nature, those being kept under the counter. John had always insisted that they should stock a good assortment of condoms, including those tied with delicate ribbons for the more discerning gentleman and others of the rougher variety kept for the working classes. He felt that this was his contribution towards stopping the terrible crisis of unwanted children being abandoned, many of whom perished when only a few hours old, left to die like so much detritus.

When he had sailed for the Colonies, London had seemed less crowded. Now, John thought, there were people everywhere. But he walked on, cheerfully enough, his mind going over the recent events at Drury Lane and then back even further, to the grim time when two savage murders had taken place there. Then he had loved Coralie Clive, the young actress, with all the passion that youth can bring. Now, with his family growing up fast, he had settled for the comfortable existence that only old acquaintance with a partner can bring.

Reaching the top of Coventry Street he glanced down the Hay Market to where Samuel Foote had his Little Theatre almost opposite John Vanbrugh's grand His Majesty's, before turning right into Shug Lane. Then he walked the few paces to his shop and thrust open the door with a cheerful shout of 'Good morning'.

When he had gone to the Colonies he had left behind Gideon Purle, managing the place as a qualified apothecary. His apprentices had been Robin Hazell and Fred, a street boy, as general assistant. Now Gideon was concentrating on running the sparkling water business and as soon as John had returned to England he had employed a sharp, dark, intelligent being called Julian Merrett to take over in Gideon's place. It had turned out that Merrett had fallen on hard times, his late wife having gone down with some mysterious illness which had cost him a fortune in medical fees and left him having to sell his shop and his home and live in a rented room. But he had been made Free of the Society of Apothecaries by Redemption and nobody could take that away from him. Liking the man, John had immediately employed him.

Now he was busy serving a customer and Robin, aged twenty-five, who had also recently been made Free of the Worshipful Society but was staying on in Shug Lane to gain a little more experience—and because he liked the company—was also engaged.

A lanky youth with the face of a merry monkey, who was pounding a simple within an inch of its life, looked up. "Master," he shouted, and putting down the pestle and mortar, rushed to the doorway where he kissed John's hand in a sweet and profound gesture. It was Fred. Remembering their first meeting when the tiny boy—grown somewhat since that first occasion—had robbed Robin Hazell of a letter suggesting that he should become John Rawlings's apprentice—still tugged at John's heartstrings. He had never been able to grant that wish as Fred was a child who had been left at the Foundling Hospital's gates and had no parents who would pay for his apprenticeship. But he was content, just to have a home and friends, to be given a wage, to have somewhere warm to sleep.

"How is it going, my boy? Are you keeping well?"

"Oh yes, sir. Where have you been this last week? We've missed you."

Before John could answer, Robin came up, an attractive youth grown into a fine-looking man.

"Hello, Mr. R. I've been wondering where you were."

"Investigating a peculiar incident at Drury Lane."

Julian Merrett came to join them and John had a brief but amusing idea that the three of them looked like a team of surgeons.

"I am sorry to have deserted you but I have been rather involved with some other business. But judging by the look of the place I feel that my presence is not really necessary." Realising that this sounded petulant he added, "You are all so competent, you see."

Merrett gave a dignified bow. "We work to the highest standards possible, sir."

He had been so glad to find a job that his relationship with John was strictly as a good employee rather than a friend, something that had to be altered it seemed.

"Capital! I wondered if you were busy on Saturday night."

Merrett looked thoroughly startled. "Why no, sir. I had nothing particular planned."

"Then I would be delighted if you would do me the honour of dining with me at my house in Chiswick and staying until Sunday. You live in Compton Street I believe."

"Yes, I do have a room there."

"Well then, if you make your way down The Strand to White Hall and then to Privy Garden Stairs I will send a local man to collect you and row you down to Strand-on-the-Green. Would that suit you?"

"Very much, Mr. Rawlings."

"Good. Then shall we say four o'clock? You can take the afternoon off. Young Hazell will deputise."

"I am honoured indeed, sir."

Having hurried home to fetch Rose, John made his way to Privy Garden Stairs. Since Irish Tom, his former coachman, had decided to remain in the Colonies, nowadays one of the male servants drove the equipage which still remained in the stabling block near Nassau Street. He deposited them at the less frequented landing stage just downriver of the new and magnificent Westminster Bridge. The truth was that John enjoyed passing beneath one of its curving arches and shouting so that his voice echoed back hollowly. Today he and Rose sang in unison and giggled and nudged each other as they did so. Fortunately the tide was flowing in their direction and young Alfred, who was pulling at the oars, was strong as an ox. The journey itself was one of which John never tired, and he was happy to give the work to a Chiswick fisherman and help the local economy.

Rose said dreamily, "There's an important letter waiting for you at home."

John glanced at her. "Your second sight?"

She smiled at him. "Of course."

And when they finally landed and went into the house there was indeed a communication lying on the hall table. John picked it up and went into the drawing room to open it. It was headed, 'To my gallant Saviour of the other Night.' It read:

'My very dear Sir

It would be too Distressing to discuss the Other Terrible Night on

Paper so I am asking you if out of the Goodness of your Heart *You*

Would be Prepared to Call on me when you are next in Town. I am

Always Ready to Receive between the hours of eleven and twelve midday. It would be So Good of you to Call.'

It was signed Phoebe Feathering.

He was delighted with the invitation. Ever since the incident he had been thinking about it and wondering how anyone could inflict such an embarrassing punishment on a hapless woman. His brain had not switched off since. There was obviously something behind such a cruel act and the Apothecary was determined to find out what. He looked at the address from which the letter had come and penned a swift reply promising to call on the following Wednesday. Then he picked up the newspaper. But this was not to be a quiet evening. There was a loud knocking on the front door and a few seconds later his jolly servant Toby appeared.

"There's someone to see you, sir. Shall I say you're in?"

John smiled his crooked smile. "I would imagine that they have guessed that I am by now. Who is it anyway?"

"It's an apprentice. Says his name is Nathaniel Hall."

"Ah yes. The brave young man. Show him in, please do."

A second later and Nathaniel was bowing in the doorway, hat in hand. "Please forgive me, Mr. Rawlings. I was just passing and thought I would call and enquire after your health."

John stood up, thinking it kind of the boy. "Never better, thank you. And how are you after your dramatic dive?"

"Quite well, sir. Forgive me, Mr. Rawlings, but in fact there is a question which I wonder if you can answer for me."

"And what might that be?"

Nathaniel paused, looked all around the room and then at the floor, then said, "No, it's too trivial to bother you with. Please forget that I mentioned it."

John, slightly puzzled, answered, "You must do what you think best, of course. Have you time to converse a little?"

"Yes, sir. May I sit down?"

"Of course, my dear boy, please do."

And it was at this awkward moment with both men wondering what to say next that Rose burst in like a sunbeam.

"Oh, forgive me, I didn't realise you had company, Papa."

Nathaniel, who had sprung to his feet, looking extremely dashing even while becoming somewhat flushed in the cheeks, gave a terribly deep bow, reminding John of himself in earlier days.

"Don't worry, sweetheart. This is Nathaniel Hall who jumped in the river and pulled out that little girl t'other day. Remember me telling you about it?"

"Yes, indeed." She spun round to give him a smile but the poor boy was still bent in half. "How do you do," she said primly. "My name is Rose Rawlings."

She curtsied as he stood straight. John, watching, thought it was

27

like looking at a couple of marionets and hid a swift grin. But then the pair gazed at each other and his daughter smiled again, and John knew for absolute sure that it was Rose's destiny to break hearts. She was as engaging as a warm summer's day, as delightful as a sparkling brook. Nathaniel—like Jem before him—was absolutely enchanted.

"And mine is Nathaniel Hall, Miss Rawlings."

"Oh Rose, please. I do think that people waste so much time on formalities. I would like to sit down with you and find out as much as I can. That is with my papa's permission of course."

John laughed and said, "Of course, my dear. It will be so much more interesting with you adding to the conversation." He rang a small bell for the jolly servant to come.

The apprentice meanwhile was fishing in the pocket of his jacket and producing a bottle of amber coloured beer.

"This, sir, is a sample of our latest brew. I brought it especially for you to try."

"Well that is exceedingly kind of you. Ah, Toby, could you pour two glasses of this delightful brew for myself and my guest. And what would you like, my dear?" He turned to his daughter.

"I would like to try it as well."

"It might be a little strong for you, Miss Rawlings."

"I shall just have to take a chance on that Mr. Hall," she answered and gave the poor boy—already completely under her spell—a smile that would have melted an iceberg.

Chapter Four

It was a neat house in George Street, which led off The Strand and ended up by the River Thames. John, approaching from the main thoroughfare, thought that it seemed slightly too gracious for an occupant of the Slips in Drury Lane and wondered if the woman merely worked here. This idea was endorsed when a footman answered the door and on hearing that he had an appointment politely told him to wait while he sought out Miss Feathering. A minute or two later she appeared in the doorway, fully clad the Apothecary was pleased to see, and gushed enthusiastically.

"Oh my dear rescuer, how can I ever thank you! You saved my life, you know. I would have died had I been left much longer." She clasped her hands together as if praying for inspiration. "You must be rewarded. But how, I ask myself."

John spoke. "Madam, there is absolutely no need. I just did what I could. I am an apothecary but when I saw the state you had been brought to I took you to the nearest hospital for treatment. It was they who saved you."

"You argue prettily but I know the true facts. But now, my dear sir, if you would be good enough to step into the salon—which my employer says I can use on important occasions—there is much I want to tell you about that night."

"I'd be only too delighted to hear."

She walked ahead of him and John, studying her, reckoned her to be about forty-five years old with hair from which the grey had been fiercely tinted by dark dyes. She was also of a slightly nervous inclination and her plump little hands fluttered like two captive birds, while her speech was high and light and incessant.

"You will be wondering no doubt what I was doing sitting in the Slips."

"Well, I …."

She raised a chubby finger to her lips. "Ask me no questions until we are private together."

John's mobile eyebrows rose but he made no comment, merely indicating that he understood by giving a short nod. Inwardly his imagination ran riot. Could this be a case of a love affair that had gone wrong—or something more sinister?

"Now before I begin, would you like a glass of sherry, Mr. Rawlings? I thought I might just moisten my lips."

"That would be most delightful, Miss Feathering."

He took a good sip, thinking that he needed a bracer before hearing the facts she was about to reveal.

"I know that I can trust you completely, Mr. Rawlings. You have such an honest countenance."

"I'm glad you think so," he answered, keeping his face extremely straight.

"It was love that took me up there," she whispered. "A mad passionate love affair."

John took another sip—larger—of his sherry—and waited.

"You do not guess to whom it was that I had lost my heart?"

The Apothecary spread his hands, slowly shaking his head. "I have no idea, madam."

"Why it was the young actor, Robert Miller, of course." Her voice pulsed with emotion.

John hastily ran through the cast list and remembered a slight young man in a minor role who had been called Miller. He had not thought him impressive.

"I see."

At the very mention of her man friend's name the lady went the colour of a peony and flopped rather ungracefully onto a small chair which squeaked in disapproval.

"Yes," she said in a tiny voice. "Yes, yes, it is he who I love." She raised an admonitory finger. "Say nothing, sir, about the difference in our ages. Say nothing of the forbidden side of our differing social classes. We love each other—and there's an end to it."

John merely nodded, sitting in silence. Warming to her theme, the woman continued.

"You wonder, perhaps, why I sit in those terrible Slips. The reason being that it is from there that I can look in private on his beautiful face."

"I don't quite understand."

"With the aid of my monoculars, sir."

The word was entirely new to the Apothecary and he looked at the panting female in some surprise.

"I see that you do not know what they are. Mine were imported from Holland, sir, and have been in my proud possession some time."

"They are some kind of optical instrument?"

"They allow one to focus on a person and show you all his gestures even though you are a mile away."

"Some type of small telescope are they?"

31

"Yes and no. They have been developed into a pair of decorated glasses. Suitable for taking to the theatre and so on. But alas they have been stolen from me. Yet by whom I have no idea. I was sitting peacefully, watching the play, when outside the outer door I heard a thump. Next thing I knew two ruffians had crept in—knocking the guard senseless—and set upon me. I remember as one villain secured my ankles together—even while I was still sitting—another was stealing my money and my precious monoculars. Oh, the horror of it. And then they lowered me over the railing, my dress fell over my face, leaving my bare body for all the world to stare at. I could die of the shame."

"Madam, you were still in your stays which covered a great deal."

Having said that the Apothecary immediately wished that he had kept quiet as a horrid kind of roguishness crept over Miss Feathering's face.

"I blush, sir, that there were so many gentlemen present at Drury Lane that night."

The old dog had been eyeing the audience through her spy glasses, he thought. She rather fancies herself.

"You did not notice much, did you, Mr. Rawlings?"

"I am a professional apothecary and was trained long ago to see the human body as a mere instrument in need of healing," he answered, keeping a stern expression.

How many times, he wondered, had naughty thoughts gone through his mind when passing a female in the street? Dozens probably. Admittedly he had been too highly trained to regard a patient in that manner but other ladies—most certainly. Miss Feathering, in common with all her sex, wore no underwear except for the corsetry that gave most of them their delectable shape. When wishing to answer the calls of nature they just hoisted their many skirts and petticoats and did so. Nothing further was required. But Miss Feathering was not particularly attractive, dressed or otherwise. John wondered, somewhat cynically, on the feelings of young Robert Miller.

She must have read his mind because she gave a gusty sigh and said, "Oh, my poor darling boy, I wrote to him but have not yet received a reply." She turned to John in a rush. "Say nothing about my clandestine lover, Mr. Rawlings. Not a word, do you hear."

"You secret is safe, madam, be assured. Now can I help you any further?"

"Could you—would you—assist me in finding my stolen monoculars? I would be so delighted if you say you could."

John's eyebrows shot up. "But they were taken by whoever assaulted you."

"Yes, but the blackguards won't know what they are. They are bound to offer them for sale somewhere."

He paused. There was a certain truth in that. "Well I can look out for you," he said.

"Oh, bless you, bless you," she cooed. "And now let us speak of more joyful things. Tell me, how do you rate my darling Robert as an actor?"

It was with a great deal of relief that John finally left the house in George Street. Miss Feathering was quite clearly being used by Mr. Miller as a fine supplier of money and other things and was making hay while the sun shone. As for the lady herself, John realised that she was happy after a fashion and it was not his place to criticise the actions of others. Without giving it too much thought he found himself—almost automatically—crossing over The Strand, dodging carts and conveyances as he did so and making his way up the shadowy confines of Half Moon Street. At the top he turned right into Maiden Lane, then cut across Southampton Street to Tavistock Street. It was just as he was entering Charles Street that he saw, strolling in his direction, a figure so familiar that he let out a shout.

"Joe. Joe Jago."

The figure paused, turned its red head in his direction and called out, "Why, bless me, if it isn't Mr. Rawlings."

John felt as if twenty years had fled past as he started to run in Joe's direction. "It's so good to see you again."

"And I you, sir.

"Why it's been an age."

"I've been in the Colonies."

"Got out just in time, eh sir?" Joe chuckled, a melodious sound.

"Yes. Feelings were very tense when I left. But enough of that. What have you been up to?"

"Quite a bit. But do you have time for a cup of coffee, Mr. Rawlings? We could go to Will's and catch one another up with all the latest."

"By all means. I would like nothing better."

So the two old acquaintances walked the short distance to the corner of Bow Street and Russell Street and, entering Will's Coffee House, ascended to the first floor where they took two seats beside the balcony. A waiter approached carrying a large black pot of coffee and poured them out a couple of cups. John insisted on paying the tuppence charge for these.

"Now, Joe, tell me all. Are you still working for Sir John Fielding?"

"Part time, I am. Another—younger—man has been appointed head clerk but I deputise for him on the odd occasion when he does not attend."

"And I heard that dear Elizabeth—Lady Fielding—died while I was abroad."

"It was terribly tragic and so sudden. She had gone north to visit relations in Carlisle and was staying with some of them in a nearby village. One night she complained of a headache and retired early, next morning she was dead. Her body was brought back and she is buried in Chelsea Parish Church."

"And what of Sir John?"

Joe's features took on the foxy look that the Apothecary remembered with such fondness. "He married again—very quickly."

"Really? Gracious me. To whom may I ask?"

"A rather plain lady called Mary Sedgley."

"Do you mean plain of feature or manner?"

"Both," Joe answered heavily.

"Oh dear," said John, and meant it. Elizabeth Fielding had always been so lovely to him, in fact to everyone. Replacing her would have been almost an impossibility.

"And what of his niece, Mary Ann?"

"I have heard a rumour that the young miss finds her step-mother boring."

John roared with laughter and a couple of wits sitting at a nearby table frowned that their earnest conversation had been interrupted. Then he asked, "Would you agree with her?"

"Shall I just say that the first Lady Fielding is very sadly missed."

The two men looked at one another and John answered, "Enough said."

The conversation turned to the Principal Magistrate.

"And how is Sir John? I really must go and see him."

"He is very busy, sir, with his Special People."

"I see. Is that branch of the Runners doing well?"

"Very well indeed. They are an orderly bunch of thief-takers and add a great contribution to the work that Sir John undertakes."

"I am very pleased to hear it. Which reminds me that a most peculiar event took place at Drury Lane Theatre the other night."

And John went on to describe to Joe the extraordinary mishap that had befallen Miss Phoebe Feathering. Despite his attempts to look serious Jago's features broke into a grin.

"Do you mean to say that the wretched woman revealed all?"

"Nothing was left to the imagination, my dear sir."

"Phew!" Joe mimed wiping his brow.

"Indeed. But, joking apart, the poor soul was unconscious and I took her to hospital, otherwise I think she would have died of a suffusion of blood to the head."

"Any idea who the villains were?"

"None except…" John's voice died away as a thought struck him. "Why did they pick on her? It can't have just been a sadistic streak, can it? And they didn't take anything except her monoculars. So why?"

Joe Jago shook his head. "Beats me. Monoculars, you say. Aren't they imported from Holland?"

"Yes. Very few people have them."

"I'll warrant they come up for sale shortly."

"Meaning?"

"That the thieves will take them to a fence and get rid of them fast. I can look round for you if you want. Like as not it will be old Samuel Gottlieb. He's well known in the Seven Dials area."

"That, my dear Joe, would be of great help."

"Anything to be of assistance, Mr. Rawlings. After all, we've worked together a great deal in the past."

"We have indeed."

Chapter Five

Next day, while still in London, John decided on a brisk visit to Coralie Clive to update her with the latest news. But alas, on calling at her fashionable address—Berry Street, near the delightful St. James's Square—where she had a suite of rooms, he was to be disappointed. The actress had gone out. The distance to Shug Lane was a mere stone's throw so the Apothecary walked briskly up Piccadilly and was just turning into the alleyway when an urchin, barefoot and snotty-nosed, tugged at his sleeve.

"You Mr. Rawlings?"

"I am."

"Letter for you from Joe Jago."

The child put on a woe-begone face and John—typically—tipped him two pennies because he felt sorry for him.

Having entered the shop, been greeted by the staff, with Fred shouting 'master' as usual, the Apothecary put on his long apron and went into the compounding room to read the letter's contents. It said: 'Just as I thought, Samuel Gottlieb has put on his daily notice board that a rare set of monoculars are offered for sale. Enquires to his premises at White Lion Street, Seven Dials. I shall go tonight. Meet me at Will's at eight o'clock if you wish to accompany me.'

John experienced a thrill of excitement. Once more a mystery in which he was involved was unfolding. He looked up as Julian Merrett came into the compounding room, a place redolent with the smell of all the drying herbs that were hanging from the beams above. He spoke at once.

"I am so looking forward to dining with you, sir. It is this coming Saturday, isn't it?"

"Yes. I suggest we travel to Chiswick together. I have been detained in town longer than I anticipated. My daughter Rose will arrange the transport. I will write to her tonight."

"That would be splendid. Don't worry about the shop. I can do all that for you."

John gave a wry smile. "The trouble is, my dear fellow, that I don't really like being semi-retired. I am an apothecary in my very bones. That is where my heart truly lies."

"I had thought from what I have heard that you also enjoyed another pursuit," Julian replied, grinning a little.

"You refer to my work with Sir John Fielding?" There was just a hint of amusement in the tone.

Julian backtracked. "No, not really. In fact I'm not sure what I meant. I was just rambling on."

"Of course, it was all highly confidential."

"I quite understand, sir."

Inwardly John smiled. As far as he was aware it was common knowledge that for several years he and the Blind Beak had been on the best of terms and that John had in the past been quite a lynch pin in his investigations. Now as he remembered the various scrapes he had been involved in—and the various people he had met as a result—he realised that it had been a huge part of his life and that he missed it.

* * *

38

Will's Coffee House was full of whirling clouds of blue smoke as the great men of the day puffed on their pipes and discussed matters of wondrous moment and importance. Voices were raised, the loudest being those of the pretty dandies trying to sound more intelligent than everyone else. Joe Jago rolled his eyes and said, "Talks most, says least, I always think."

John nodded. "It was ever thus. But you're on the trail of the missing monoculars. How interesting."

"Indeed Mr. R., it is. So now let us go to that den of iniquity—the Seven Dials."

The Apothecary—who could not consciously remember ever having set foot in the place—was appalled by the rank atmosphere and squalor of the entire area. Separated from Covent Garden Market by a road called Long Acre, the Dials consisted of seven streets, all equally seedy, leading from a dilapidated central roundel in which a few wretched plants struggled for life.

"Careful where you put your feet," warned Joe as they made their way to White Lion Street where, swathed in shadows, lay the shop of Samuel Gottlieb. Pushing the door open set a bell above their heads clanging and then a shape, covered in shawls, sitting behind the wooden counter, stirred.

"Good evening, gents," intoned a liquid voice. "And vot can I do for such a pair of fine gentlemen who have come to see me on a night as dark as this?"

It was Charles Macklin playing Shylock—or so John thought for a mad moment—until he realised that the great actor had perfected the Jewish accent so well that Shakespeare's immortal lines had been given its intonation.

"Good evening, Samuel," said Joe, stepping forward into the dimness of the candlelight.

The bundle of clothes gave a visible jump. "Vie, if it isn't Mr. Jago. How are you, my very good sir? It has been a long time since you graced my poor establishment with your excellent presence."

"I've come because I want your help. Did you hear about the recent rumpus at the Theatre Royal?"

The shawls shimmered as the man shook his head. "No, I did not, Mr. Jago. I rarely leave these premises, you see, so word of vot goes on in the big world beyond rarely reaches my ears."

"Committed to your work," Joe replied drily.

John spoke up. "Good evening, Mr. Gottlieb. I believe you are advertising the sale of a pair of monoculars."

Samuel shifted himself and regarded the Apothecary with a pair of eyes dark as winter's night. "And you are, good sir?"

"He is a friend of mine and I can vouch for his character. Not that you've ever let that bother you in the past, Samuel," said Joe reprovingly.

The nest of talliths twitched slightly. "And what might your interest in them be, kind sir?"

"Merely that I believe they belong to an acquaintance of mine who was robbed of them in the theatre t'other night."

"Oh dear me. But of what help can I be in this matter?"

Joe Jago suddenly slapped his palm down hard on the counter. "That will be enough procrastination, Gottlieb. You are one of the best-known fences in London, information of which Sir John Fielding is more than aware. If I so chose I could have you closed down tonight. It is only the fact that you are willing to share the information you receive with those in the Public Office that keeps you going. Now produce those damned eyeglasses and tell us who sold them to you immediately."

Samuel actually hissed with annoyance, his hand shooting to a box beneath the counter. For a moment the Apothecary wondered if he was going to produce a pistol but instead saw that the man had brought forth something incredibly rare and beautiful. John bent forward to examine it more closely, delighting in the brilliance of the first pair of monoculars he had ever seen. They were just as Phoebe Feathering had described them. A duo of tiny telescopes joined together by a bridge which went over the nose. But more than that, the workmanship that had gone into them literally took his breath away.

The fence spoke. "Look well, gentlemen. These were made in Venice by a craftsman called Salva and brought to this country by someone who had visited that city. I know this because I have many books of reference and when the two ruffians brought the eyeglasses in I wanted to know exactly what was their purpose. And now it breaks old Samuel's heart to have to sell them. Oy vey."

Joe, who had recovered his equilibrium, said, "You knew these were stolen property when you received them. By law you should have handed them in to the authorities."

Samuel swelled with wrath, whether assumed or natural John was not certain.

"And how was I to know their origins? I trust all my customers. I think you are against me, Mr. Jago, because of my antecedents."

"Mr. Gottlieb, that would not be fair. I treat all who consort with criminals equally, regardless of their origins. You admitted that this was sold to you by rogues."

"They looked a little uncouth but when they offered me this thing of beauty I asked no further questions. I did not enquire as to its history."

Having said this the fence picked up the monoculars and slipped them beneath his mantle of coverings. Then he looked malevolently, first at Joe Jago, then at John.

"How much do you want for them?" the Apothecary asked.

"Five pounds cash."

It was an eye-wateringly enormous sum. "I'll give you two. That is the highest I can go."

"I have other people interested."

"Then you must," John answered with great dignity, "seek them out."

He turned towards the door and Joe, reading the situation, did likewise. Then he spoke. "Sir John Fielding has expressed a personal interest in this case, by the way. He has asked me to investigate it on his behalf."

Behind them they could hear the rustle of Samuel's shawls.

"Gentlemen, come back," he called.

In the darkness of the doorway Joe Jago gave a wink then, as one, the two men turned and went back into the shadowy interior of the fence's shop.

It was a relief to get back to the quiet of Strand-on-the-Green after the shocks and smells of London. As soon as John had refreshed himself from the journey he hurried next door to see Zoffany, only to find the painter laughing in his living room with none other than Rose and young Nathaniel, who had dropped in unexpectedly - yet again. As the Apothecary made his way inside, Zoffany turned to him, as full of life as ever.

"My dear friend, you have been in town for an age. Come and tell us all your news."

John gave them a heavily edited version, omitting any reference to Phoebe Feathering's desperate quest for her monoculars and cutting out completely the visit to Samuel Gottlieb's den of deception, which had in fact ended on a satisfactory note. Samuel had, after whining a great deal about the cruelty of both Jago and Sir John Fielding, decided that if you can't beat them it might be better to co-operate. He had promised on the life of his mother—it was difficult to imagine her somehow—that if anyone should contact him about the glasses he would get in touch with Joe immediately.

"Did you see them? What were they like?" Zoffany asked John.

"A work of art, my friend. Not just beautiful but practical as well."

"And they can magnify the thing you are looking at."

"Yes, just like a telescope. But the beauty of them is that they are so small and at the same time so exquisite."

"Describe them," said Rose.

"Well, they were blue enamel, covered all over with a delicate array of birds and flowers. Really someone in this country ought to copy the design and put them on the market. They would make a fortune."

"I shall mention them to my grandfather," said Nathaniel unexpectedly.

"But I thought you said that he was a brewer and that you were following in his footsteps by being apprenticed to such?"

Nathaniel's eyes, which had wandered round to Rose, focussed on John once more.

"Yes, I did. But he likes to sponsor various ideas. I think the monoculars might appeal to him."

"What did you say his name was?"

"Sampson Hanbury."

John clutched at the threads of his memory. "He owns a brewery down Essex way, doesn't he?"

"Fairly recently inherited. But he's always been a bit of a dilletante. Likes to collect things and so on."

"You must tell him about them. Or perhaps we can persuade Miss Feathering to show them to him. That is if she ever gets them back again."

"But she will, Papa. Now that you are on the trail," Rose said with confidence.

Chapter Six

The weekend with Julian Merrett passed pleasantly enough while John, half amused, half anxious, watched Rose's incredible power over the opposite sex. He comforted himself with the thought that his daughter was more than capable of looking after herself and was also gifted with an ability to see coming events. Nonetheless, she was his child and he wanted to keep her safe. It seemed to him almost unbelievable how Julian—whom he had taken on as a sober-sided young apothecary—had blossomed beneath his daughter's delightful chatter. He looked younger—in fact he turned out to be only twenty-six years old—had laughed a great deal, and even indulged in a small amount of idiotic behaviour. When he had taken his leave on Sunday evening he had looked thoroughly depressed.

It was during this pleasant twenty-four hours that John received a letter from his old and dear friend Samuel Swann. In it was a request for the Apothecary to visit him at his country residence, Foxfire Hall. Even as he read the name John conjured up a vision of that great and wonderful house which Sam had acquired through his marriage to the dark and slightly sinister Jocasta Rayner. It was as old as time and quite definitely haunted—somewhat like Jocasta herself John had always thought. But now he reread the contents with pleasure and sauntered next door to tell Zoffany of the invitation. He found the painter deep in conversation with a mysterious woman who the Apothecary presumed to be his wife, though she merely smiled and scuttled away despite the fact that John always bowed to her handsomely. Zoffany waved a deprecating hand at her disappearing back.

"Very shy," he announced.

"I wish my daughter were," John said, more to himself than to the world at large.

"Ah, daughters. I have many of them," Zoffany announced, then immediately changed the subject. "So how are you, my friend?"

"I have had a wonderful invitation to visit an old friend in Surrey. He has a country place called Foxfire Hall which is exceptionally beautiful."

"A man of means I take it."

"Yes, he is a goldsmith so quite wealthy. But the house came to him through his marriage. Not that he married for money, bless his good-natured soul."

"And his wife?"

"Bit of a dark horse. Powerful and extremely thin. I think she bosses him about."

Zoffany sipped a glass of claret and looked thoughtful. "I would like to accompany you on this journey. I can stay in a nearby hostelry but perhaps could see the house at your friend's convenience. The fact is that I want to paint the landscape of your beautiful countryside in all its finest detail. Besides I want to get away from this harem of females for a while."

John, who had no idea how many women lived under Zoffany's roof, nodded in silent agreement. He could not think of a better travelling companion. Good hearted and kindly natured, a lover of his victuals, always ready for a good gossip, there could be no more genial a person with which to set forth.

"What a simply splendid idea. I shall write to Samuel forthwith. I know he will be delighted to offer you hospitality. It is a large old house with plenty of rooms - and also a very exciting place to be."

"I cannot wait to paint it."

"Now that is a splendid notion."

The Apothecary returned home full of good cheer, humming a song to himself, and calling for his personal servant to help him pack his clothes. In the end he decided to take two portmanteaux because, as always, he could not make up his mind as to which of his many colourful ensembles he should carry with him. In this way he ended up taking at least eight. These were carefully rolled and placed in the two cylindrical leather cases, which could be easily fitted behind the saddle of a horse when he and the painter hired mounts.

Downstairs, Rose awaited him, for once sitting quite subdued, staring into the flames.

"Why so pensive, sweetheart?"

"I don't know really, Papa. It's just that I have such an ominous feeling."

"About what?"

"I'm not sure. Whatever is happening it is going to be much bigger than you think."

John's thoughts flew about but could come up with nothing. The Phoebe Feathering incident had been wildly embarrassing for her and the search for the monoculars not without incident, but there was nothing particularly menacing about it. He backtracked to the child who had fallen into the Thames, declaring that she had been pushed. That statement had been put down to the vivid imagination of a little girl. There was nothing of great menace about either unrelated incident. Yet Rose did not make such claims lightly.

"But nothing *is* happening, my dear. Other than for poor Miss Feathering nothing exciting has happened for months."

She looked up and he saw that her forget-me-not eyes had become clouded. "I realise that. But something is about to happen. I feel it so strongly. Be careful, dear Papa. Please guard yourself."

She slumped back and he could see by looking at her pale face that whatever she had just envisaged had gone away. He sat down beside her and took her into his arms.

"My dear girl," he said.

"I'm sorry, Father. It was just a premonition. But promise me that you will take care on this excursion of yours."

"I give you my word. Besides I'll have Zoffany to guard me."

Rose's naughty grin appeared. "Perhaps that is what I am worried about."

As the route to Foxfire Hall took them to Bagshot and from there onward required a driver and trap, John and Zoffany had decided to do the first leg of the journey on the public stage. This left from the Gloucester Coffee House in Piccadilly which was the starting point for all journeys to the West Country. For the sake of an easier trip they spent the night before departing in Nassau Street. It was a strange event because John could have sworn that shortly after midnight someone knocked gently but firmly on his bedroom door. When he called out, "Come in," there was no answer. Eventually, very curious, the Apothecary got out of bed and pulled the door open. Sir Gabriel Kent stood there, his great three storey wig shining in the light of John's candle, his immaculate black satin coat contrasting with the white ruffle of his neckpiece, a stark glittering brooch of jet at his throat.

"Father!" John exclaimed.

But even as he spoke the figure was growing transparent and the Apothecary realised that he was staring at nothing, that there was nobody there. Yet he *had* seen something. Just for a few seconds the ghost of his beloved father had looked at him and given the suspicion of a wink before the vision had faded. John slowly went back to his bed but found himself unable to sleep. Was Sir Gabriel trying to tell him something? Did some strange fate await him in Foxfire Hall? He remembered the picture in the Long Gallery to which he had been so attracted. The Tudor woman and the sad little monkey, both with the same expressions on their faces even though the very thought of such a shared look was almost inconceivable. Behind that picture had lain a secret room, a priest hole, for Foxfire had been built by a Catholic nobleman in the dangerous reign of Elizabeth, when the sound of approaching horses would send the priest conducting mass scurrying to the nearest hiding place. Eventually the Apothecary fell into a deep slumber and was awakened by a servant. Glancing at his pocket watch John saw that there was only an hour left before the Poole Stagecoach departed at eight o'clock.

As usual the conveyance was packed with people. Inside were four persons who were probably going to Poole itself and who had booked their seats well in advance. On the roof was a jostling crowd of nine; one sitting beside the coachman, two squashed in directly behind them, the other seven distributed amongst the top and the basket at the back. Zoffany, handing his easel and brushes to the porter, gave him a generous tip to find a good place amongst the piled-high luggage and John did likewise as he handed over his two portmanteaux. Then the two of them squeezed into a place for one, offered to them by an unsmiling woman taking a child of about five onto her lap. John thanked her profusely and she smiled with her lips, her eyes remaining cold. Punctually at eight o'clock—the ostlers having pushed the team of four fine horses into the traces—there was a loud blast on a horn, the coachman cracked his whip, the passengers clung onto whatever they could find, and they were off.

John, with one hip pointing towards the sky and the other wedged between Zoffany's redoubtable knees, could think of few times that he had been so horribly uncomfortable. To make matters worse the small son of the unsmiling woman decided he wanted to pass water and insisted on doing so over the coach's side. As they were travelling fairly fast the results of this were predictable and John was never more delighted than when she and her brood alighted at Staines. Squeezing into her seat, John breathed freely for the first time on this outing.

"I swear before the bar of heaven that I shall always hire a post chaise in future."

"That is because you can afford to do so, my dear friend. But look around our fellow travellers. They are perhaps not as affluent as you and I."

"That is very true."

"But I agree with you wholeheartedly," Zoffany chuckled, then continued, "but consider, every one of these poor wretches came into the world with nothing and in the same fashion will leave it. So why do people strive and scrimp and save. What for?"

"So that they can ride in a post chaise instead of like this," John answered, and burst out laughing. A sound so marvellous to hear on a particularly nasty morning that several of the other passengers joined in. Zoffany—caught in mid-philosophy—looked momentarily askance, then bellowed a guffaw. And so it was that they arrived at Bagshot shortly before noon and descended to the cobbles below to supervise the handing down of their luggage.

They were in the courtyard of the Old Crown Inn which looked at one glance both hospitable and welcoming. With jovial accord the two friends made their way inside. Two hours later they emerged, somewhat the worse for wine, and tipping a porter—who oversaw their luggage then found them a man with a trap plying for hire—they set off into that golden afternoon. Sunshine was everywhere, throwing its brilliant points of light on towering trees, on the ebony glisten of the horse that drew them, on the pond that danced with a million flames, on the curling fragrance of sweet-smelling blossom. It was so beautiful that the two men sat in silence, drinking in the pleasure of that impeccable moment. Then the trap turned and went through two tall wrought-iron gates, past a lodge where a small child waved at them, and up a splendid drive.

"We're here," said John.

"Mein Gott," Zoffany gasped as Foxfire Hall came into view.

"Indeed."

Shaped in the letter E for Elizabeth, the monarch who had ruled all England when it was built, the house gleamed mellow in the late-day light. Smoke rose lazily from its curling chimney pots and a feeling of languorous warmth hung over the place. Yet it was the fact that Foxfire was smothered with a mass of rambling roses that drew the eye to its outer walls. Whoever had originally planted them had obviously had an eye for glorious colours, for crimson draped over damask with white and pink throwing them into sharp relief. Even as they approached nearer it was obvious that their arrival had been monitored by someone, for the front door was thrown open and Samuel Swann's broad figure appeared in the entrance, larger and with a certain gravitas that had been acquired with the passing of the years.

John stood up in the trap and swept off his hat. "Sam," he called out. "I'm here." And then he was forced to sit down rapidly as they bumped over a stone. Zoffany, lost in admiration, made small exclamations in his native German meanwhile.

They drew up at the vast arched doorway and John paused just for a moment to commit the scene to his pictorial memory. Samuel's great frame, the superb mixed shades of the roses, the softness of the Tudor brick, all combining in the glory of that vivid afternoon. Zoffany had clambered down and was busy introducing himself to Samuel, who had clearly heard of him and was obviously somewhat impressed. John followed more slowly, clutching his hat, tears starting in his eyes, full of memories of his boyhood, none of which would have been as joyful if it had not been for the tall and comfortable personage of Samuel Swann.

Jocasta, sinuous as ever, silently came to join her husband. Never a beauty—her eyes being too small and her body too bony—she had nonetheless a cool attractiveness about her, and her dark hair was lovely. She gave John a half-smile of welcome, her actual thoughts, as always, hidden and secretive.

"John, my very dear fellow. How absolutely wonderful to see you again." Samuel clutched the Apothecary against his silken waistcoat. "It's been far too long. I was utterly delighted when I got your letter. I hope you and Zoffany—I hear he's your new neighbour—can stay a while."

"About five days if that would be in order."

"It most certainly would. Now come in, do. We country folk dine quite early. I hope that suits you."

"Most certainly. Remember that I spend a lot of time in the country as well."

"Ah," Samuel answered wisely, "but that is only an escape from your London home."

"Whereas you have given up yours." John looked round the splendour of the Great Hall in which they were now standing. "And I can't say I blame you."

Samuel looked a little shame faced. "I call in at my business once a week. But what about you? I hear that you've made so much money out of your bottled water that you no longer need to work."

51

"That isn't quite true."

"And what news of Sir John Fielding? How is he, do you know?"

"Well, as a matter of fact I do."

And leaving Zoffany to entertain Jocasta, which—with his eye ever-ready to explore any member of the female sex, young or old— the painter found no difficulty in doing, John told Samuel all about his latest adventure in the Theatre Royal and all that it had led to.

"By Jove, so you've met up with Joe Jago again. You lucky devil. I remember all the times I helped you solve those devilish murders. Gad, but they were exciting days."

Inwardly the Apothecary winced. Samuel had slowed him up so frequently when he had been assisting the Magistrate with an enquiry that he had almost wished the goldsmith far away. Yet he had been so fond of the large young man that it had been impossible to do so.

"Yes, indeed they were," he said now.

Later, after they had partaken of a truly excellent meal, served by quiet unobtrusive servants, and the evening candles had been lit, John turned to Zoffany, who had already been commissioned by Samuel to paint Jocasta, to say nothing of the beauty of the house, and said, "May I show Johan the famous painting?"

"As far as I am concerned you have the freedom of the house," Samuel answered heartily, and Jocasta gave a small nod of assent.

"I find the portrait quite fascinating," John remarked.

"Yes, I remember that you were one of the few people who could set off the hidden mechanism hidden in the panelling. None of us could ever find it," Samuel answered.

"It's true enough," said Jocasta. "When I was a child, my two sisters and I used to play for hours trying to discover the priest's hole that lay behind it. But we never could. It was such a bore. In the end we gave up trying."

"This painting I must see. Who is the artist? Do you know?"

"I'm afraid not, Herr Zoffany. His identity is lost in the mists of time."

"It all sounds very romantic."

"Come on," said John, "let's have a look at her before the light fades."

They went down the length of the enormous Long Gallery and even as they approached the portrait John felt its fascination grip him. As they drew nearer and the face of Lady Tewkesbury, a remote relation and ancestor of Jocasta's family, emerged from the shadows, John felt her enchantment reach out and touch him. It was an angular face, staring out from beneath a Tudor headdress, her knowing dark eyes utterly absorbing the person looking at it.

"Mein Gott," said Zoffany, holding up the candle he had been given, "this is quite remarkable. The artist has given her so much character, so much vitality, yet at the same time she is utterly motionless, like an animal preparing to pounce."

"Have you noticed the monkey?"

"No, where is it?"

"Down there, beside her skirt. It has one of the most tragic faces I have ever seen."

"It is her soul, of course. She has transferred herself into the animal rather than face the cruelty of life."

"Now," John stated robustly, "you are being fanciful. Do you know who the artist is, by the way?"

Zoffany leant forward and put a pair of round spectacles on his nose. "I'm not sure. It could be Isaac Oliver."

"The man who painted the Rainbow Portrait of Elizabeth?"

"Yes, the very one. That portrait is extremely mysterious, many now believing that the rainbow the Queen is holding is in fact a symbol of something else."

"Really?" said John, surprised. "I've never heard that before."

"That, my friend, is because you spend your time amongst dried out herbs and mysterious potions. We artists have a wider vision."

"Then it is your duty to educate the ignorant classes. Tell me."

"In that particular portrait the queen was sixty years of age yet the face is flawless, the hair long and loose. It represents her in all her glory. But look more closely and you will see that her dress is covered with eyes and ears, showing that she is conversant with all that goes on, that she is wholly cognisant of the workings of everything, including the Secret Service. I could talk for hours but I can tell you that Elizabeth was a canny old witch, a very clever woman. She let nothing—I repeat nothing—get past her."

John looked once more at the closed face of Lady Tewkesbury and her unbearably sad companion.

"Not as dramatic as the Queen but with a tale to tell."

"Of what?"

"Of love, despair, treachery and finally mystery."

"I think, my dear fellow, that you could be describing anyone's life. For we all of us endure those things in varying degrees before we are called before our Master."

"True. Very."

"And now are you going to show me the amazing mechanical device?"

But though the Apothecary ran his hands over the spot where he remembered the spring had been, this time he found nothing. It was as if it was guarded by some mysterious means. In the end he had to shake his head.

"I'm sorry, Johan, it seems to have vanished. I don't understand it. I think the lady is playing tricks on me."

"I believe she is," Zoffany replied comfortably and smiled as John followed him back along the Long Gallery.

Chapter Seven

John did not sleep well despite the luxury of the room in which he stayed. The bed was an old-fashioned four poster which seemed to swallow him up. Ridiculous though it was, he had the strangest impression that there was somebody sleeping beside him. In fact, he could have sworn that once a ghostly arm reached out and rested on his chest. He struggled free and sat upright, wide awake. After that the Apothecary merely dozed fitfully and was glad when the morning light lit the place, and he heard the servant's tramping feet as he approached with hot water and washing accoutrements.

Breakfast came as a great relief, the night's shadows banished. The three men ate together, John as usual having an enormous helping of everything on offer.

"Jocasta apologises but she always has breakfast with the children."

"How many do you have?" asked Zoffany.

"Two, both girls. Jocasta did not want any more."

"Girls! I have lost count of how many I have."

It was on John's mind to mention some of the condoms of which he always had a goodly supply in his shop, but he thought better of it. It was impolite—unless being professionally consulted—to talk about things of such a delicate nature. Particularly at breakfast time. But it was just at this moment that his thoughts were brought back to the present by a huge thundering on the door. All three of them looked up.

"Good gracious," said Samuel, thoroughly startled. "Whoever can that be?"

"Sounds like something urgent," John answered, and as he spoke had that strange premonition that a chain of events was about to unfold that was peculiar in the extreme. A second later a footman hurried into the room.

"So sorry to disturb you Mr. Swann but there is a man at the door asking for help. Apparently there has been a bad riding accident and we are the nearest place he could find to come to."

John was on his feet almost as a reflex action. "Where is the injured person?"

"I don't know, sir. But his companion is in the Hall. He's in a terrible state."

That was a slight understatement. The poor creature was cloud white and shaking from head to foot.

"My dear fellow," said John, and reaching in his coat pocket, found the bottle of salts which he always carried on him. The other man inhaled deeply, gulped, then recovered slightly.

"Oh, it was the worst thing I've ever seen. The bone was sticking right out of the flesh. The poor devil must be in agony."

Over his shoulder John shouted to Samuel, "Sam, fetch my bag of medicaments. It's in the bedroom."

For a hefty fellow his host could move quickly. He sprinted up the stairs, followed by a couple of servants who could not keep up with him. A few minutes later he reappeared with the Apothecary's hold-all in his hand.

"Where did the accident happen?"

"Over in the far spinney apparently. It seems his horse shied at something and the rider fell off only for the horse to walk over him. It sounds pretty grim, Sam. How do we get there fast?"

"We'll take the gig. We'll just about squeeze into that."

The wish was father to the thought, John considered, as he clambered into the small vehicle and watched a reluctant horse—with much snorting and baring of its teeth – being pushed backwards between the two long shafts. Surprisingly it took off the moment Samuel cracked the whip and went with a great deal of alacrity, swerving down the drive and then to the right where in the distance John could see a spinney of trees. It pulled up with a halt that practically sent the Apothecary flying to the ground below had he not clung on to his companion and his medical bag in one great bear hug. Jumping out he hurried to the figure lying inert in a pool of blood, the grass around the man dyed a sickly shade of decaying vegetation. A piece of white human bone was sticking out through the soft leather of his riding boot. A vast black horse grazed contentedly nearby, looking quite incapable of wounding anyone so grievously as the poor wretched fellow. As John slipped his folded coat beneath the man's head, he opened his eyes.

"Oh God help me," he groaned.

"Try and lie still," John answered. "We'll get you back to the house as soon as possible. Can you tell me where you've come from?"

But the poor creature was slipping in and out of consciousness and further speech was beyond him. John searched in his medical bag and produced a little bottle with the words 'Hemlock, compounded by J. Rawlings' and a date. This was the strongest pain killer of them all but an overdose could produce paralysis and death. But this case was beyond doubt the worst that the Apothecary had ever witnessed and the poor creature lying on the ground was almost in extremis.

John pulled the cork from the little bottle and held it to his patient's lips. The man choked it down.

Samuel, who had been hovering in the background said, "That seems to have eased him. What is it?"

John glanced up. "It's powerful stuff. I've never actually administered it before."

At that moment the man who had brought the terrible news to Foxfire Hall arrived on his horse, both he and the animal looking thoroughly depressed.

"Is he still alive?" he asked tremulously.

John stood up. "Yes, but he needs urgent medical attention. Now who is he and where does he live?"

"His name is Humphrey Warburton and he is a Sir. And he's staying at Lynton Park with the Duke and Duchess of Derwent."

"A good address indeed," said Samuel. "It is an exquisite house. A glorious Palladian mansion."

"Well, we must contrive to take him there. But being doubled up in the gig would be far too painful. He'll have to travel by coach where he can stretch out on a seat."

"I'll go back and get one of mine," offered Samuel.

"And I'll go and inform His Grace that there has been a terrible accident," said the servant.

"What are we going to do about his horse?"

"I'll lead it," the man answered, with more bravado than sense, John thought.

They set off on their various missions, leaving the Apothecary alone with the broken man who had started life that morning as a hale and hearty individual. He was now lying very still, the pain dulled, his consciousness coming and going in short moments only. John, leaning over him, decided to administer nothing further to the luckless devil and went to a tree stump and sat uncomfortably on it, looking around him.

His eye was caught by something moving in the spinney of trees, not only moving but bobbing about as if it had life. Puzzled, John walked cautiously towards it. It blew on the breeze as he drew nearer and he realised that it was only the air currents that gave the illusion. But what an illusion. It was a life-sized paper skeleton—the sort that a father might cut out for his inquisitive child on the eve of all Hallows. Attached to a branch it would dance in the wind and surely be enough to spook any animal. He knew in that split second that someone had placed it there in order to frighten Sir Humphrey's mount and either end it or ruin him for life.

The Apothecary was deep in thought when his friend Samuel appeared with a coach and driver, which drew up just short of the spinney. Between them—and with the greatest care possible—they carried the groaning Sir Humphrey down to the conveyance and there placed him as comfortably as possible on one of the seats.

"I'm coming with you," said Samuel as they started off slowly. "There's something fishy about this accident. I feel absolutely positive of it."

"You're right," said John, pointing to where the paper skeleton still danced listlessly in the breeze. "That thing was hidden in the trees."

Samuel looked at him, horror-struck. "To scare the horse," he said, putting John's thoughts into words.

"Precisely," came the reply as the Apothecary cut it down.

Lynton Park turned out to be even more spectacular than John could have imagined. It stood, absolutely square, in the morning sunshine, basking in the Italianate style of the movement's founder, the morning light reflecting warmly off its mellow brick. Built in the fashion begun by Andrea Palladio, its very symmetry appealed to the Apothecary who loved its long lean lines, whereas Samuel said, "All right if you like that sort of thing but give me Foxfire Hall any day. The Tudors, they knew how to build all right."

"But surely every era is allowed to have its own style, Sam. This one is so modern, so aggressively now. It is a masterpiece. You must see that."

"Well, I don't, sorry. Now which of us is going to ring the bell? That poor devil in the coach must be near death's door."

A gently curving staircase of about a dozen or so steps led on either side to the front entrance which stood, windowed above and totally magnificent, beneath its grand and imposing pillared entrance. John hurried up the stairs and pulled the wrought-iron bell rope. It was answered almost immediately by a stony-faced footman in a vivid scarlet livery.

"Yes, sir?" he said in a voice that meant, "And what do *you* want?"

"I have Sir Humphrey Warburton in a coach." John gesticulated with his arm. "He is in a critical condition having sustained a riding accident which has shattered one of his legs. Can we please get help and carry him inside?"

"I will fetch His Grace. Please be so good as to wait."

The door was shut again in a highly meaningful manner. It opened a few minutes later during which time John had changed places with Samuel and had entered the coach to tend to the injured man. He watched over his shoulder as Samuel was finally given permission to enter and disappeared from view. Sir Humphrey's eyelids flickered.

"Oh God help me."

John made a small joke about not being the Almighty but doing his best. Sir Humphrey did not respond. Staring at him closely, the Apothecary considered that he was not an unattractive man. He had a thinning amount of brownish curls on the top of his high-domed head and a large pair of velvety eyes. But these at the moment were creased with pain and his entire face glistened with sweat. Looking at him, seeing that he was regaining consciousness, John took a bottle containing opium from his medicine bag.

"Here, have a little of this. It will ease your pain."

Sir Humphrey would have taken the whole dose but the Apothecary stopped him. "Not too much I beg you. It could only make you unconscious."

"I don't care."

"No, but I do."

Samuel reappeared at that juncture, running down the staircase, this time accompanied by a large dark thunderous-looking man and a flock of servants. The newcomer's eyes were two black gimlets, darting hither and thither, turning his angry gaze in the direction of the coach and shouting, "Where is Warburton? In the carriage, d'you say?"

Samuel, extremely flustered, answered, "Yes, Your Grace. He is seriously injured."

The conveyance rocked as his lordship put his foot on the step and peered inside.

"Warburton," he shouted. "I hear you've had an accident."

John interposed. "He can't answer you, sir. The poor devil is in extremis. Can your servants help me carry him into the house?"

"No they cannot. The whole place is packing up tomorrow. I cannot receive anyone. Who are you anyway?"

"My name is Rawlings. John Rawlings," the Apothecary answered, thunderstruck by the man's attitude.

"Well, I'm Derwent. And as I've said my wife and I are shutting the house tomorrow morning. Going to my residence in Bath for a few weeks. Sorry I can't help."

"Yes, and I am sorry too, Milord. If Sir Humphrey dies, which he well might—and I speak as a qualified apothecary not just some interfering fool—I hope you will be able to sleep with a quiet conscience."

The duke shot him a malevolent look. "What do you want me to do? Cancel our trip?"

John made no reply, merely giving the man an unreadable glance, and hastening back into the carriage from which could be heard the sound of Warburton's low moans. It was very much as the Apothecary had thought. The man could not live much longer with such terrible injuries. He turned back to the Duke of Derwent.

"My lord, if it would not be too much trouble, I would ask you to write a note and despatch it this evening. If you could address it to William Bromfeild of Conduit Street, London. He is a master surgeon and if you could request that he comes immediately to wherever you suggest I take Sir Humphrey next, then I would be mightily obliged to you."

"Can he not go home with you?"

Samuel spoke. "It is quite a long way, my lord. I think, for the sake of the patient, somewhere nearer might be better."

Derwent raised a mighty pair of shoulders in a shrug. "Oh, take him to Oakridge, that's not far from here."

Samuel chimed in again. "But that is an old Tudor place and owned by an eccentric foreigner. Do you really think it will be all right?"

The duke boomed a huge laugh, though he did not smile at all. "Baron Rotmuller, a German financier, lives there. He apparently won the whole estate on a single game of cards. Obtained it from the poor young Earl of Alston, who then went outside and shot himself as a result. Nowadays the baron lives there all alone. But he is philanthropic and won't turn you away."

Realising what he had just said, the man had the good grace to flush an unattractive shade of beetroot. John and Samuel exchanged a glance and then, simultaneously looked up at the balcony above the stairs. A woman stood there, an elegant figure tricked out in deep burgundy shades.

"Frederick," she was calling. "Where are you?"

A chill shot through John as something in his memory stirred. He had seen her before somewhere—but where? He racked his pictorial memory, that indefinable thing that had first proved to John Fielding that here was someone worth employing, albeit part time. But for once it was letting him down as no answer came. Yet he knew he was right. If only for a fleeting second, he had glanced on that exquisite creature before.

"Frederick," she called again, "is anything the matter? Who is in that coach parked outside?"

"Nothing to worry you, my dear. It is Sir Humphrey. He has been wounded. These two men are going to take him on to Oakridge because we are leaving first thing if you remember."

"Yes, of course. Is it serious? Has he been in an accident?"

She stared at John, long and hard, her eyes full of questions and thoughts.

"We've got to move on," he muttered to Samuel. "The longer we stay the better the chance of the poor wretch dying." Raising his voice, he called, "We'll be off, Your Grace, madam ..." He bowed charmingly in the woman's direction. "Thank you for promising to write, my lord, and please send your letter tonight—without fail. Sam, you'd better come with us to Oakridge. I feel certain we must go there immediately."

That said they bowed yet again in the woman's direction, gave the curtest of salutes to the duke, and jumped into the coach. With a crack of the whip they were off, the wretched Sir Humphrey groaning with each turn of the wheel.

John called up to the coachman. "Drive us through some town or other if you can. I must get some opium from an apothecary. Don't worry, they will sell it to me. One of the useful things about being in the trade as it were."

Samuel chuckled. "You will never cease to amaze me, John. You don't change at all, do you? Not even one tiny little bit."

"What do you mean by that exactly?"

"Just what I say. You'll enter that shop with a long face, deep voice and a reassuring manner. The poor fellow will hand you the stuff and know that he will be safe in doing so. Yet I know you as someone entirely different, the chap who has always known the way to make me laugh."

"I'm a split personality, Sam. Remember I was born under the sign of the twins."

Shortly afterwards they entered a large village and there, sure enough, was an apothecary's shop arrayed with a rather small display of bottles. Calling to the coachman to stop, John leapt out, and emerged some ten minutes later carrying a small green phial.

"I knew I was right," Samuel crowed in triumph. "Why did he sell it to a complete stranger?"

"Because I discussed with him the way he had obtained it. Named the supplier from whom it was bought. Told him I used the same shipper myself."

"And do you?"

"Yes, of course." There was just the faintest hint of annoyance in the Apothecary's voice. "I'm not an out and out liar, you know."

After that there was silence and the coach rolled on into the darkness.

Chapter Eight

The silence was broken as the great sweep of what had once been a beautiful and splendid Abbey came into view. Now the former home of the Brothers of Penitence—or Bonhomme as they were generally known—stood out as a mass of neglected arches and silent walkways. With the sun just beginning to make its westerly descent, the stark black skeletons of what had once been fine old buildings rose in dilapidated anguish before their eyes. So much so that they barely noticed the outline of those which remained standing, formerly the living quarters of the Abbot and his brothers of the cloth. Yet, beyond these ruins stood another—a house of considerable proportions.

"I believe," said Samuel, "that that was once the dwelling place of Elizabeth, before she became queen."

"Really?"

"Yes, so I've heard. It was apparently left to her by Henry VIII's will. She lived here until she was arrested by her sister Mary."

"Lovely family that. They spat their poison everywhere."

"Yes, the cause of all this ruin." Samuel gesticulated to the remains of what had once been a beautiful and holy place. "Henry VIII was a particularly vicious old swine, don't you think?"

"I hope you mean that as a rhetorical question, my dear Samuel. Because in my opinion there can't have been a worse one."

"And all this terrible ruination done so that he could marry Anne Boleyn. And how long did that marriage last?"

"I think when she gave birth to Elizabeth, Anne signed her own death warrant."

"I think you are more than possibly right."

"Meanwhile unless we can beg some accommodation for our poor passenger, he won't survive the night."

It was a very weird experience, so John thought as he crossed the walkway that separated the coach from the former quarters of the Bonhomme. When Henry VIII had dissolved the monasteries, seizing their wealth and power for the royal treasury and at the same time conveniently placing himself as the head of the newly formed Church of England, he had altered for evermore the way that the country had functioned.

A strange silence had fallen since their coach had turned up the ancient drive and John felt it even more deeply at this moment, standing on the doorstep of what must once have been the Abbot's lodging, now converted into a glorious mansion by Henry VIII's wily daughter. Trying to find someone who would have a good enough nature to take a hideously wounded man in was hard work indeed. He was dimly aware that more candles had been lit inside as the ancient fastenings creaked and the door slowly swung open.

"Baron Rotmuller?" he asked tentatively.

It was like a scene from a play as an old man standing in the entrance cupped his hand round his ear and said "Eh?"

The Apothecary felt hysteria rise and fought back an overwhelming urge to burst out laughing. "Is your master in?" he shrieked.

The servant stared at him blankly but then the situation was mightily relieved by the arrival of a tall being wearing a long robe and saying, "I am he of whom you speak, my good sir. How can I help you?"

John bowed low. "I have come to ask you the mightiest favour. There is a wounded man in my carriage, a man who must have urgent medical attention or else lose his life. Can I beg you that we carry him within?"

The man's face flickered momentarily, a rapid range of expressions crossing it. He was deciding, or so the Apothecary thought, whether to be welcoming or otherwise. Fortunately he came down on the side of good.

"Of course, of course. Who am I to turn down a fellow human being in dire straits? I'll raise the servants." Turning to the deaf old man, he bellowed, "Job, wake the household. We are going to need help. Quickly now." He wheeled to face John again. "My dear young friend, please come in. I've an army of staff who can help with your wounded friend." He was charm itself, his heavily accented voice reassuring somehow.

"A bit more than simple wounding I'm afraid. A surgeon from London has been sent for and told to come here immediately."

"Really? Well we shall have to cross that bridge when we arrive at it."

"May I ask your name sir?"

His host bowed from the waist most graciously. "I am Baron Rotmuller." He flashed an apologetic smile. "I realise I have a strong German accent but I speak English perfectly. And that is because I was born in England and raised here until the age of five. Because she—my lady mother—the Honourable Letitia Smythey, don't you know, was visiting her people in England at the time. They were the Clarences …"—this added with a slightly roguish smile—"… and my mother considered that they would give me a far better education than would be possible in my father's country, so—"

But he was interrupted by the sound of anguished cries from the hall as a host of heaving servants were seen carrying the shattered body of Sir Humphrey Warburton aloft, followed by Samuel who appeared absolutely drained. Just for the briefest moment the baron looked aghast then he readjusted his features.

"Take the wounded man to the second guest suite."

"If I might interrupt, baron, I presume that this house has a Long Gallery."

A slight frown teased Rotmuller's brow. "Yes, one was installed by Queen Bess herself …"

"Then may I suggest that Sir Humphrey is taken straight there. The best surgeons—of which number I can assure you Mr. Bromfeild is one—like to operate where there is as much daylight as possible. So it would be a great courtesy on your behalf if the patient was placed there immediately."

The baron, who had been pursing his lips, instantly became more attentive. "This surgeon you mentioned. Bromfeild was it not? I think I have heard his name before somewhere. From which I take it that he operates on gentlefolk?"

The Apothecary smiled. "I believe he operates on those who need it. But the Dowager Princess of Wales is his patron if that helps."

Rotmuller nodded solemnly. There was an awkward silence broken by Samuel saying in a pathetic voice, "Do you mind if I sit down?"

The baron's mood changed and he now emerged fully in his element, grace and charm oozing from him, as with a great many hand gestures he ordered his servants about, enunciating with great care when he spoke to deaf Job. The staff, obviously used to this, hurried about their tasks so that five minutes later a groaning Sir Humphrey had been removed to the Long Gallery where the Apothecary had, with enormous care, removed his soiled and saddened riding clothes and placed him in a flowing shift, meanwhile giving the man another small dose of opium. Praying that Mr. Bromfeild was hurrying through the night, John finally left him in the charge of a sensible valet and went to find Samuel.

He discovered the baron and his guest in a small and comfortable room—clearly used at one time as the Abbot's private reading space—where Rotmuller was amusing the exhausted Mr. Swann with a series of anecdotes about life in the former priory. John, watching them, decided that the Baron was a man of substance.

"Thank you very much, my dear sir, for handling this unwelcome intrusion so splendidly."

Rotmuller turned his face in the Apothecary's direction. "Oh there you are, my friend. I was wondering what kept you. How is poor Sir Humphrey?"

"Wretchedly ill, I fear. I think if Mr. Bromfeild does not get here within the next twelve hours the poor wretch will be a dead man."

The baron rose from his chair, his robe sweeping round him as he did so. "Is there anything I can do to help? Should I send for my own doctor?"

"It is kind of you to offer but there is nothing he can do. Only a surgeon can save the day now, I fear."

The look on the baron's face could have been that of an actor, ranging through every emotion in about three minutes flat. In fact so grim was it that Samuel called out, "Please don't worry so much, sir. I am sure he will get here as soon as he receives the Duke of Derwent's note."

Rotmuller raised his brows. "So that villain is involved in this. I might have guessed. If indeed he wrote such a letter. I don't trust that man further than I can throw him."

"Are you well acquainted?" John asked.

"I play cards with his wife." And Rotmuller rumbled a laugh.

John raised a mental eyebrow but said nothing; Samuel looked frankly astonished.

Half an hour later, drowsy with port and dozing through sheer exhaustion, the trio were awakened by a peal at the front doorbell and it was Rotmuller, drawn to his considerable height, who answered it in person. Fully prepared to welcome the eminent surgeon with a fulsome speech, the wind was taken out of his sails by Bromfeild rapidly climbing out of the conveyance, shouting to his assistants, "Get inside, boys. It's cold enough to freeze the bollocks off a grizzly bear," and plunging straight past his host and into the warmth within. The baron appeared momentarily put out but changed his features to a smile before he followed the surgeon into the parlour.

"Welcome, Mr. Bromfeild. I am honoured to have the pleasure of your company."

The surgeon looked up from beneath a pair of formidable eyebrows. "And you are?" he said.

Rotmuller looked extremely hurt. "I am the owner of this property, sir, and as such am your host."

"Really," Bromfeild put out his hand to receive a glass of gin which Samuel had thrust into it. "I thought it was that rascal Derwent. Where is he? Sound asleep I dare say."

"The duke does not live here," the baron put in, by now highly aggrieved. "I believe he wrote to you and begged you to attend one of his guests who he then directed on to my address, God alone knows why."

"Because he was shutting down his home and travelling the next day. Oakridge—the baron's dwelling—was the nearest place he could think of," said John, hoping to clear the air.

Rotmuller wrestled with his obvious desire to throw the lot of them out but somehow managed to spread a smile over his reluctant features.

"Of course, I have known Derwent for many years, better or worse luck." He gave a half-hearted grin. "But he knew that he could rely on me in a crisis." For the first time John felt desperately sorry for the poor fellow.

"I see." Bromfeild downed his drink. "It sounds as if I should visit the patient immediately. Derwent said something in his letter about there being an apothecary present."

He looked round the room and John took a pace forward. "I am qualified, sir. I have a shop in Shug Lane, Piccadilly."

Bromfeild looked him up and down. "Very well. Let us go to the poor devil."

They climbed a staircase that obviously had not been altered since the days of the Tudors. John had a mental picture of a richly amber-headed young woman walking regally before them then gliding down the corridor and out of their sight. He gave an involuntary shiver. Bromfeild shot him a look from beneath his formidable eyebrows.

"I trust that you will assist me during the operation." It was more a direction than a question.

"Of course, sir. It will be fascinating to watch."

"Fascinating—but bloody. I do hope that you're not the fainting sort."

"I don't think I am."

"Well, I've two medical students accompanying me and I'll have to recruit the rest from the youngest and strongest of the baron's household."

"You will require seven people all together?"

"That is the bare minimum with which I can contemplate such a feat of surgical skill."

He turned and began his examination of the injured man. Fortunately Sir Humphrey had lost consciousness and only stirred and muttered as with enormous skill Mr. Bromfeild undertook the delicate task of looking at him.

"This is a brutal wound," he said to John over his shoulder, "look closer boys." He gestured to the medical students.

They leant over Sir Humphrey's leg, discussing points in lowered voices.

Bromfeild sniffed Sir Humphrey's breath, raising his brows then looking sharply at John. "When did you give this patient opium, Mr. Rawlings?"

"About two hours ago, sir. He was in mortal agony."

"Well, that is how he will have to remain. I do not believe in giving my patients any anodyne drafts whatsoever. Fortunately this will have worn off by tomorrow morning so we can proceed as soon as it is light enough." He straightened and looked John directly in the eye. "No more medicaments, do you understand?"

"I do indeed, sir."

At midnight, when he finally retired to his room, John thought that he would drop off to sleep immediately, instead he lay awake, his brain feeling it would explode with all the facts that surgeon Bromfeild had rattled off at him. It seemed that the Apothecary had been granted the unlovely task of holding Sir Humphrey's shattered limb as it was removed from the rest of the poor chap's body.

Yet again he recalled all that he had learned as an apprentice to a master herbalist. First and foremost had been the fact that the dead could not hurt anyone nor, presumably, could any part of them. Secondly, when he had— aged seventeen—served as an assistant to a leading surgeon of the day, he had passed the test and had earned praise for his cool head and good behaviour. Now, as a grown man, surely he could behave as well, though he had to confess he was hardly looking forward to the ordeal.

Next morning he saw that Samuel, clothed in a loose shirt and a pair of borrowed breeches, was already at his station behind the chair in which wretched Sir Humphrey would shortly be seated. John, similarly dressed, immediately took up his position. Two burly fellows who worked in the baron's stables and a young man in his early twenties, plus the two medical students, made up the rest of the team. Bromfeild arrived in the Hall in the flurry of importance which always surrounds any great man of medicine. John, watching him, decided that the surgeon himself was unaware of the power of his personality as he gave orders to his acolytes, who hung upon his every word as if it had been delivered by the Almighty himself. Finally, tying on an apron which the Apothecary was delighted to see was freshly laundered, he gave orders for Sir Humphrey to be carried to the operation. Deprived of his opium concoction the poor man was rigid with fright.

"There, there, my good chap, relax. I will do my utter best for you. There is no need to fear a thing. But I think we will give you an enema just in case."

"Already been done, sir," one of the medical students answered briskly. "That and being bled by leeches. Taken care of first thing this morning." He winked at the other young assistant who nodded his agreement.

Now, with no regard for what was left of Sir Humphrey's dignity, the poor man was stripped naked and sheets were wound round his torso before he was strapped into the chair over which a pale Samuel, sweating but steadfast, had control. The stable hands were given the task of washing the wounds on the patient's leg while the young chap from the kitchens shaved the hair off Sir Humphrey's thigh. With a nod to Samuel, who was doing his absolute best, the operation began.

Bromfeild walked round the chair and Sir Humphrey, in an agony of fear and pain, still managed to give him a sickly smile. The great man acknowledged this with a curt bow and without further ceremony spread the patient's legs wide before applying a tourniquet. Samuel held the poor devil's shoulders, the medical students rushed to assist while Bromfield drew down the arteries, cutting, tying and cauterising. John was fascinated, lost in admiration for the surgeon's enormous skill but at the same time realising the tremendous pain that the gallant Sir Humphrey was enduring. When the tourniquet was finally secured, the skin and muscle were pulled back and it was time for the first cut. The assistants held fast, Bromfield made a rapid incision in a circular motion near the knee and round the lower thigh, and the patient let out a scream that was terrible to hear. The surgeon, nothing daunted, worked on at speed. John, lost in wonderment, clung on to the leg until, at last, a brief order came from Bromfeild, and the shattered remains of what had once been a human limb was lowered into the sawdust. It was done. A successful amputation had taken place.

The wretched patient had fainted with the shock and so was spared the sight of what happened next. Bromfeild now had to secure the blood vessels in what was left of Sir Humphrey's leg, a technique he had studied with the great William Hunter—the most eminent doctor of the day. Seizing an artery with his fingertips he bound it tightly, but to avoid the danger of it bursting open he tied several more ligatures, each one slightly slacker than the last. At last he was ready to close the wound. Eventually, after the most precise work that the Apothecary had ever watched, Bromfeild attached to the still bleeding stump absorbent bandages of linen mixed with flour, a washed calf's bladder adding the final sealant. Then and only then did the surgeon stand fully upright and allow a medical student to wipe his brow.

"My work is done," he announced shortly. "The rest of you can clear up. Mr. Rawlings, stay with the patient and keep the pressure on the stump. I don't suppose you have your medical bag with you."

"I'm afraid not, sir."

"Then can you make haste to an apothecary and get a compound of the juice of moneywort. There's nothing better for staying blood flow in my opinion. On second thoughts write a note and give it to the boy to take. I would like you to remain with the medical students and watch over Sir Humphrey. I am going downstairs now. Mr. Swann you may accompany me."

John thought that though they were being ordered around like a bunch of schoolboys the great man had earned his right to assume the role of headmaster. For what skill, what knowledge, what wealth of learning and understanding had just been exhibited. He felt that it was unlikely that he would ever again meet a man who he would hold in so high a regard.

"Before you go, sir, I have one question to ask you."

"And that is?"

"May I add some opium to the note for the apothecary? In other words, would it be advisable for Sir Humphrey to have small doses to relieve the pain now that the operation is over?"

Bromfeild smiled. "Yes, I think so, provided that it is properly regulated. You probably thought it cruel of me to order nothing during the procedure but I have experienced it having some very odd side effects and that is why I have come out against its use."

"I understand, sir. And may I say that it was a privilege to watch you work. Something I shall remember always."

"Thank you, my friend. Adieu."

And with those words the surgeon left the room.

Later that evening, both having been relieved of their posts by two doctors who practised locally, Samuel and John sat in deep conversation.

"I think he chose me for the chair job because I am quite power-fully built, you know."

"I am sure of it. I know I couldn't have held the poor devil in his place. I think you did admirably, Sam."

"Do you really? Thank you so much. This reminds me of the old days when I used to assist with your murder cases. I so enjoyed them, you know."

John, recalling how the Blind Beak would rumble a laugh whenever he was informed that Samuel was taking a keen interest in a case and he—revelling in Samuel's company as he usually did—could wish most heartily that his friend had other interests. But all that had changed when Samuel had finally married the somewhat intense Jocasta Rayner, a very wealthy woman in her own right. Foxfire Hall and all the glories of living in such a place had made John's friend happy at last—or had it? There had been a certain boyish enthusiasm about the way in which he had decided to join in on the ghastly trip which had recently ended. The trip in which Sir Humphrey Warburton's leg had been amputated in Oakridge, the ancient Tudor residence of both holy brothers and a devilish queen.

Sam sighed. "I suppose I'll be having to get back tomorrow. I do dislike leaving you, John."

"I'll probably head for town myself. What shall I do about Zoffany?"

"Oh, leave him with us. He will amuse Jocasta and take her mind off my absence."

"He's a great flirt, you know."

"Good."

John silently wondered about that answer but did not pursue the conversation further. He changed the subject.

"I've been having a very odd time lately. A run of most peculiar events. If I were superstitious I would think someone was wishing me ill luck."

Sam looked interested. "Tell me more."

"Well, it all started when a little girl fell into the Thames just outside my house."

And before he could stop to think about it the Apothecary had launched into a description of the various happenings which had led up to the time when he had visited Samuel in order to introduce him to Zoffany, the famous artist. Sam sat, looking just as he had when he was a child, mouth slightly agape and eyes big as moonstones.

"Good heavens," he said, when John had finished speaking, "what a strange run of fortune. Do you think the incidents were related in any way?"

"No, how could they be?"

And then John paused, bringing into play his pictorial memory, not used so frequently these days. He saw again the china-blue eyes of the four-year-old and the certainty with which she had shaken her wet curls and lisped at him, "I was pushed. I did not fall." Next he saw the terrible sight of the naked form of Miss Phoebe Feathering—every bone of her stays doing its duty—lowered over the Slips and left to swing slightly above the audience at Drury Lane Theatre. Finally there was the life-sized paper skeleton impaled amongst the trees which would make a passing horse shy and in all probability throw its rider. But how could these three totally different occasions be linked in any way? It was not possible. Or was it?

"It's simply not possible—unless?"

"Unless what?"

"There's some malevolent mind seeking revenge for something or other. But that couldn't be."

"Why not?" said Samuel simply. "The world is full of lunatic people."

"Which reminds me. I've yet to show you this."

77

And reaching into his portmanteau John produced the set of cut-out bare bones that he had found near the scene of Sir Humphrey Warburton's accident. Taking it from him, Samuel turned it in his hands and said, "Do you think this was placed deliberately?"

"Yes, I do. It was fastened amongst the tree branches, not dangling as if it had been blown off by the breeze."

"Then there's something behind all this, John. I really think you should go and report it all to Sir John Fielding."

The Apothecary pulled a slight face. "I haven't met the new wife yet. I must say I have been putting the moment off."

"Well don't let any fear of her put a stop to it. My dear old friend, it is your duty to report these odd occurrences."

"Sam, you've persuaded me. As soon as we get back to town Bow Street will be my next port of call."

"I am delighted to hear it."

Chapter Nine

John thought, roving his eye round the rest of the crowd jammed together in the public gallery of the Principal Magistrate's courthouse, that time had made little difference to the audience. Fashions had changed, the great hooped skirts, so well-beloved in the middle of the century—when women had taken up three times the space of men— had disappeared. On the other hand there were three Macaroni's sitting in the front row of the gallery, wearing enormous wigs upon their heads atop which were the tiny *chapeau bras* which they all affected. They were talking loudly in mewling voices throughout the proceedings and eyeing people up through their ridiculous pendant quizzing glasses, meanwhile blocking the view of those unfortunate enough to be sitting behind them. The sound of their mincing effeminate chatter was clearly audible to the entire court room. Suddenly Sir John Fielding turned his sightless eyes upward and stared—if it had been possible for him to see—at the place in which they sat. The Macaronis let out an audible giggle and continued their meaningless conversation.

After a few seconds Sir John spoke. "Silence," rumbled from his mighty chest.

"My dears," said one of them loudly. "I do believe Sir is addressing us."

"Shush," answered a second one and let out a hysterical laugh.

"I think the Chief Magistrate is cwoss wiv us," said the third, deliberately lisping like a child.

"And I think," answered Sir John, "that the Earl of Harlington's sissy son is causing this disturbance. Arrest him now—and his cronies—and let us see how a term in the cells cools their ardour."

John drew breath. It was said that blind Sir John could recognise over a thousand villains from their speech alone and once again it seemed that it must be true. There was the sound of heavy footsteps on the stairs and two Runners appeared at the top and without apology thrust their way past the seated audience. Then there was applause and cheers from all present as one of them swung a small Macaroni high into the air by his vast wig, which flew from the fellow's head to present a silly shaved crown for all the world to see.

"That's the stuff," shouted someone. "Punch his lights," yelled someone else.

John roared with the rest of them. This was London, this was society at its roughest, this was the people having their say, this was what he had been brought up to understand. A third Macaroni attempted to escape but was stopped by a strapping man who—if his clothes and demeanour were anything to go by—came from the highest ranks of social standing. The Macaroni put his hand to what passed for his sword but the other man, laughing the meanwhile, crashed his fist to the fellow's chin and watched as he slithered to the floor, unconscious. He then stepped over him but nonchalantly took the man's wig as a souvenir. The crowd cheered with a mighty voice.

Sir John, meanwhile, had been listening with obvious enjoyment to the rumpus overhead but now decided that enough was enough and banged with his gavel. The gallery subsided and the Runners dragged the bodies of the Macaroni's down the stairs to the cells below the courtroom. The whole uproarious incident was over.

Making his way into Bow Street later, the court having risen for the day, John thought long and carefully about his plan to visit John Fielding. He had not seen the Magistrate since his return from the Colonies, who had now declared themselves independent and were engaged in a bloody war with Britain as a result. During the time when they had not seen each other Fielding's wife Elizabeth—a sweet and friendly soul of whom the Apothecary had been extremely fond—had died whilst visiting relations in the north. Somewhat scandalously, Sir John had married again barely ten weeks later, his bride a certain Mary Sedgely—daughter of a man quite wealthy, or so John believed. It had all come as rather a shock to polite society. But then—if one weighed matters up—the magistrate, though brilliant in mind, was nonetheless impaired in body. It was difficult for a blind man to look after himself and the only practical thing was to marry again, which the lady—in exchange for a title and a home perhaps—was prepared to do. Remembering Joe Jago's lukewarm appraisal of her, John Rawlings hesitated, then took himself to task for being a coward and, entering the Public Office, sent up a note. Some while later a bowing servant approached and invited him to join Sir John in the rooms above.

As he climbed the curving staircase to the private quarters of the Principal Magistrate, John was flooded with memories. The first time he had ever seen the famed Blind Beak had been in one of the smaller rooms. The recollection of an early morning, of sitting alone and hearing the sound of a cane tap-tapping as it approached, of the iciness in his heart as it stopped outside, of the door being flung open and that vastly tall figure looming in the entrance, even now brought an involuntary shiver. The Magistrate could cause a thrill of fear that resonated to this very day. But afterwards they had become firm friends and now John looked forward to seeing his former companion again.

It was not so much the look of the woman already seated in the small parlour but her slightly stuffy smell that struck the Apothecary as he made his way in. The second Lady Fielding—for that was who it had to be—was nondescript to say the least and had the odour of one who had spent many years sewing indoors. A pair of timid eyes looked up nervously from an embroidery frame and then hastily darted their gaze to the floor as John entered. Inwardly he sighed. He knew at once that she was the daughter of some old boy who had been more than anxious to marry her off and had meanwhile used the poor creature as the worst kind of unpaid servant while she remained at home, growing more ancient by the minute. Small wonder indeed that the proposal of marriage from anyone as eminent as the Blind Beak, albeit only a scandalous ten weeks since the death of his first wife, had been seen as a God send. Poor creature, John thought, she had no looks to speak of and no fine clothes to hide herself within. She was like an essay in mouse brown. He gave her a splendid bow and a brilliant smile.

"Forgive my intrusion, Lady Fielding. It was most kind of you to allow me to call."

Her eyes widened with a look of complete panic. "I thought it would be what Sir John would wish."

The Apothecary briefly wondered whether he should kiss her hand but decided that it would probably frighten her even more. He stood, regarding her, waiting for an invitation to sit down. She accidentally dropped her embroidery.

"I am sorry, sir. I do not know where Sir John is. He should be back from court by now. Would you like to be seated while you wait?" she added as an afterthought.

"Yes, I would indeed. How kind of you."

She relapsed into silence once more, snatching her handiwork up from the floor and nervously plucking at the stitches.

"What are you making?" John asked.

"Oh, nothing very important, I'm afraid. I really stitch to give myself something to do."

"You find time weighs heavy on your hands?"

He had not meant it to sound quite so brusque but remembering how Elizabeth Fielding had bustled about the place, busy and merry as a bee, the question almost asked itself. The new Lady Fielding shot him a nervous glance.

"Truth to tell, sir, I am not quite used to this life yet. There are several servants here who seem more than capable and I do not like to interfere."

"You have not settled in perhaps?"

"I don't know for sure. Sir John is so very different from Papa."

John hardly felt in a position to point out that there was a vast difference between a husband and a father when the door opened slowly to reveal the great man himself. But instead of entering, Sir John just stood there, sniffing the air.

"It can't be," he said.

Lady Fielding sat riveted, not choosing to move, while John was gazing in awe. Everyone knew the legend that the Magistrate could recognise a thousand villains by their voices alone but throughout their friendship he had realised that the man could also recognise people—John being one of them—by their particular scent. But surely after all these months it was not possible. Yet Sir John stood in the doorway, his eyes bound by a black ribbon, sniffing in quite a meaningful manner. Turning to Mary Fielding, John raised his finger to his lips and she actually gave him a timid, girlish smile in response.

"You have company, my dear?" asked the Magistrate.

"Yes, yes, I have. I knew you wouldn't mind."

"Mind? Why should I mind? Yet I feel I know your guest."

John smiled and silently rose from his chair. His friend of many years standing spoke.

"Bless me, I know it can't be, but I would swear it is John Rawlings himself. I had heard you were back in this country, you rogue."

John bowed his special bow. "Sir John, it's been such a long time. May I kiss your hand?"

"No, you may not. You may embrace me instead."

And with that he was seized into a great bear hug that lifted him clean off his feet. Meanwhile Mary Fielding had risen from her chair obviously uncertain of what she should do next.

"Would you like me to go?" she whispered to her husband.

"Yes, my dear, if you would ask the kitchen staff to make a special jug of punch for my guest. And then leave us in peace for a half hour or so. I feel quite certain that Mr. Rawlings has something of interest to tell me."

"You are absolutely right in that, sir."

"Then run along, Mary. That is if it doesn't disoblige you."

"Not at all, Sir John," she answered, and hurried out of the room.

The Blind Beak turned to John. "Now, my boy, tell me all your adventures, if you please."

Half an hour later and well through their second jug of punch, John said, "So you see, Sir John, why I am so puzzled. There was nothing whatsoever to link those three incidents yet Samuel half convinced me that there must be some thread that connects them. But I doubted him. To be honest with you I just thought it was extremely bad luck for me that I was present."

The Blind Beak tipped his head back, appearing to stare at the ceiling. For a long while he did not speak, so much so that those who did not know him better would believe he had fallen asleep. Finally he spoke.

"In a way I think you and Sam are both right."

"What do you mean?"

"That it was unfortunate for the perpetrator—imaginary or otherwise—that you of all people should have been present on these occasions. On the other hand, they could just be a trick of fate that seems to have been unlucky enough to have been misconstrued."

John clicked his tongue. "Please don't tease me, sir. I came to you for advice because I am genuinely confused."

"In that case I shall let my instincts rule rather than my reason. Let us suppose that Samuel is probably right. There is a maliciousness behind them that links these three events. The child in the river, you say, was aged four and too young to have done anyone harm, therefore we must look to her parents and find out about them. Next, the unfortunate Miss Feathering strung up and baring her unappetising form all for the startled delight of the patrons of Drury Lane. What enemies had she got? Or did her father or some other relative do someone a mischief? Thirdly we come to the case of the wicked harming of Sir Humphrey Warburton. You have proved that that was deliberate. That someone who knew the route he was taking planted a frightener in the trees so that the horse would spook and throw its rider. If all this is so, then, Mr. Rawlings, you must ferret the wrongdoer out. If Samuel is correct you will be searching for a very twisted mind indeed."

The Blind Beak emptied his glass and held it up for a refill. John poured and saw that the jug was empty.

"You've had the last drop, sir."

For answer Sir John rang a bell and when the servant came promptly ordered another jug of punch to be made.

"This is like old times, sir. How I remember those great days. You and I before a fire talking of this and that."

The Beak sighed. "I miss them too and, of course, I miss Elizabeth."

John, not wishing to mention the newly arrived Lady Fielding, said quietly, "She was a wonderful woman indeed."

"And now somebody new takes her place," the Magistrate said forthrightly.

John felt embarrassed, hardly knowing how to answer. "She seemed quite pleasant to me," he said quietly.

"That is a good word for her—pleasant. The poor soul had a terrible background, of course. A beast of an old father who expected her to wait on him hand and foot. Nobody could have been more delighted than she was when I proposed."

"How did you meet, sir? Surely not through the courts?"

"Yes and no. I was visiting some old acquaintances of mine and saying how useless I was at looking after myself and how I would give a good woman a decent life if only I knew one. They laughed till they wept—I do not joke, my friend—and then suggested Mary Sedgely but warned me that I would have the devil's own job to get her away from her father, who practically insisted that she wiped his posterior for him."

"So how did you?"

"I called on him and just by way of conversation . . ." The magistrate allowed himself a small but naughty chuckle. ". . . I happened to mention that a young Eustace Sedgely had recently come up before me and asked if he was any relation. The old man went as white as a bowl of porridge and denied it. But it was true and he knew that I knew it was. After that there was not much problem about my marriage—except Mary herself."

"She did not want to accept?"

"She was afraid that she would not fit in with my style of life. Which is a shame. Because I was willing to spare her as much time as court life permits."

86

John gave a small, sad smile. It was obvious that poor Mary was an elderly virgin and Sir John had weightier things on his mind than gently wooing a nervous damsel. Perhaps he should invite them to come and stay at Strand-on-the-Green and see if the gentle murmuring of the Thames might help. He cleared his throat and changed the subject.

"So how would you suggest I proceed with my strange problem, sir?"

"I would call on the child's parents as my initial step. I presume you have a note of who they are?"

"Yes, I think I scribbled down an address at the time."

"Then call. Make some excuse—enquiring after the child's continuing health would do—and find out all you can. Then go to see the poor Feathering woman again. After that you should have enough to warrant a further investigation or realise that it was merely a series of unfortunate accidents."

As the servant appeared bearing yet another jug of punch, John stood up. "I will do as you say."

Mary came into view, hovering in the doorway. "Are you going, sir? I've been in the kitchen making a lardy cake. Would you like some?"

"No, I've thought of a better idea. Why don't you and Sir John come to stay at my country home on the river Thames? You can bring a lardy cake with you. I'm sure my daughter would love some."

The poor creature went crimson and her sad eyes, which closely resembled dried sultanas, turned in the magistrate's direction. "If Sir John would like to," she said.

"I would like to very much, my dear. I leave all the arrangements to you and Mr. Rawlings. I am expecting Jago at any moment to discuss some confidential court affairs. Au revoir, my friend. Until we meet again."

And with his head buzzing with a myriad of thoughts the Apothecary bowed his way out.

Chapter Ten

Judging by the house's exterior, John thought, as he stepped out of the coach which he kept for his use when he was in London, the family of the little girl who had plummeted into the river and whose life had been saved by the quick action of Nathaniel Hall, was of the middle-income range. The place was small but serviceable and stood not far from St. Paul's Cathedral in Little Knightrider Street. John guessed that the child's father was employed thereabouts and that she had been staying with relatives or friends when the accident had befallen her. With a friendly smile he pealed the front doorbell. A harassed girl with wisps of lemon coloured hair descending from her mob cap answered and said "Yes," through a row of insubstantial teeth.

"I've called to see your mistress. Is she in by any chance?"

"Yes, she's in the yard at St. Andrews by the Wardrobe."

John stared at her. "Do you mean that she's dead?"

"Been gawn a twelvemonth. Master don't know what to do, run off his feet, he is. I sez he ought to marry again but he don't listen to me. Not his class I'm not."

"Perhaps I could see him?"

"No, he works in Paternoster Row. Has to get up at five to feed all them kinchen their breakfast afore he starts. Poor old fool."

John had a vivid mental picture of a harassed little man thrusting a bottle of milk into a baby's yelling mouth whilst spooning some porridge into another child's greedy maw.

For answer he said, "Oh dear." Then he gave the girl a small bow and thrust a coin at her. She looked at it suspiciously.

"Wot's this for?"

"For your help. I'll go and find your master. What number in Paternoster Row did you say?"

"I didn't, but it's fifty. What d'you want with him?"

The Apothecary smiled pleasantly. "To pass the time of day, that's all."

Before she could question him further he had raised his hat and was half way down the road, realising that he didn't know the name of the man he was looking for. But as fate would have it, it was easy to spot him. A small, anxious-looking person, wearing a pair of spectacles which utterly dominated his face, was scurrying back and forth in the office, muttering under his breath as he did so. John stepped inside the publisher's headquarters smiling broadly.

"Good morning to you."

The glasses slipped down the nose a fraction. "Good morning, sir."

"A very fine place you have here. Am I speaking to the owner?"

"Unfortunately not. I am merely his assistant."

The Apothecary gave a friendly smile. "Was it your firm that was responsible for publishing that marvellous book *Robinson Crusoe* some years ago?"

"Yes, it was actually."

The sad flustered face had relaxed slightly and taken on a look that John recognised; it was the face of a true enthusiast. However ghastly his homelife at least the poor soul quite clearly adored his job.

"A masterpiece, I always thought," said John. "I have often wondered how I would fare if I were marooned on a desert island. In fact I was only saying to Zoffany t'other day …"

"Would that be the painter Zoffany, sir?"

"Yes, it would. I live next door to him, you know. At Strand-on-the-Green in Chiswick."

The strained expression had returned. "Good gracious. D'you know my little daughter had an accident there recently. She fell in the river and would have drowned had it not been for an apprentice who dived in and saved her."

John looked aghast. "Good gracious. I witnessed the whole thing. I was taking the air at the time and turned when I heard the splash. A pretty little girl she is too. Thank goodness that cub Nat Hall had the presence of mind to dive in and save her."

"You know the young lad?"

The Apothecary lied just a little. "Quite well, yes. Why?"

"I would like to reward him in some way."

John thought rapidly.

"Mr… ? I am so sorry, I don't know your name. It's …?"

"Buffitt. Thomas Buffitt."

"Mr. Buffitt, I was wondering if you could spare me an hour and let us go somewhere where we could talk more freely. Perhaps I could take you to an ordinary where we could enjoy more civilised surroundings."

The hunted look overtook poor Thomas's face yet again.

"I have a household of children to look after. Molly, the girl, goes to her dwelling in the evenings leaving my housekeeper, Mrs. Walton, to deal with everything on her own. She does not live in so when I finish here I must hurry back to help her, I'm afraid."

"I quite understand. Then let us go now. We can repair to a tavern and have whatever bill of fare they are offering. Can you be spared for an hour?"

"Josiah, where are you?" Thomas called, and a pimply boy, clearly an apprentice, appeared from the back of the office. Mr. Buffitt was suddenly decisive. "Take over, will you? This gentleman and I are stepping out for a brief while."

The pimply boy looked askance. "But what shall I do if somebody calls, Mr. Buffitt?"

"Tell them that I have had to go out on a business matter and will be back shortly."

"Very good, sir. But what if the Master comes looking for you."

"Tell him that I felt a little faint and had to step into the street for some air."

"Yes, sir. Can I say when you will be returning?"

"No, you may not."

And seizing his hat from a nearby hook, Mr. Buffitt—trying to scowl magnificently—made his way into the street showing more courage than the Apothecary had thought him capable of.

It was a sad tale he had to tell. He had, in the opinion of his parents, married far beneath him, his intended bride a humble sewing girl, but worse—far worse—she had brought a fatherless child into the world before she was seventeen years of age. But the young apprentice Thomas Buffitt—who had for his master the famous William Taylor who had indeed published that masterpiece of English writing *Robinson Crusoe*—would not be deterred. As soon as he was made Free he had married little Lavinia Gwynn and taken her bastard daughter as his own, bringing the child up and giving it a good and loving home. Four more children had followed in rapid succession but the last birth had been too much for Lavinia and she had died a few minutes later.

All this was revealed to John Rawlings after a few glasses of decent burgundy at an ordinary selling a substantial repast of soup, mutton pie with a side plate of herrings, followed by cheese and a heart cake. Poor little Mr. Buffitt shoved food in as if it were balanced on a garden implement and John's mental picture of him feeding the youngsters before himself looked as if it might be startlingly true.

Helping himself to a little more wine, the Apothecary said, "So the eldest girl—the one who fell into the Thames—is not your child then?"

"No she isn't, bless her, though I love Lucinda dearly, just as much as the others. No, I have three boys as well, and then a baby daughter of my own."

"I see. A goodly bunch indeed. I thought your little girl very charming."

"Yes. She was extremely frightened by that river ordeal, you know."

John decided to go straight to the point. "She had the strangest feeling that she was pushed into the Thames. When I told her to be careful in future she answered, 'But I was pushed.'"

"She said much the same thing to me when she returned home."

"Where was she staying did you say?"

"With my sister and her family. They live in Chiswick and had taken the children for a country walk to Strand-on-the-Green."

The Apothecary cast his pictorial memory back and summoned up a rather blurry image of a group of adult women walking in a group, of one or two children playing on the shore, and the head of Lucinda appearing above the water of the fast-flowing Thames. There was no sign of anyone loitering back. And yet … and yet … A lovely woman had come running towards him, looking anxious, but who it was he had no idea. Yet he had the feeling that he had met her somewhere. But where?

"Do you know who your sister had with her?"

Thomas, sinking his teeth well in to a pie, looked somewhat surprised. "No. She lives in a cottage in Sutton Lane. I'm not aware of who her friends are."

John hesitated before asking the question but asked it anyway. "Who is Lucinda's father, do you know?"

Thomas shook his head. "My wife would never tell me his name, though I have my suspicions. Her father worked in the gardens of the Jacquard family. And I believe that a son of the house strolled past their dwelling one day and took a fancy to the young beauty within. Seduced her, then buttoned up his trousers and walked away. All I can say is that he must have been a handsome devil for Lucinda shows every sign of turning into a beauty—and she certainly has his bright blue eyes."

John nodded. "I'm afraid it throws little light on the matter of her being pushed in unless someone from his family wanted rid of his bastard. But that is too fanciful for words. But thank you for telling me anyway."

The Apothecary's heart ached for Thomas but there was nothing further he could say and he spent the rest of the meal in cheery conversation, hoping that the pleasant surroundings would lighten the load that poor Buffitt was bearing so splendidly. But the problem of who pushed Lucinda into the river water worried him all that evening and he determined to ask young Nathaniel Hall if he had noticed anything before the fateful dive that had most certainly saved the poor child's life.

Next day the Apothecary—after having called into his shop in Shug Lane to check that all was well—set off by water for his country home. Yet all the time through that long and beautiful journey he worried over the three incidents—or were they just coincidences?—in

93

which he had become recently involved. The idea that Lucinda's dubious parentage had something to do with the matter constantly nagged at him, yet John could see no connection between that and the other two. However, when he stepped through his front door, glad to see his beautifully situated house once more, he saw a letter from Joe Jago lying on the hall table. Before he had so much as removed his travelling cloak, the Apothecary had ripped off the seal and was reading the words written in Jago's fine hand. Then he chuckled. Their plan had succeeded. Samuel Gottlieb had been contacted about the monoculars that he had recently offered for sale. It had been arranged that the interested party was going to call on the fence in two days' time. Did Mr. Rawlings wish to be present?

"Nothing would keep me away," the Apothecary muttered under his breath, then the chatter of female voices from the small drawing room had him opening the door to see who had called.

She was as fresh as morning, the girl who looked up as he went in. The scents of peony and wood sage hung in the air, the lights in the room were dappled with the shimmer of the river, a pair of eyes as deep a shade of lilac and as full of joy as any he had ever seen, gazed laughingly into John's. He gazed back dumbstruck but inside he was giving a tremendous shout. Middle-aged he might be but that did not stop the stirring of his blood, the rhythm of his heartbeat, that wonderful ecstatic motion of his feet that actually danced a pace or two on the spot. As for the girl, she smiled all the deeper, her beautiful cherry-ripe mouth curving up over her pretty white teeth.

"Father," said Rose, standing up. "May I present Miss Hyacinth Jacquard who has moved to Chiswick from school in London to join her brothers. Hyacinth, this is my father, John Rawlings."

The girl curtsied, lovely and sweet, and John gave a bow full of admiration as if he had been a young apothecary on the brink of life.

Hyacinth held out her hand and he kissed it swiftly. It was a moment cut in crystal and one that he would treasure for a long time. Yet he knew that this brief idyll must end, that dreary old common sense had to prevail. He who had loved well and not always wisely was more than aware that golden moments such as he had just enjoyed were not meant to last, that the dreams of older people were, like brittle glass, easily shattered. Yet not even this clarity of vision could take away his immense feeling of happiness and another thought that entered his brain. Jacquard? Surely that had been the name Buffitt had mentioned.

Clearing his throat, John said, "How do you do, Miss Hyacinth? I do hope that you will enjoy living in beautiful Chiswick."

She looked at him and he noticed the delicate structure of her chin. "Thank you, sir," she answered. "I find it quite delightful so far."

"How long have you been here?"

"Four weeks. Miss Rose and I met one morning when we were both out taking the air."

"How prettily put," he said, and smiled his crooked smile. After all, he thought, he could admire the view and gain some pleasure from that innocent pastime alone.

Rose spoke. "I was just going to invite Hyacinth's family and ask them if they would like to come and dine with us one day."

"An excellent plan."

Hyacinth disengaged her hand from John's and said, "I have no mama, I fear. I have moved to Chiswick to be with my brothers. My father died recently and my eldest brother is head of the family now."

"I'm sorry to hear that. Whereabouts are you living?"

"Not far from Chiswick House. My eldest brother works for the Duke of Devonshire who is occasionally in residence there as you probably know."

But John was not thinking of the Devonshires and their extraordinary lifestyle. Instead he was worrying about the name Jacquard which he knew he had heard only recently.

The day turned into a glorious evening, the sort that only a fine early summer can produce. The Thames murmured a lullaby to the setting sun and every house was bathed in a gentle glow as the great orb sank away. Walking back with his daughter and her new friend, the Apothecary turned inland towards the great Chiswick House and came to a road which led towards that extraordinary Palladian villa.

It had originally been built next door to a Jacobean mansion, but the current owners—the Duke of Devonshire and his amazing wife Georgiana—having chosen to live in the villa, had decided to build on two extra wings, one on each side, to make sufficient room for the members of their household. These were in the final stages of completion but the Apothecary, by dint of narrowing his eyes, could still make out the lines of the stark symmetrical beauty of the original structure, built by Lord Burlington, returning from a Grand Tour and deeply enamoured of the Italianate style. Yet the Apothecary's eyes were drawn to the Jacobean house which had once, in its hey-day, been a splendid place in which to dwell. Why did it—on this glorious afternoon—cause him to grow suddenly cold, he wondered.

Chapter Eleven

Samuel Gottlieb, swathed in innumerable shawls, lit another candle as John and Joe Jago made their way into his shop, peering a little in the sudden gloom.

"There, there, my gentlemen," came the glutinous voice, "this should help you see a little better."

"Our eyes are sharp enough, you old charlatan," Joe answered. "But thank you for the thought."

They made their way to the counter and stood silently, John copying Joe's action which was to stand still and wait for the fence to speak. Eventually Samuel rumbled a laugh and adjusted his coverings, throwing a strange smell of Old Araby and numerous Eastern brothels into the air. He spoke.

"Enough of playing cats got our tongues. I did as you instructed, Mr. Jago. It turns out that he was a very nice young fellow, well dressed and with a good speaking voice. Pretty much what you expected, I believe."

Joe gave a laugh. "He came in answer to your advertisement I take it."

"You take correctly. But let me just say here and now, Mr. Jago, that I think he had nothing to do with causing the affair in the theatre, honest truth to the One Above who sees all." He rolled his bulbous eyes heavenwards, displaying a rather frightening amount of white. "He had such a friendly air about him. Of course, I do not pretend to be so good a judge of character as your excellent self."

"Never mind the young man. Tell me exactly what happened."

"I put an advertisement in the Advertiser—" Samuel roared with laughter at the pun and his shawls slipped about him releasing another peculiar odour. "—and he sees it and comes to enquire, says he wants to buy them for a present. That's all there was to it. But I done what you told me to do, dear friend. I made him sign a receipt for the transaction. And here it is." A skinny arm appeared from under the coverings and thrust a piece of paper under Joe's nose. "Read for yourself."

"Good gracious," John exclaimed, peering over Joe's shoulder. "I don't believe it."

"What?" asked Joe.

"It's someone I think I know."

Joe held the flimsy note up to the light to see it better. "Robert Rotmuller?" he asked aloud.

"Yes, unless Rotmuller is a more common name than I thought. Also it is very similar to Miss Feathering's light-o'-love—Robert Miller."

"It gives an address here, Oakridge House."

"That proves it. He must be related to the baron. Is it merely a coincidence?"

Joe smiled in the candlelight. "Well, well. Ain't it just a small world—or is it? Just you keep your ears and eyes open and then I'll be obliged if you would seek me out. We must have a further discussion about matters."

"This," answered John Rawlings, trying to resist the sudden coldness of his spine, "is getting too interesting for belief."

* * *

John entered the home of Miss Hyacinth Jacquard, feeling fairly certain that amongst her brothers was a worthless scoundrel, the father of the wretched child who had been pushed into the Thames. During the night it had come back to him. Of course! Poor little Mr. Buffitt had told him that his late wife has probably been the victim of one of the sons of the family. However, the person whom John particularly wanted to meet had made his apologies and was absent. Mr. Giles Jacquard, so his sister Hyacinth informed John and his daughter, had been called away on urgent business and therefore could present nothing but his regrets. Her other brothers, however, loomed large. The eldest and very much the head, was Sir James Jacquard. It turned out that he had a tiny wee wife, a rather dismal little creature John thought her, with very dark hair pulled back tightly from a waxen face and a pair of huge, staring eyes. Her name was Louisa and she spoke softly and with little inflexion. Next came brother Paul, a sturdy ox of a young man, but who had nothing of interest to add to the conversation. Next had come the missing Giles, followed by Charles, the youngest of the brood, a lanky tall youth with a sweet smile and an engaging manner. This last named quite lit up when he saw Rose and engaged her in a conversation about hunting dogs, in which she had no interest whatsoever, for the remainder of the afternoon. John felt slight boredom as the host, Sir James, launched into a story of his family's exploits, none of which seemed particularly exciting. As soon as the meal was finished he asked politely if he could look round the garden and Louisa, staring and startled, gave him permission to explore.

"Do you want someone to accompany you, Mr. Rawlings?" Paul asked politely.

"No, no, please don't break up the party. I shall be back in ten minutes. I only want a breath of air."

He had really wanted to look at Chiswick House more closely, and wonder at the wilder exploits of Georgiana, Duchess of Devonshire, and try to discover whether she was in residence. The gardens of Lovegrave House, one of the several grace-and-favour dwellings that stood close to the main building and in which dwelt the Jacquards, were near his objective and he broke into a rapid stride. But then his attention was caught by the gloomy magnificence of the Jacobean mansion that lay beyond Chiswick House, its façade dark and empty, its size and grandeur a hollow reminder of earlier days. And yet, a solitary candle was flickering inside the building as someone walked by an unshuttered window. The Apothecary's interest was immediately aroused and he could not help himself, breaking into a fast trot as he passed the villa and drew closer to the magnificent old building. Uninhabited it might officially be but there was definitely someone within because as he drew nearer John could see that several candles had been lit inside. He was just approaching the vast old doorway when to his surprise it flew open. A female figure stood there, peering anxiously into the twilight.

"Can you help me?" she called to him.

"Of course. What's the matter?"

"My companion has fainted and I cannot lift her up off the floor."

"I'll do what I can."

He had entered the house by the great front door—or middle entry—and a quick glance to the right revealed a wonderfully carved musicians gallery with intricate fretwork situated high above, a beautiful example of Jacobean craftsmanship. John could just picture the players, sweating profusely, as beneath them the guests danced. At floor level were two doors each situated at the furthest corners of the room. And it was in one of these that—just for a second—something hovered, something dark, hardly there, but which sent a shiver down his spine. The next second it was gone. He stared, wondering if he had imagined it, but his attention was drawn immediately to a woman lying unconscious on the floor. John stooped and raised her top half in his arms. Her eyelashes fluttered and she groaned.

"Madam, you look very poorly. Let me lay you down on this chaise longue."

Her companion, who had called him in, spoke. "The dear soul has been much taken up with strolling round the building works at the villa. I fear that she has overdone it."

Thinking to himself that she must have put in a lot of travelling in the last few hours, as he had last seen her near Dorking—unless this was not the Duchess of Derwent but her *alter ego*, her identical twin—the Apothecary scrabbled in his pocket and drew out an ancient bottle of salts that had been nestling there since he last put the coat on. He held it beneath the lady's nose and she obligingly coughed and opened her eyes. She stared at John blankly.

"I do not know you, sir," she said.

"Well I most certainly know you, madam. Lady Derwent if I am not mistaken."

Her companion laughed. "A common mistake, sir. This is her twin sister, Lady Lovell. Her husband is the viscount."

The Apothecary stared. "Forgive me. You are an exact image, which is something you must tire of hearing."

"I am a little but it cannot be helped." She tried to sit up but put a hand to her forehead saying, "Oh dear, everything is going black again. I don't know what is the matter with me." She reached for the salts.

"I do," her friend answered robustly, "if you will spend the afternoon wandering about during your first three months you have only yourself to blame."

Lady Lovell rolled her eyes. "La, so my secret is out. You are such a chatterbox Penelope. Now everyone will know what is going on."

101

John bowed. "I am hardly everyone, dear madam. Nor am I particularly talkative. I am in fact a trained apothecary and used to dealing with those members of the opposite sex who are *enceinte*. Indeed in my time I have delivered the odd babe or two. Your secret as far as I am concerned is perfectly safe."

A tiny little smile pulled at the corners of Lady Lovell's mouth. "I stand corrected, Apothecary. Please excuse my ill manners. I must say these salts of yours are damned fine." She took another sniff then handed him back the bottle.

"Thank you for saying so. Now, my lady, if you would be kind enough to let me give you some advice. Let me suggest that in your present condition you eat nutritious food, exercise sensibly, and cut back on the amount of alcohol."

She wrinkled her nose. "Sounds deadly dull."

"But wise."

"Oh pouffe! Who wants to be wise? I never am."

And looking at her sharply for a moment, the Apothecary thought that under all her obvious beauty there did indeed lurk a slightly ruthless streak.

He returned to the party to find that—thanks to several bottles of extremely decent claret—it had warmed up. Hyacinth was playing the piano and singing a rather risqué duet with a male friend of one of her brothers, while Rose was having a very amusing conversation with Charles Jacquard. Louisa Jacquard sat alone and so it was to her side that John made his way.

"That's a wonderful Jacobean house I came across. A splendid building."

"Yes, it is rather fine. Alas, though, doomed. The duke has ordered its demolition."

"Really? Why?"

"Because they are building two extensions on to the villa. The house will, frankly, be in the way."

"So it stands empty—or does it?"

"Oh yes, officially. Though I have heard rumours that Georgiana—the duchess—lets some of her friends stay there."

"I think I met one of them tonight."

But the conversation was abruptly terminated as Sir James, very much the genial host, joined them, pressing John to have some excellent brandy and commenting on what a beautiful young woman Rose was.

Later—the evening finished and done and extremely revealing—the Apothecary and his daughter walked home beneath a gigantic sweep of stars that shone and glistened not only in the late spring sky but reflected in the gurgling flow of the Thames. It looked as if a magician had fallen into the river and his star bespangled cloak was glittering just beneath the surface. There was the murmur of the water whispering a strange mystic song and Rose cupped her ear in order to hear it better. But the sound was drowned by a burst of laughter coming from one of the riverside inns and the moment of mystery was shattered and gone. The girl smiled at her father but he made no reply, too intent on thinking of the extraordinary events that he had recently witnessed and wondering if there was any possibility at all that in some mysterious way they could indeed be connected.

Chapter Twelve

The following morning was splendid and fine, and John was pleased to hear at about eleven o'clock the sound of Zoffany and a boat-load of canvases returning. He hurried to the front door and was immediately greeted by the painter who kissed him enthusiastically on both cheeks, ordering the boy who was helping him to carry the paintings into his house, and asked John if he could come in for a cup of coffee.

"Most certainly, my dear friend. I have a great deal to tell you."

"And I, alas, very little to recount. Except that I flirted delightfully with your friend's wife Jocasta while he was away with you."

"Good. I am sure she enjoyed it. Now come in and settle down."

Several cups later Zoffany was totally up to date with all that had transpired since the moment they had parted company. He sat in aston-ishment and finally asked breathlessly, "You say that Sir Humphrey's horse was deliberately caused to rear? And the other two incidents? That poor child that could have drowned and the attack by strangers on the woman at Drury Lane Theatre—what a bunch of villainous people are abroad these days."

"I don't know for sure, Johan, but it seems to be a terrible series of events. Yet there is nothing that I can grasp together. Do you have any thoughts?"

"No, nothing. But if I were in your shoes I would try to find out which one of the Jacquard boys fathered that small girl."

"But," John answered wretchedly, "Buffitt—her adopted father—only told me that it was the son of a family with a big house in Chiswick. It could be anyone. It's not necessarily the Jacquards, though I admit that I do suspect them."

"Amateur though I may be, I shall work on your behalf, believe me. People gossip, you know, when they are sitting still to have their portraits painted."

Mentally the Apothecary raised an eyebrow but he could only thank his neighbour and ask him to do his best. Then he retired to his study to think. This, however, proved to be useless and eventually he went downstairs, put on his hat, picked up his walking cane, and strode out to the riverside. As he paced along he thought hard. It occurred to him that the only possible connection between these three completely random victims—the child Lucinda, Miss Feathering and Sir Humphrey Warburton, none of whom knew each other—was that they were all three connected with some incident which had happened in the past. But what could be so terrible that some shadowy figure could now be wreaking revenge on them all? What monstrous thing could they have done? And if—IF—his mad conjecture proved correct, however could he find the person responsible?

Who was the one who could tell him most? It had to be Sir Humphrey. Lucinda was too young, Miss Feathering too delightfully silly, but Sir Humphrey might be the best bet. John gulped in a great breath of fresh river air and decided that this very day he would write to the man's address in London and ask if he may call on him to enquire about his health. This being decided, the Apothecary, his mind much clearer as to his plan of action, headed for home.

A few days later and he had returned to London and had a street directory in his hands. Running his eye swiftly down the addresses—they were arranged alphabetically—he came upon what he wanted: 4, King Street, Piccadilly, Sir Humphrey Warburton, Bart. John wondered as he strode out from Nassau Street whether there was, or had been, a Lady Warburton at some stage, though he rather thought not. He was still wondering when he rang the bell a short while later but did not glean any further information other than that Sir Humphrey was not available. Putting on his 'Honest Citizen' face, the Apothecary was informed that Sir Humphrey's destination had been Hanover Street in the Long Acre, to which he had been carried by servants. Recollecting immediately that the great actor Samuel Foote had walked on a false leg made for him by a puppeteer in that part of the world, John hailed a passing chair and was carried in state to Covent Garden.

The shop outside which he was standing had the most incredible things in the window—a great and glorious mixture of the surgical and the silly. Puppets, fantastical and funny, jostled strange-looking prosthetic instruments, together with clay pipes for smoking. There was everything, John thought, to see one through from the cradle to the grave. Before he had left Baron Rotmuller's house he had chatted with one of Mr. Bromfeild's assistants and found out that the great man always ordered false limbs from a shop in Hanover Street—once he had ascertained whether his patient was going to survive the operation, of course.

The Apothecary had thought the place's proprietor most likely to be a man of serious mind, but indeed not. He was a puppet master first and foremost. Grinning clowns, cheeks adorned with two spots of red paint, cuddled up to Jack Tars, whose mobile legs could obviously do a hornpipe in the hands of a master puppeteer. A milkmaid, fully articulated, was accompanied by a cow with long eyelashes, who allowed herself to be milked for a few seconds and then raised an elegant leg and kicked over the pail. John's eye wandered on to the prosthetics. Legs, arms and disembodied hands made rather a grisly collection, the hands in particular being squat, the colour of tanned flesh. It was difficult to imagine their usage. If someone had been unfortunate enough to lose a hand in an accident, then the fake one could be strapped on at the wrist. But movement in it would have been impossible, it would merely have been for show. The Apothecary was pondering this when a familiar cry came from inside the shop which prompted him to open the door and walk in. The shout was from Sir Humphrey Warburton and came from a back room. John hurried towards it but was stopped by a young assistant.

"Please sir, no further. One of our clients is in there with Mr. Bromfeild, the surgeon, and Mr. Addison, the proprietor."

"I was present and indeed assisted when Sir Humphrey recently underwent surgery. I am sure he would not mind me joining him," the Apothecary answered, speaking above the level of his normal voice.

As he thought a shouted answer said, "Is that Mr. Rawlings? If so, please step in and see what marvellous contraption Mr. Addison has made for Sir Humphrey."

"Thank you, sir. I should be most interested to observe." He looked at the assistant politely. "If it is alright with you."

Somewhat disgruntled, the other gave a curt nod.

In the adjoining room Sir Humphrey, the stump so well healed that it was barely recognisable as that earlier mass of torn and ragged flesh, was struggling into two circular leather shoulder straps which were joined onto the prosthesis at its top. Surgeon Bromfeild, examining the artificial leg through a magnifying glass, was clearly delighted with Mr. Addison's work.

"This is excellent, my friend. I am delighted that the knee bends so splendidly. What do you think, Sir Humphrey?"

"It is masterly—all I need is to be able to walk on it."

"Go on, sir," urged Mr. Addison. "Take a step forward. I will catch you if you fall."

But Sir Humphrey didn't fall. Instead he took one faltering step after another until he had slowly but surely paced the length of the room. The three men watching him burst into spontaneous applause.

"That was excellent," said the Apothecary. "A brilliant piece of work from all three of you gentlemen. I am honoured to be in such accomplished company."

"Thank you for your help, young man," said Bromfeild, and waved a careless hand.

John was more pleased with the soubriquet than anything else. Once outside he helped Sir Humphrey—limping but determined—into his coach, then stood looking a little helpless. As he had hoped, the baronet leaned forward.

"Can I give you a lift, Mr. Rawlings? Or are you taking a stroll?"

"I would very much appreciate a ride back to King Street. As a matter of fact, I was on my way to see you."

"Really?"

"Yes, sir. There is something important—but private—that I wish to tell you."

"Now," said Sir Humphrey, "what on earth can that be?"

John came straight to the point. "Your accident, sir. Your horse reared and threw you because it was deliberately frightened. A childish cut-out skeleton—life size—had been planted and was blowing in the trees. Your animal saw it and reacted violently. And you weren't

108

the only one. Two other people—of whom you probably have never heard—were subjected to violent treatment at roughly the same time and I can't help wondering if all three incidents are related."

Sir Humphrey looked extremely puzzled. "But how could they be if I don't know the people concerned?"

John tried a new tack. "Do you come from a large family, sir?"

"No I don't as a matter of fact. I had one sister—Cecilia, known as Cecily. After my mother died my father did not marry again. I personally have not married…" John wondered why he was not surprised "… but I have a great many harum-scarum nephews and a couple of nieces. Does that help you? Now who were these people who were also discomforted?"

Though he had been taught by the Blind Beak when he had first started to work assisting the Runners never to reveal too much, now John broke the rule. In as brief a way as possible he described how Lucinda had been pushed into the river and Miss Feathering had been hanged upside down in Drury Lane theatre. At this last description Sir Humphrey had winced.

"Poor wretched woman. I'm sorry but the mental picture is excruciating."

Shortly afterwards John left the conversation, almost empty handed. The one piece of information he had received was the name of Sir Humphrey's sister's family. They were the Redwoods and if John's distant memories were correct they had quite a reputation in the gaming hells. He made a mental note to himself to call on Serafina, who at one stage of her life had occupied every gaming establishment in London, to see if she could give him any information.

Yet he was in a strange mood when he hired a wherryman at White Hall Stairs to take him upriver to Strand-on-the-Green, remaining silent through most of the journey. There was some connection between the incidents—he felt sure of it—yet it was going to be a puzzle almost impossible to solve.

He arrived at home to find Rose buzzing round the kitchen like a bee, making cakes and puddings and giving instructions to the cook who looked terribly put out as a result.

"I didn't realise you were interested in domesticity, darling."

She waved a flour covered wooden spoon at him. "I do vow and declare that you had forgotten the twins are coming back from school tomorrow. You really are quite hopeless, Papa."

"I admit it—and all I can say is beg pardon."

She whirled round and planted a kiss on his cheek and John, remembering how she had winked at him when she had first been presented, lying on a cushion, freshly washed and dressed but only a few hours old, grinned at her and said, "I know I'm not very good but I do try."

"Very trying," she answered, and winked at him once more. "By the way, the woman you attended the other night—the one who is staying in the old house, a friend of the duchess—has written to you. It is on the tray in the hall."

The letter was brief but to the point. Lady Lovell begged the Apothecary to come to her once more. The fear that she might lose the child was preying on her mind and so far nobody other than a few close friends knew of her pregnancy. Could he come as soon as he returned from town? John called out to Rose.

"I am going out again. As soon as I have packed my medical bag."

"And whom, may I ask, is this in aid of?"

"Never question a man of medicine when he is about his private affairs," John answered, attempting to look severe.

"Oh I see, it's a secret. I shall return to my cooking and say no more."

"Then that's as well," he answered, and made her a mocking bow.

The house looked gracious but grave on this dank and downcast evening. John had walked the short distance to Chiswick House and had got thoroughly soaked as a result. Trying to manage an umbrella and a bag of herbal remedies had not been easy in the steady downpour which had now set in. Therefore he was glad when a servant answered the bell of the neighbouring Jacobean mansion and promptly showed him into the Great Hall. As before, John was left alone and once again a feeling of deep unease descended on him. For all its decaying beauty he was not comfortable in the house's once impressive surroundings. He sat down on the edge of a chair and looked about him. And then his attention was drawn to the vast window opposite which he was sitting. It stretched from ceiling to floor, bringing light to the Great Hall, covered with an intricate design of coloured glass. And pressed against the glass, two pale hands resting on either side, was a face. Yet it was not a human face but a parody of such a thing.

John froze with fear, staring motionless at the creature gazing inward. It had two eyes above a husk of nose and a twisted terrible mouth that seemed to be shaped in a permanent grin. It was female, that much he could make out. Yet, afraid though he was, it seemed that the creature was also frightened. Its damaged eyes widened, one hand flew to its contorted mouth, and before it fled into the rain-filled afternoon it pulled a veil over its satire of human features, then vanished.

The Apothecary stood up, shaking uncontrollably, and the next minute a voice said, "You seem somewhat out of sorts, sir."

He wheeled round to see that Viscountess Lovell had entered silently and was regarding him with a rather strange expression on her face.

"I am sorry, madam. I thought I saw someone staring in at me. Probably my imagination."

It wasn't, of course, and he knew it but she—after a sharp intake of breath – played along with him.

"Yes. It is the pattern on that window, particularly smudged on a dull evening with the rain pouring. Guests often think that they can see things. But thank you for coming in such terrible weather."

John pulled himself together. "It's my pleasure, viscountess. Now tell me exactly what is bothering you."

"I had a slight discharge but that seems to have gone now."

"And that is all?"

She sat down and motioned to him to do likewise. "Actually, I need someone to talk to. Someone outside my social circle but someone I can trust." The Apothecary remained silent. "I feel that perhaps you might be the right person."

He nodded and spread his hands. "I am bound by certain rules that govern all of us who deal with the sick."

"And they are?"

"Not to speak of things we learn about them to any other individual."

"If what I say remains private between the two of us it would be very much appreciated."

"Let me assure you that anything you say will be treated as utterly confidential."

"I fear that I will lose this child and I need to have it desperately."

"Because of your husband's title?"

"Partly that but also to bring back his waning attention to me."

"Good gracious. Has he met somebody else?"

She smiled and shrugged her elegant shoulders. "No, it is not that so much, though I expect he has. It's more his addiction to the gaming tables."

"That seems common enough," John answered and smiled a little wryly, wondering how many women had uttered the same words to him in his time.

"He is rarely at home," Lady Lovell continued. "I see him at most about once a week. It is a miracle that this child was conceived at all."

She said it in such a dry voice that the Apothecary had to hide a sad grimace, despite his earlier frightening experience. He thought how beautiful a creature she was, never to have been loved alas.

"But do you care for him still?" he asked.

"It was a marriage of convenience for both parties, arranged by our parents. And then, more fool me, I fell passionately in love with the wretch. Heaven alone knows why."

"What is his background?"

"He is the Viscount Lovell, heir to the Earl of Cumbria, though that has only come about by two feeble cousins of his dying of fever. He was just plain Michael Redwood when I married him, with no title in sight."

"And did that worry you?"

"Not in the least."

"I see," John answered, and nodded again.

"I would gladly renounce the whole title business and have a true lover—and now I am anxious about his baby."

"The baby," the Apothecary answered firmly, "will be quite alright if you take care of yourself, madam. And that I most certainly will see that you do."

They smiled at each other, an understanding born between them.

Chapter Thirteen

A letter from Samuel brightened the next morning. It announced
that he was coming to call on the Apothecary and would take the
stagecoach to London and another coach to Kew where he would
stay the night. He would then make his way by water and arrive at
John's in time to have a midday snack. Glancing at the date the letter
was written, the Apothecary realised that Samuel would be arriving
today and laughed aloud at the way his old friend took it for granted
that he would be welcome, which of course he always was. Then John
remembered that his twin sons would be coming home from school
this same day. Cursing himself for being so forgetful, he called out
to Rose. She appeared, somewhat to his surprise dressed in a smart
blue cloak and matching feathered hat.

Before he had had time to speak she said crisply, "I'm just off to
town to meet the boys, Papa. Don't worry, Wilkins is coming with
me. We shall pick them up at the Gloucester Coffee House and bring
them back by boat. And please don't apologise. You are the best of
parents and the worst of them as well."

"I don't know whether to beam with pleasure or break down
and weep."

"Try doing both," she answered, smiling despite herself. "And be sure to order a good dinner to be served tonight. We don't want Samuel going hungry."

John caught her hand. "My darling girl, please don't be angry with me. I know it was very remiss of me to forget that my sons were returning, but quite honestly I had rather an eerie experience last night that has put me somewhat out of countenance."

Immediately she was all attention as he had guessed she would be. "Tell me about it—but be brief. I want to be there waiting when the stage pulls in."

"It was while I was attending Lady Lovell. I was alone in the Great Hall of the old Jacobean mansion that stands close to Chiswick House. It was pouring with rain and as I looked out of the big window that runs from floor to ceiling something looked back at me from outside."

"What do you mean exactly?"

"It was a face—but a grotesque one. Its features had been knocked all awry. Quite honestly, it terrified me."

"Was it a human being?"

"I don't know. I think it could have been. Why?"

"Because Nat mentioned something to me the other day."

The Apothecary raised a mental eyebrow but said nothing other than, "And what might that have been?"

"That he was taking a short cut through the extensive grounds of Chiswick House and saw something that scared him."

"Go on."

"It was a woman. He caught a glimpse of her face before she covered it with a heavy veil. He said it was ghastly."

"In what way?"

"Like you described. But, Papa, I dare not talk about it now. I will be late for the boys. Next term is their last at school, then they leave

115

for Oxford remember. If remembering will not be too foreign to your nature." This last said with a cheeky grin that wrinkled her nose so that he could not take offence. "Now I'll be off. And you await the appearance of the great Mr. Swann." And Rose departed leaving John no option but to smile and shake his head.

The arrival of Samuel an hour later, was—as always—not without drama. He slipped on the landing stage and would have plunged into the Thames had it not been for the quick thinking of the boatman who—with almost superhuman strength—grabbed him and straightened him up before any damage could be done. John, hearing the commotion, stepped out of his front door and seizing his friend firmly by the elbow guided him indoors. Samuel straightened his wig and wiped his sweating face with a large handkerchief.

"I say, that was a near thing."

John smiled as he bent over the decanter and poured out two shots of brandy. "Here, drink this old friend. And sit down do. That was quite an entrance you made."

"I thought I was going to have to swim for it."

"Not easy when fully clad."

"No." Samuel emptied the glass in one go and held it out for a refill. "My goodness, John, what a splendid position this beautiful house is in. You must be tremendously happy here. I quite envy you."

"But Foxfire Hall is glorious."

"Yes, you're right, of course. But I do miss the good company of yourself and my other friends."

"Yes, I'm sure. You must come and visit London more often."

"I should like that." Samuel looked around. "But where is young Rose? How old is she now? I was trying to work it out the other day."

"She's twenty-two and has several youthful suitors yearning for her."

And John proceeded to describe to his old friend the apprentice Nathaniel Hall, together with the master shoemaker they had met on the night of Miss Feathering's embarrassment, and the young widower who was now running the Apothecary's shop for him.

"And those are the ones I know about."

Samuel chuckled. "A beautiful woman has many admirers, John. It's something you will have to get used to."

"When the beauty is one's own daughter it is not so easy."

"I wish I had a guinea for every father who has thought the same."

With this lively banter the afternoon passed pleasantly and then at six o'clock when both he and Samuel had gone upstairs to change for dinner there was a noise from the hallway below. He heard the delightful voice of one of the twins saying, "I love this house. Papa chose well when he bought this," and slipping into his satin coat, John raced down the stairs to meet them.

They looked up as they heard his footsteps and John saw—somewhat to his chagrin—that they were now taller than he was. They were also deliciously alike and darkly handsome, far more like Elizabeth than their father. They both swept a bow as he approached—good manners never forgotten—then rushed to embrace him. Temporarily lifted off his feet, the Apothecary laughed with indescribable joy. Two pairs of eyes creased with amusement as James and Jasper squeezed him tightly, adding to the general delight. Then Samuel came hurrying down the stairs with cries of, "I don't believe it. You've grown into veritable grenadiers. Gracious me alive." And there was much more mirth and jollity—and a few merry japes.

The boys were now sixteen years old with identical velvety dark hair, each tied back in a tail and adorned with a smart bow. Their eyes were bright but had a slightly knowing look which their father had not noticed before and which set him wondering a little. They were highly protective of their half-sister, Rose, who in comparison with their muscularity and manliness seemed as if she were made of porcelain.

"Well, chaps, what are the plans for the future?" Samuel asked.

"We leave school at the end of next term and then start at Oxford in the following autumn."

"What are you reading?"

"Law," answered one of them. "We both are."

"It appeals to us," added the other.

"So no-one is going to follow in your footsteps, John."

"It would appear not, Samuel. But frankly I don't care very much. As long as the twins are happy they can put on wigs and gowns and frighten the life out of the hapless victims who appear as witnesses for the other side."

There was a shout of laughter and John felt a moment of such intense joy that he had to blow his nose to hide the fact that tears were filling his eyes.

It was a delicious, wine-filled evening, during which the twins teased Rose about her marriage plans.

"I have none," she said, her cheeks very pink and her eyes luminous in the candlelight.

"So who is this Nat person you keep referring to?" asked Jasper, leaning back in his chair, his face quizzical and amused.

"He is an apprentice in his final year."

"And also the son and heir of a wealthy local brewer," added John. "Learning his trade from the bottom up, which I think is admirable."

"Hear, hear," chorused the twins, who were by now slightly tipsy and thoroughly enjoying themselves.

"Do you remember how we used to see our mother swimming in the sea, Papa?" asked Jasper.

Rose moved very slightly, ready to stop the conversation if it were going to upset anybody.

"It's all right," John said to her. Then, "What were you going to say, my dear?"

"That the last time we saw her swimming was the final time. I think it meant that we were growing up and adults don't have the same ability to see things as children."

Thinking of the terrible face that he had glimpsed on the previous evening, John replied, "I'm not sure that I agree with you about that. I believe that certain people have a gift which remains with them all their lives."

James took up the story. "The school had a trip for the older boys to study seaside history. There was a telescope rigged up on shore and we all took turns looking through it. When it came to my turn I saw Mama, she was quite far out but swimming strongly. I called her name and at that she looked at me and blew a kiss. But it was rather sad because I knew it meant farewell. Then James looked and he saw her too and she did the same to him—and that really was goodbye."

In his mind's eye he saw again the face of the woman who had for so many years of his adult life obsessed him, and who had taken her own when the cruel crab of cancer had bitten too deep. She and her old horse Sabre had leapt towards the sun, over the cliff edge and into the sea below, to end it all before the pain became too much to bear. And ever since her twin sons—though they never knew the exact details of Elizabeth's suicide—had imagined they had seen her swimming in the sea. Or was it imagination? John deep in his heart hoped that those wonderful young men had glimpsed her and that the experience had somehow enriched their youthful lives.

That night he slept in a happy house, filled by his family and his faithful friend. He lay awake for a few brief minutes, listening to the sounds of the place settling down, creaking wood from the stairs, soft snoring from Samuel, then he was lulled to dreams by the gentle voice of the sweet-banked Thames as it lapped at the walkway which ran beside the river.

As soon as he had breakfasted, John made a call to the dwelling next door where he discovered Zoffany yawning over a cup of coffee. Once he had uttered the ritualistic morning greetings, John accepted a cup himself, then sat down opposite the painter.

"Tell me," he said without preamble, "everything that you can about the twin sisters, Lady Derwent and Lady Lovell. It is not that I am being inquisitive but have been called in about a medical matter—nothing serious—by Lady Lovell. What do you know about her husband? And also that ogre of a man, the Duke of Derwent?"

Zoffany gave a snort of laughter and droplets of liquid fell upon the tablecloth. "I take it you don't like him?"

"I think he is one of the most overbearing creatures I have ever set eyes on."

And briefly John told the painter the story of all that had taken place since they had last seen one another, including the riding calamity which had smashed Warburton's leg.

"Poor Sir Humphrey. What a terrible thing. But you say he has been given a false leg now?"

"Yes. Surgeon Bromfeild is a genius. He ordered a prosthetic to be specially made for him by a puppet master in Covent Garden. It fits him like a glove. Samuel Foote, the actor, also has a wooden limb, well concealed I think."

"Well, well, I never knew. How interesting too that you have met Baron Rotmuller. Apparently he is a member of a large banking family who are well known throughout Europe. What is he like?"

John laughed. "Quite likeable in his way. But it's not him I came to talk about. I really want as much information as you can give me about those two extraordinary women. Everything you know."

Zoffany smiled. "Of course. Let me start with Lady Derwent's husband, the duke. He is indeed one of the nastiest people in the world, or so rumour has it. He was according to his old nurse—who I painted once—a spoilt and ridiculous brat, rude, without manners, but a good dancer. Anyway, the girls' father—who is Winterlight, the jobbing painter—was more than anxious for them to marry well and was delighted when the heir to the Duke of Derwent made an offer for his daughter's hand. She was miserable, of course. Tried running away from home but was caught and locked in her room, so rumour has it. Apparently she wept all though the wedding ceremony. The other sister, your patient, did not react so violently. She was completely cool with her husband—treated him more as a joke than anything else—but he, lucky fellow, unexpectedly, after the death of two sickly cousins, came in line for a title."

"So she told me."

"An incredibly effete young man who spends his entire life gambling."

"And whoring?"

"Not that I have heard. And you can believe me that when painting a portrait, the artist hears all."

"I can imagine. So is the viscount a lily-boy or just not interested?"

"The latter I believe. I have not been told anything to the contrary."

"I see. Thank you for the information. It will remain entirely confidential."

"You sound very professional, John."

"Ah, that's the old apothecary talking. Instilled into us when we begin our apprenticeship. Is there anything further that would help me in my treatment of the Viscountess?"

"I don't know what you are treating her for," Zoffany answered, with a naughty smile. "Can't think of anything unless she is still depressed."

"About her marriage? A little perhaps."

"No, all women hate their husbands at some point in their lives. No, I meant about her sister. The dead one."

John gaped at him, looking rather silly. "I don't know anything about a dead sister. Enlighten me."

"The twins had an older sibling, apparently one of the most beautiful creatures that ever walked the earth. It appears she was attacked one night and died of her injuries. The girls went absolutely insane with grief. Their mother had died when they were born and this older sister brought them up. She was their entire world it seems."

The Apothecary was silent for a few moments, thinking that the two women had not known much happiness in their lives despite title and money and position.

"How very tragic," he said eventually.

"Yes, a terrible tale. It just shows that females are not safe walking about without an armed servant at their side."

"But surely the dead woman was accompanied by one."

"I think the servant was a woman and was done to death as well. The sister's name was Arabella by the way. There is a famous painting of her somewhere or other but for the life of me I can't remember where. But for pity's sake say nothing of this to anyone. The story is kept very quiet you understand."

"Perfectly. As I told you, keeping secrets is part of our training."

And it was with a very straight face and his mouth drawn into a hard line that the Apothecary left the place of his friend and went back to his own dwelling. But the happy noise coming from Rose and the boys was too much to contend with when he was in such a pensive mood, and within a quarter of an hour John had left again and asked a local wherryman to take him for a row upstream where he could watch the banks of the river slide quietly by. But the harder he thought the less sense anything made. Not that the cases of horror and suffering he had heard or witnessed had any relation one to the other. Or had they?

Oliver's Island was an eyot in the River Thames, where it had stood uninhabited, abounding with legends, beautifully laden with elegant trees and mystery, since time began. John had ordered a small wherry boat and by offering the owner a further good tip if he could get him there quickly, fairly skimmed to his destination over the water. The sun was just above the high point and the world was transformed into a roseate glow when he first caught sight of the eyot. But to make the occasion truly enchanting a masculine voice rang out over the water singing 'A Lover and His Lass' to the accompaniment of a flute. It was as if the whole scene had been plucked from fairyland, as if they had gone back to some mythical time when all the world sang for joy. Life stood still as for a crystalline moment the scene of the sweeping trees, the golden river and, above all, the sheer beauty of that lyrical voice dominated everything. The wherryman shipped his oars and listened, John closed his eyes and put his head back to hear the more clearly, and the Thames joined in the song. In after years the Apothecary always swore that just for a moment the river had a clear voice, deep and beautiful, that took part in that marvellous experience. And then it was over. The song came to an end and there was the gentle buzz of conversation and the sound of clapping from Oliver's Island.

John landed to find Miss Hyacinth had joined his family party and was standing, flute in hand, beside his son James. They were smiling at each other, and the Apothecary knew then that his life's pattern was about to change. That he had not lived through all his many adventures, nor experienced his affairs of the heart, to arrive at this juncture without a certain touch of sadness but also a great deal of joy. Sweeping his hat to the ground he bade the company much cheer and took the glass of sparkling wine that Samuel had thoughtfully poured out for him, then proceeded to get a little tipsy and wallow in the general atmosphere of love and harmony.

Finally, having invited everyone back to dine with them, the meal was eaten, and John and Samuel sat outside the front door and watched the young people—Rose and Jasper, James and Hyacinth—stroll on an evening promenade up the towpath. They were laughing and chattering, James talking with much enthusiasm to the pretty girl who had accompanied his singing with her delicate flute.

"Do you remember when you were his age?" asked Samuel reflectively.

"Of course. Both you and I were apprenticed and busting out of our breeches."

Samuel guffawed heartily. "Speak for yourself. I was as good as gold."

"How sad," John answered, catching the other's eye and both laughed until they wept.

"So how did you get on today?" Samuel asked when they had quietened down.

John refilled their glasses. "Very well once I had dried the lady's eyes."

"By the way," Samuel put in, "I heard the most interesting piece of gossip from one of Jocasta's friends who came to dine the other day. I can inform you that the Baron Rotmuller has reared his formidable head again. Apparently he has a much younger brother who has entered the theatre under the name Robert Miller. I saw him in *The Way of the World*. He was appalling."

John had had just enough to drink to see the funny side of everything and he chuckled joyously, the sound rolling down the river, disturbing a heron who was standing silently at the water's edge waiting for a fish to appear.

"A visit to Drury Lane is indicated, I think. Besides, it's high time I saw Coralie again."

"How is your relationship with her? It seems to have cooled down somewhat?"

"Settled down, rather than cooled. I love the woman, always have and always will. But she wants to continue with her stage work and living here would put paid to that. One day when she finally retires she will no doubt decide to leave the theatre behind her and move in with me."

"And until that lucky day comes you will stay here and make eyes at the various pretty girls."

"Ah well, you know what they say. A woman is as old as she looks, a man is old when he doesn't look any more."

Samuel seemed very slightly put out. "I wouldn't dare. Jocasta is quite a determined woman."

John, deeply fond of his old friend, patted Sam's robust shoulder. "She is the right wife for you, my friend. She keeps you on your toes."

"I know she does. It's when she treads on them that I object."

John, serious suddenly, said, "Well Sam we are where we are. We have done things that we remember with fondness and other things that make us unhappy. But, together, we have arrived at a point in our lives where we can sit like good friends of old acquaintance and feel the sun on our faces."

He looked along the tow path and saw that the young people were coming back. John observed James slip his arm briefly round Hyacinth's waist and smile at her. He looked so like Elizabeth at that moment that it wrenched the Apothecary's heart and a solitary tear, quite unbidden, ran down the side of his nose and into his wine glass. Nobody noticed and all was jollity once more as the party came to join them in the last rays of that joyful day's end.

Chapter Fourteen

Nothing had changed in the home of Miss Phoebe Feathering other than for her appearance. She had dyed her hair a vivid shade of red and had piled it high upon her head topped with a bow made of puce satin. The effect was eye watering, to say the least of it. John, accidentally staring, felt it beholden on himself to make some kind of comment.

"How are you, Miss Feathering? In good health I trust. I see you have changed your hairstyle."

"Quite well, I thank you. Do tell me, do you like my new coiffure? It was done by Monsieur Jacques of Pelham Place. You don't think it is ageing, do you?"

It was. In fact poor Miss Feathering looked freakish, her white maquillage garish beneath the vivid fire of her head. Trying to guess her age was difficult but John felt that he was not being unfair when he considered that she would not see her sixtieth birthday again.

However, he lied when he made an answer.

"Not at all. Perhaps you could wear a trifle more rouge as the blazing hair makes your skin appear somewhat more delicate."

The second part was a fact and Miss Feathering clasped her hands together in delight, dancing on the spot with pleasure.

"Oh thank you, thank you. I have nobody to ask about such matters, you see. My friends are too prim and my maid is too grim." She gave a light-hearted laugh. "Prim and grim, I've never thought of it before. Why, I'm a regular poetess."

"Indeed you are, we'll have you writing for the theatre next. Which reminds me, how is your young actor friend? Robert Miller? The one at Drury Lane?"

John had returned to London with his family and while there was continuing with his enquiries and making a few calls on various people connected with the case.

Miss Feathering went scarlet, her skin and her hair suddenly matching one another. She sighed gustily. "Alas, I have seen nothing of him since that terrible night. I have felt too ashamed to contact him. For him to have glimpsed me like *that*. I cannot even bear to think of it."

"My dear madam, please don't distress yourself. It was not your fault. Besides he might not have been on stage at that particular moment."

"Oh, but he was. The last thing I saw before those ruffians set their hands upon me was him, looking so young and so gallant. Very much the man about town."

"His name is Robert Miller, so you said. But would he also be Robert Rotmuller in private life?"

Her hand flew to her mouth, her eyes expanded to twice their normal size, and the colour drained from her face leaving her looking like someone who had tramped through a snowstorm. Her lips moved soundlessly, the whole vision of a despairing woman enough to make John feel thoroughly ashamed of himself.

"I'm sorry," he lied.

A voice croaked back at him. "How did you know?

"I didn't really. It was a lucky guess."

This was not the moment to tell her that the most notorious fence in London had handled the sale of her monoculars and had indeed put an advertisement in a London newspaper offering them for purchase.

Miss Feathering wept, loudly and spectacularly, throwing herself at John and beating with feeble fists upon his chest. He made comforting noises; speech was practically impossible in the racket she was creating.

"There, there, dear lady. Your private life shall remain so, I promise you. Your secret is safe with me. No-one will ever know," he managed to gasp out.

The sobbing showed no signs of lessening and her considerable bosom heaved with emotion. "You will tell the world," she hissed. "You will bring ruin down upon him."

"Nonsense," John answered loudly, growing more than a little tired of the heavy drama in which Miss Feathering was indulging. "I give you my word that no mention of this will be made to the general public though it may be that I shall have to see the Baron Rotmuller about the matter, unless you decide to quieten down that is."

She stared up at him. "You know him? The baron?"

"I have stayed in his house," John said sneakily.

"You are friends?"

"Not exactly, more acquaintances."

"Then we are done for, Robert and I. You will tell the baron everything."

She began to pummel him again, little fists flying.

"Any more of this nonsense and I will indeed go to see him. If you cease all weeping and wailing now, I can assure you that I will not say a word to him."

"Do I have your pledge of honour?"

"Yes, you do. Now stop it."

She collapsed heavily in a nearby chair, which was small and creaked in protest.

"Now," John said, kindly but firmly, "tell me the whole story."

She gulped, then said quietly, "I first admired him at the theatre. He was playing a small part but I thought he far outshone everyone else involved. As you know…"

Which the Apothecary did not.

"… he appears under the name Robert Miller, thinking the other sounded too Germanic for a British acting company."

John nodded thoughtfully.

"Of course, that is where the family's roots originally lie but they have adopted a very English way of life. Anyway, Robert's sibling is, of course, the head of this particular branch of them."

"He looks old enough to be the young man's father—but I believe they are actually brothers."

"Yes, these great banking tribes tend to have several children. The baron is the eldest, then come another ten of mixed sexes, and Robert was the final joy."

"All from the one mother?"

"So I believe."

"Gracious me, the poor woman scarcely had time to breathe," the Apothecary answered, thinking to himself of the condoms that he had in plentiful supply in his shop. Surely they were available in Europe as they were supposedly invented by Casanova himself, a legend which he personally doubted. Yet these enormous families continued, particularly amongst the working class. Silently John shook his head. Miss Feathering was speaking again, her voice steady once more.

"So what action are you going to take?"

"I told you, none. And now l must bid you good day, Miss Feathering. I believe our interview has reached an end. Farewell."

He swept an elegant bow and left her looking startled.

"Mr. Rawlings," she called out as he hovered in the doorway.

"Yes?"

"Remember your promise."

"Don't worry. Your secret is safe I assure you."

And with that he hurried back to his London home in preparation for an evening at Drury Lane, this one more peaceful than the last, he hoped.

The dressing room for the male actors who played minor roles was packed to suffocation. The sweat was beading through the makeup of many and—in one or two cases—had started to run. The smell of unwashed human parts was overpowering, so much so that the Apothecary was forced to raise a silk handkerchief to his nostrils and breathe through it. Young Mr. Miller—as he styled himself— seemed immune to all the disturbing odours and sat squeezed into a corner gallantly dabbing some brown substance on places where his greasepaint had started to melt away. In between these forays he was trying to catch every word that John Rawlings said over the buzz of loud human chatter.

"I beg your pardon. Did you say you are a friend of my brother's?"

"Yes. I spent several days at your splendid place in the country. He told me all about you …" John lied gallantly, "… so I was wondering if you would care to join me in a drink after the play has ended."

Robert flashed his eyes in the Apothecary's direction. They were large and very seductive and it was quite understandable that Miss Phoebe Feathering had lost her middle-aged heart to their owner.

"Oh! Well, I don't see why not," the actor answered casually.

"Right. I shall await you at the stage door."

"Oh, I wouldn't advise that. There's always a milling crowd. I usually go to a little tavern round the corner, The Bunch of Grapes. I'll see you in there."

The Apothecary smiled and made his way out, glad to get away from the stifling smell of unwashed human anatomy. This night he had visited the Theatre Royal at Drury Lane on his own, feeling in one of his solitary moods. An earlier call on Coralie Clive had revealed that she was out and was not expected back till late, having been invited to play cards. So John had booked a single seat and laughed his head off as that delightful comedy *She Stoops to Conquer* had proceeded at a cracking pace. Robert had only a few lines to say but he spoke up and pulled faces and thus endeared himself to the audience, who were happy to be so easily pleased. Afterwards in the hostelry, which was packed with the theatre crowd, both actors and audience alike, John felt his sleeve being tugged and turning found himself staring into the face of one whom he considered to be a great and good friend, Louis de Vignolles.

"My dear soul," he said loudly, as the background hubbub was deafening. "How wonderful to see you. It's been an age. Let me buy you a drink. I'm actually waiting for a young actor who was in the play but do please stay and meet him. Is Serafina with you?"

"No, she is at home gambling." He smiled a trifle ruefully. "I am afraid that I could never break her of the habit."

"I should hope not indeed. The most feared player in London. Yet despite that, you were the envy of every red-blooded male in town."

"And still am, I fear. There are one or two I can think of who would gladly push me down the stairs should they ever get the opportunity."

"Bad luck to them, whoever they are."

At this moment Robert Miller appeared, looking quite young and vulnerable without his fearsome layer of greasepaint.

"Am I interrupting?" he said.

"Not at all. This is my old friend Louis de Vignolles …"

131

"Not the husband of the celebrated Serafina de Vignolles?"

"You were right," Louis said. "Her admirers are everywhere." Louder, he added, "Yes, sir, I do have that privilege. But let me tell you how much I enjoyed your performance. You were most amusing. Were you pleased with everything?"

"Yes, it went very well. To celebrate may I buy you gentlemen a drink."

"I have a far better idea," Louis said. "Let you both come home with me. There you can meet the lady in question—and renew your acquaintance with her, John. She is having a private card party tonight and that is why I have been disposed of and attended the theatre alone."

Robert showed his Germanic ancestry by clicking his heels and giving a wonderful bow. "What a splendid notion. I should be honoured indeed."

"I'd be delighted," added John.

"Then let's not waste any more time."

The laughter from the upstairs salon was immediately audible as the three men went into number twelve, Hanover Street. Above all they could hear Serafina's deliciously husky voice saying, "Your turn I believe, Lord Hunter," and the other replying, "I am still perusing my move, dear lady."

"He's frightened she is going to fleece him," said Louis, *sotto voce*.

Robert laughed nervously as they made their way up the graciously curving staircase to the room above. The place had been set for cards, a half dozen little tables with four players at each one, scattered about. Serafina rose at the sound of people arriving and her eyes widened at the sight of John. He, looking at her, thought that the hand of age had been laid upon her graciously. The hair was more silvery now than dark, but the beautiful eyes, with the look of knowing in their depths, were as lively and lovely as they had always been. She hurried towards him, arms outstretched.

"My very dear friend, I have not seen you in an age. Have you given up on us poor people who dwell in town? Why I could swear that you have become quite the country gentleman."

John seized her hand and gave it a lingering kiss, for truth to tell he had nursed a secret longing for her for years. But as he straightened up he felt certain that someone was staring at him with a certain amount of amusement.

"Of course you know many people here," Serafina continued— and John, looking round, certainly did. For Coralie was gazing at him with her cool green stare, and, as he returned the glance, raised a questioning eyebrow. He refused to be drawn further and instead greeted other guests with pleasure, finally going to where she was sitting and kissing her hand.

"Well, my friend," she said, "I haven't set eyes on you in a while."

"Nor I you, madam. Unfortunately, other commitments have kept me in Chiswick. But, sweet lady, if I may dare to say it, you know that my house is open to you at any time you care to mention. When your theatrical engagements will allow you to leave London, of course."

She opened her mouth to answer but at that moment Robert Rotmuller dashed up and, after kissing her hand fervently, said, "Madam Clive, I do not suppose you will recognise me but I am a very junior member of the company at Drury Lane. Can I just say that I watch your performances whenever I possibly can and am positively thrilled."

The famous glance swept over the young man and eventually a slow smile which meant she had finally recognised him appeared.

"Mr. Miller is it not?"

"My stage name, madam. Actually I am a member of the Rotmuller family."

"Yes, of course, the bankers."

"My cousins are. I am but a humble actor fellow. Whereas you, madam, are a star that glistens above us all."

John cleared his throat and gave Coralie a sideways grin. "I must do my duty by the other guests. I see Louis beckoning me. I shall leave you two fellow thespians to your backstage chatter. Adieu."

He felt rather mean as he walked away, realising that Coralie was probably squirming beneath the young actor's fervent gaze. On the other hand she could be enjoying it thoroughly. One never knew with women however old one became. He crossed over to Serafina.

"My very dear friend. Do you know that you look as lovely as the time I first saw you, which was quite a considerable while ago?"

"And which role was I playing, the Masked Lady or the sickly Countess?"

"Both. Exquisitely."

But his string of compliments was cut short by a strange whooping sound as Robert Rotmuller leapt lithely from where he had been standing alone—Coralie Clive having politely abandoned him—and dramatically fell on one knee before Serafina.

"May I kiss your hand, Comtesse? You are the most famous woman in the world, the greatest gambler of them all. Please, allow me. It would be such an honour."

She nodded, too astonished to speak, and Robert ran his lips luxuriously over her outstretched fingers. Raising her eyebrows in astonishment, Serafina simply stared. The Apothecary thought the Rotmullers were a highly eccentric bunch of people, judging by the two members of the family he had so far come across.

Eventually Serafina, temporarily rendered speechless, removed her hand and said, "Have we met, sir?"

"No, madam, I have never had the good fortune until this moment.

Allow me to present myself. Robert Rotmuller. But perhaps you have glimpsed me when I have appeared on stage under the name of Robert Miller. But there again, perhaps you have not."

"I am sure I would have noticed you, sir," Serafina answered. "Unfortunately, my husband and I do not get to see the play as often as we would like. My daughter is about to become a mother for the first time so we are very much on call as it were."

"Good gracious," put in John. "I cannot see you in the role of grandmama. You are not old enough."

"What a ridiculous statement. Italia has been married a twelve month at least." She shot him a brief appraising glance. "Come now, Apothecary, you can't say that the thought of being a grandfather has not crossed your mind."

"It has—and I drove it away upon the instant. I was too busy thinking of myself to worry about future generations."

Serafina gave him a cool stare and—after a second or so—burst out laughing. "I know you of old, John Rawlings. You cannot fool me with your ridiculous chatter."

He kissed her hand and went off, leaving her to the mercies of Robert Rotmuller who was begging her for a game of cards. But, truth to tell, he could not mingle, his mind being constantly drawn back to the conversation he had had with Zoffany. A germ of an idea had come to him then and now it pursued him with full force.

Before Samuel had left him they had discussed the case and Samuel had said, "Tell me more about this Rotmuller chap. What with helping at the operation and the general march of events I hardly had time to speak to him."

"There is nothing particularly interesting to say. He is German and apparently won the property on a roll of the dice. His youngest brother is the actor who you considered so terrible."

"Oh he was, believe me."

"Sam, I am stuck. It is this strange series of events. I have a feeling that they must be related. But how in the world *can* they be?"

The goldsmith had shaken his head. "I just don't know and, believe me, I would help you if I could. My only suggestion is to go and see Lady Lovell again. I am suspicious of her husband, though heaven knows why?"

John had sighed deeply. "I will do as you think."

Now, though, he was brought back to the present moment by Coralie's voice. "My dear, you are frowning deeply and your lips are moving without speaking. In other words, what is the matter?"

"I was thinking about a problem I have to solve."

"Ah, another one. What is it this time?"

As briefly as he could the Apothecary outlined the story to her. Coralie rested her head in her hand while she listened. Eventually she said, "The answer has to lie with those two sisters—the twins. You'll have to get them to talk to you more openly."

"The wish will be father to the thought."

"Now, now, John. You could get the Sphinx to tell you the secret of the Pyramids if you really put your mind to it."

"Thank you, madam. By the way, I still remember you running in your high heels in the direction of a villain at Vaux Hall Gardens."

"Those were wonderful days. But, alas, I am getting old now. I can't run so fast."

"That is what makes you completely irresistible."

Knowing that his children were more than capable of organising his house in Nassau Street, John decided at that moment to go back to Chiswick and talk to Zoffany. Even though the night was moonless and black as dead water, John managed to hire a boat at Whitehall stairs and make his way up the Thames's inky darkness. It was a horrible journey, lit here and there by some dim lights from the embankments and occasional village illuminations. But other than for that, nothing. John's heart was in his boots but he was delighted to see that Zoffany's house was a blaze of light and the yellow beams struck the water with inviting rays when they finally drew alongside Oliver's Island.

"Pull over there," John instructed the boatman.

The man did so, grumbling under his breath.

"What's the matter?" asked John.

"I don't usually work this late."

The Apothecary handed over an extra-large tip. He could have argued but decided against it. The boatman was a burly type and John did not fancy ending up at the bottom of the river. He hurried to take his first step on dry land and without hesitation gave a loud knock on Zoffany's front door. It was answered by a woman, of which a great many lived in the painter's house. Behind her came a bellow of raucous laughter and John, handing her his long coat and fashionable hat, made his way into a room packed with good-humoured male company. Then he nearly dropped with surprise. For there, his face suffused with wine and guffawing to display a great mountain of teeth, was Baron Rotmuller, of all the people in the world. Zoffany rose to his feet.

"Ah, my dear John. Come and meet the company. I believe you know the baron, in fact have stayed with him at the unfortunate time of the removal of Sir Humphrey Warburton's leg. Allow me to present my other guest, Viscount Lovell. The rest you probably know. All of you, this is my great friend and neighbour, John Rawlings."

So, thought the Apothecary, here he is at last, the famous Lovell, whose mother is Sir Humphrey's sister. He raised his quizzing glass for a discreet gaze. It was a slim creature that he was looking at, with a face that could have been beautiful had not the early lines of dissipation showed clearly upon it. Lovell had plucked off his wig and a lot of fair hair clung round his ears. His eyes had dark shadows beneath but the eyes themselves were of a smoky blue that gleamed in the candlelight. If he drank less and paid more attention to his diet the young man could have been stunningly good-looking. The Apothecary bowed.

"Delighted to meet you. But please accept my sincere good wishes on the return to full health of your uncle."

Lovell stared. "Great heavens! How did you know that I was related?"

The Apothecary put on his professional face. "I attended Sir Humphrey at the scene of his accident and afterwards acted as an assistant during the removal of his irretrievably broken leg. May I assure you that it was a brilliant operation."

"But how did you know we were kinfolk?"

"Sir Humphrey told me that his sister married a man called Redwood and had several children by him. I believe that was your name before you became a member of the nobility."

"How pompous that sounds. The nobility? I can tell you I was a nobody when two of my cousins caught some fever or other and died within days of one another. I suddenly found that I had some money to spend." The smoky eyes glistened in the candlelight and John saw that humour lay in their depths. There was hope for Lady Lovell after all!

"Really? How interesting. It just proves that there is some almighty plan at work, don't you think?"

"No, I don't. It was just plain luck. But good fortune—it would seem—has been eluding me once more."

"Oh dear. Why is that?"

"Because I am losing cash again. Playing with that old devil over there."

The smoky eyes indicated Baron Rotmuller.

"But surely the baron just gambles for amusement."

"That's as may be. But you know that he won that magnificent pile of his on the throw of a dice."

"I had heard something to that effect."

"Well, it's true."

The Viscount looked round the room and while his attention was drawn elsewhere John tried wildly to think of a cunning plan by means of which he could bring the dissipated young man back to the arms of his pregnant wife. But he couldn't. It was beyond him. The baron, meanwhile, feeling himself stared at, flashed a great smile. John wondered if his teeth were false and regarded them seriously.

"Ah ha, I see two of my friends are here. Lord Lovell, come and throw some dice with me. My dear Mr. Rawlings, I had quite forgot you live next door to the painter fellow."

"Who's that calling me a painter fellow? I am *the* painter fellow," said Zoffany good-naturedly.

Surprisingly, Lord Lovell looked over his shoulder at John and winked one of his brilliant eyes. "You won't find any shrinking violets here," he whispered.

The party drew to its inebriated close in the small hours of the morning. The baron had fallen asleep where he sat and was snoring loudly, his great teeth gnashing as he did so. The Viscount had insisted on walking home accompanied by a couple of servants who had been aroused from the kitchen. John had made his way in the darkness of the next day and crept up the stairs, aware of the fact that his house was empty. But he had woken early after only a couple of hours sleep and having washed and shaved away the signs of the party, he stepped out into a beautiful morning.

139

The sun had risen and everything was crisp and fresh and newly-painted looking. Most surprisingly he had no hangover and felt both alive and alert. Unerringly he found his feet leading him in the direction of Chiswick House to see Lady Lovell—or at least that would be his excuse—even though she would most probably still be asleep at this early hour. Even more important was to try and get her wretched husband to come to his senses—which was about as likely as getting men to walk upon the moon. Nonetheless the Apothecary determinedly trotted at speed through the glistening morning towards the Jacobean mansion in which the Lovells were currently staying.

The house looked bleak in the early sun and had an air of fin-de-siecle about it. It was condemned to be knocked down as soon as the extensions to Chiswick House were begun. John Rawlings could not help but think it would be a pity as his eye ran over its fine lines and immense grandeur. But though neglected, the building was alive. Smoke rose through the chimney and from the bakery came the delicious smell of baking bread. The servants were up and busy even if the master and mistress were still abed.

Wandering round the building John drew level with the enormous window through which he had seen that terrible face staring in, and glancing through it, he saw another grim sight. Viscount Lovell was slumped in a chair, his head back and his mouth gaping, before him on the table stood an empty bottle of wine and a glass, a drop of fluid still in its depths. He had drunk himself into a fitful sleep.

John never knew what made him act as he did. Perhaps it was a deep, cold fury that the young idiot should be throwing his life away, perhaps it was the look on his wife's face when she had spoken of her love for him. Whatever it was, the Apothecary found himself sprinting round the house to the front door which opened beneath a mighty shove. Without a word he rushed up to where the viscount sat sprawled and heaved him up over one of his shoulders. Then, with no hesitation he made for the disused stables where stood a decrepit pump and, plunging the young man under it, let him have jets of icy water right over his head, soaking his body and clothes in the same gushing spray.

"What the hell …?" started the viscount, just about regaining his senses, but was cut short by a gallon of water descending on him. He did his best to punch John hard but was still too enfeebled to make contact. The Apothecary, almost frenetically, pumped till his arm ached and until the figure standing in front of him was transformed into a sodden wreck, pale of countenance and sobbing. Then he stopped. Before the other could say a word, John spoke.

"You wretched man. You silly, foolish creature. How can you carry on living as you do and then die after ten miserable years of a completely wasted life? You should be ashamed of yourself, sir. Deeply and bitterly ashamed."

Lovell shook himself, his actions terribly reminiscent of a soaking wet dog. Then he spluttered a cough but still said nothing. From out of his mess of hair a bloodshot blue eye looked wretchedly.

"You wife is in love with you, you asinine little creature. She is expecting your child and she is desperate not to miscarry. If you pull yourself together and turn your life around, the whole of your future will turn around with you. You're drinking yourself to death, don't you understand that?"

"It helps me forget," Lovell said, his voice shaking, though whether through emotion or the recent soaking the Apothecary could not tell.

"Forget what?"

"That I owe money right, left and centre."

"And whose fault was that?"

"Mine. I've been a damnable fool. God, sometimes I hate myself."

"Come here. Let's get you dry."

John picked up an old rag lying on the cobbled floor and as Redwood stepped towards him applied it vigorously to the young man's head. The blond hair caught the glimmer of the sun and John said, "You will ruin your looks you know if you continue to drink so much."

Redwood looked at him wearily. "I know. I realise that everything you say is a fact. But at the moment I am so messed up that I cannot help myself."

"Let us go indoors and order some strong coffee, then we can discuss your problems and see if there is any way at all of sorting them out."

They walked in silently, John feeling exactly as if he were punishing one of his sons. Redwood sank into a chair and John said, "Where are the towels? I'll go and get some."

"No, I can fetch them."

"You stay exactly where you are. I don't want you to move until you've told me the whole story."

"Don't you trust me?"

"No," the Apothecary answered—and meant it.

A few minutes later he returned with a selection of towelling. As he had suspected, the Lovells slept in different rooms—he had seen the young man's bed unslept in and with not a sign of a woman anywhere, not a promising omen for the future. The viscount meanwhile had stripped to his drawers, throwing the rest of the clothes into a soggy heap upon the floor. Taking a large towel, he rubbed himself dry and John was interested to see that the fair hair—usually hidden by a wig—was naturally curly. He took a mouthful of coffee, which had been served by a tactful man servant, eyes averted, but nonetheless very aware that the master of the house was entertaining wearing only a pair of smalls. The viscount was beyond caring, staring straight in front of him, the vivid eyes clouded and sad.

"I presume they are gambling debts," said the Apothecary, opening the conversation.

"Mostly, yes."

"To one specific person or do you spread yourself about?"

The viscount looked up sharply to see whether John was making fun but the Apothecary's face was absolutely straight.

"No, it's one particular man—and you know who it is. That old rogue Rotmuller, who is as rich as Croesus anyway and even won his estate on the throw of a dice."

"So I have frequently heard."

"It's true enough. He and the whole of his wretched family are all born to make money. They are very well known for it."

"In Europe perhaps. Not quite so much over here."

"That's as may be. The fact remains that he is after me."

"But I would have judged you to be friends seeing you together last night."

Redwood gulped down the rest of his coffee. "We are, socially. But when it comes to cards it is a different matter."

John was silent as the basis of an idea formed in his mind, aloud he said nothing of it. "Tell me about your marriage," he said.

The young man's eyes had lightened and now looked slightly amused. "What is there to tell? What is there about any society marriage that is worth talking about?"

"The fact that—regardless of whether you be a prince of the blood or a simple cow hand—there is someone else's feelings to consider. Oh, don't give me that supercilious look. However hard-hearted you are—and I do not believe that you are at all, quite the reverse—the wretched woman, your wife, has had the misfortune to fall in love with you. God knows why! And for that reason alone she is to be treated with some respect. Moreover, she is fearful of losing the child—your child. I know this because I am an apothecary and your wife has consulted me professionally."

Redwood turned to look at him. "Is this a fact?" he asked slowly.

"Of course it's a fact," John answered tersely. "I don't say things for the sake of conversing."

The viscount shook his head silently and John thought that with his fair hair and smoky eyes he really was most pleasing to look at. Then there was a noise on the stairs and both men turned their heads to see that the viscountess was making her way down wearing a simple muslin chemise adorned with celestial blue ribbons. She looked very fresh and lovely yet delicate, the rounding of her body just beginning to show. Redwood watched her silently for a moment, then he stood up.

"You're wearing your drawers—and nothing else," she said, and gave a quiet laugh.

"And you, my lady, have come downstairs in a state of undress."

"I did not realise that we had company but when I saw that it was Mr. Rawlings I came down anyway."

"And I did not realise you were on such intimate terms," said Lovell, but he was smiling at them both.

There was a sudden lifting of the Apothecary's heart as he saw the Viscount's arm go out as he helped his wife into a chair. Could it be that the session under the pump had done some good or were those lucky incidents reserved for story books alone? It would appear to have had some benefit, however, as Redwood suddenly raised her hand to his lips.

"Promise me to be careful," he said.

She looked at him in some surprise. "I always am."

"That's not what I heard. Rumour has it that you tramp all over the estate regardless of the weather."

"Exercise is good for the child." And the viscountess put her hand down to her—as yet—small rounding.

"I don't know about exercise but something is making you very beautiful, Arabella."

She gazed at him in surprise. "You've never said that before."

"Only because I hadn't really looked."

This, thought the Apothecary, is my cue to go. He stood up and neither of the couple were aware of him. It was quite definitely the time to leave. He bowed.

"Please excuse me. I really must return home. It has been a pleasure to be in your company."

At last the viscount gazed at him and there was an expression in the smoky eyes that made John chuckle to himself, though outwardly his face did not do more than give a polite smile. Redwood extended a neat but useful hand.

"You must come and dine with us, Mr. Rawlings."

"Thank you, my lord. I await your invitation with pleasure."

And he was gone, wondering to himself whether that old pump had contained some kind of magic spell. However, he had not walked for more than ten minutes when he saw Lady Lovell coming towards him. Just for an instant it frightened him that she could be in two places at once until he realised that it was her identical twin sister, Lady Derwent. They were so stunningly alike that it was as if the very fact of twins was nature's way of saying that it ruled everything. Yet one thing it could not do was produce identical expressions. For Lady Derwent in repose was quite a sight. She looked hawkish, her mouth turned down into an ugly line, great purplish shadows under her eyes, yet for all that she was still undeniably beautiful. John recalled the last time he had seen her. Sir Humphrey Warburton had lain near death in a nearby coach and she had allowed her husband to send him away. On that occasion she had given the Apothecary such a strange look.

"Good morning, Lady Derwent," he said, and swept a small, studiously polite, bow.

She peered at him. "Oh, it's you. The man with Sir Humphrey. Where have you been?"

"Visiting your brother-in-law, madam."

"Indeed. Was he sober?"

John concealed his smile by pretending to cough. "Excuse me. Very much so. He and your sister were somewhat weary after a late night, however, and have gone to bed rest."

"Oh, I was hoping to call on her."

"I wouldn't advise it, my lady."

And the Apothecary gave her a crooked grin and raised an eyebrow. She did not smile back, in fact she looked positively frosty. Inwardly John felt a surge of immense pleasure at her reaction, at the same time thinking how strange it was that two people, so alike on the surface, could be so different within.

"Then I'll say good day, Rawlings."

"Thank you, madam. Grateful indeed."

He gave her another, deeper, bow and stood thus, bent double, until she had swept from his sight. Then he began to hum a triumphant little tune and was singing quite loudly by the time he got home.

Chapter Fifteen

Jasper and James were most anxious to savour the delights of London—a thought which made John somewhat uneasy. Remembering himself and Samuel at the age of sixteen and how difficult it had been to keep to the rules of being apprenticed—one of which was that apprentices were not allowed to fornicate—gave him much cause for concern. They were not only his sons but Elizabeth's. And she was the most passionate woman that the Apothecary had ever met, with her dark hair and wild unruly ways. There was so much of her in them, with their enticing eyes and gorgeous smiles, that there was nothing he could do to stop them being what they were—normal, beautiful young males. So he did what he hoped was a sensible thing. He took them to his shop and asked Julian Merrett—apothecary in charge when John was not present—to show his sons everything they sold. His eyes had lingered momentarily on the drawer in which were contained what John considered essential to the world in general. Julian caught his glance and gave a minute nod. John disappeared into the compounding room and happily got to work.

As he was back, staying in Nassau Street, he thought he might call on Sir Humphrey Warburton and see how well the man was managing his prosthetic leg and also to find out any scraps of information he could further glean about the Redwood family. Despite the fact that he now had a sneaking regard for Lord Lovell—the eldest Redwood—who had stood up to his ordeal beneath the pump very well, John wanted to know if his new-found fondness for his wife had stayed the course or disappeared as quickly as it had come. He accordingly visited one morning and sent in his card. The footman returned after a few moments and told him he could step inside the small salon.

A woman was seated in a comfortable chair near the window and Sir Humphrey had risen to greet his visitor.

"My dear Rawlings, how are you? You're looking well. May I present my sister?" John bowed. "Mrs. Redwood, I would like to introduce my good friend, John Rawlings. He was one of the young assistants at my recent operation. A brave fellow indeed."

She rose slowly to her feet, a huge puce feather in her hair swirling as she did so. She had about her an air of greatness, of being someone of importance, which immediately made John certain that she came from fairly humble stock. Genuinely significant people never assumed anything. He bowed once more.

"How dee do?" she said eventually.

She stood very still—to be observed more easily perhaps—and John, looking at her, thought she must have been quite a beauty in her heyday and was certainly aware of it. Her face was oval, surrounded by a mass of deeply dyed hair, and her eyes were cast upwards, giving her rather a pained expression as she gazed wistfully at the heavens above. The Apothecary had the vivid impression that she had once posed for a portrait using an identical gesture.

"Madam, I am honoured," he said in a deep theatrical voice.

Her eyes did not move, still gazing at the heavens.

148

"Cecily," said Sir Humphrey irritably.

At last she looked down. "I am sorry. I was far away. Thinking of a poem I once read. So you assisted at my brother's operation. How noble spirited of you indeed."

"I am an apothecary, madam, and quite used to seeing surgical cuts."

"Surely you don't perform them."

"Not unless you consider fiddling about with loose teeth as one, no. But when I was an apprentice we used to go with our masters to all kinds of accidents and see some rather grim sights."

"Oh dear," she answered, and fluttered her eyelashes at a tremendous rate.

John gave a half-hearted smile. "Tell me about your family," he said.

Sir Humphrey spoke up for her. "Three boys and three girls. The eldest male is Viscount Lovell, who will one day become the Earl of Cumbria. I think you know him, Rawlings."

An image of the sodden wreck shivering beneath the pump shot through the Apothecary's mind and he couldn't resist a small smile. "Yes, we have met," he said.

So there *was* a connection, he considered. Sir Humphrey was Lovell's uncle. But what did that prove? Nothing. As far as John knew it didn't alter anything. Or did it?

"Of course the viscount is my favourite child," Cecily was speaking, this time staring at John fixedly. "He is such a dear boy. The other two are scallywags. Always getting into scrapes but wonderfully kind and handsome for all that. Their names are Roderick and Percival, known as Rod and Val in the family. Then come my three daughters—Matilda, Maud and Maria. Wonderfully beautiful gals, all of them."

Behind her Sir Humphrey rolled his eyes but remained silent. John struggled on bravely. "I would like to meet your family at some time in the future."

"The viscount—my son—and his wife are shortly going to a new home so cannot receive company at the moment. The house is not quite ready but is being built in the environs of Berkeley Square. Meanwhile they are staying in a Jacobean mansion nearby. This of course is by special consent of Georgiana, Duchess of Devonshire, who is currently abroad. The viscountess is one of the famous Winterlight beauties you know." She gave a deep sigh.

The Apothecary felt suddenly tired of Mrs. Redwood and her wretched snobbery, to say nothing of the obvious relish with which she discussed members of the aristocracy. He glanced at his pocket watch surreptitiously, then said politely, "My dear Sir Humphrey, would you mind if I take my leave? Else I shall be late for my next appointment."

"Not at all, my friend. Hope to see you again shortly."

Mrs. Redwood stuck out a small claw which John dutifully kissed, then with much bowing and waving he made his way to the street outside, glad to be away from the pretentious old dame.

Feeling in desperate need of a good book, John hailed a hackney coach and was driven to the bookshop in Carter Lane on the off chance of meeting Mr. Buffitt. There, indeed, the earnest little man was busily serving a customer. John made eye contact, smiled and settled himself on a chair with a copy of *Evelina* written by—of all things!—a woman, a Miss Frances Burney. He liked the style of it very much. As soon as Buffitt had finished and the satisfied customer had left the shop, John rose from his chair.

"My dear chap, how nice to see you again. I would like to buy a copy of this for my daughter."

"Certainly, Mr. Rawlings. And how are you keeping, sir?"

"Very well."

"And the family?"

"My boys are getting to the…er… inquisitive age, I fear. Children don't remain children for very long, do they?"

"My Lucinda is growing fast."

"I'm so glad to hear it. How is she in herself?"

"She's away at the moment. Gone to stay with my sister-in-law in Chiswick."

The Apothecary received one of those moments of dread which always alerted him that something was moving in the shadows.

"Would you mind if I called in on her?" he asked, and there was a note of urgency in his voice that Buffitt picked up on.

"No. But why? You don't think anything's wrong do you?"

"Of course not," John lied. "But I am going back home shortly and may as well. Where is she staying exactly?"

"With my sister in Sutton Lane. Nothing terribly grand but very homely. She's in one of the old cottages there."

"I'll make a point of visiting."

"Give her my fondest love, won't you? Please excuse me. How may I help you, sir?" And the neat little man turned to his next customer.

John sped back to Nassau Street to find that Miss Hyacinth had called—also visiting town it seemed—and all four of his brood had gone out.

"Damnation," he said. "I must get to Chiswick urgently." He turned to the footman. "Now, Markham, you are to tell Miss Rose that I put her in charge of her brothers. I don't want any trouble from them."

The footman fought to keep his features under control. "I am sure she will do her best, sir."

John suddenly burst out laughing. "Dammit, Markham, what will be, will be. But keep a fatherly eye on them for me. Don't let them go wild."

"I promise you, sir. Now would you like a chair to the Stairs?"

"Yes, that will just give me time to throw some things into a bag."

Despite his best endeavours he did not arrive at Strand-on-the-Green until the shadows were lengthening on that summer's day. Yet something made him decide to press on and check that Lucinda was safely in Sutton Lane. Dropping his portmanteau at home he set off on a series of meandering paths until he eventually arrived in the shady confines of rural Chiswick. Here the sound of children's voices reassured him and he hastened towards the happy group, looking for the small girl. She was not amongst them.

"Where's Lucinda gone?" he asked in what he thought was a kindly voice.

They looked at him, mouths open, frankly terrified. What he had taken for playful laughter had been something entirely different. A boy spoke up.

"She be gone with the Straw Man, mister."

"He frightens us," added a small girl.

John felt the icy grip of fear. "Who is he, this man?"

"He lives in the woods. He watches us play."

"He touches himself down there," said one of the older children, lowering her eyes and indicating.

John could almost picture him, striking terror into the children's hearts.

"How long ago did he take her? And which direction did they go in?"

"About ten minutes," answered the boy who had spoken first. "And he dragged her off over there." And he pointed to a small copse of trees.

The Apothecary did not stop to ask them why they hadn't shouted for their mothers but took off at a fast pace in the direction of the boy's indicating finger. As he neared the spinney he heard a faint cry and redoubled his efforts, though he did not move quite as fast these

152

days as once he had done. He nonetheless must have made a noise as he approached because as he hurried through the trees he saw the man look round. Lucinda had been pushed to the ground, her clothes all awry, the youth was gaping at her, open-mouthed, his hand frantically working his penis, while he muttered something under his breath. John moved so fast that he even surprised himself. Rushing up to the Straw Man he landed him a blow on the jaw which felled him to the ground so hard that what was left of the wretched fellow's teeth rattled in his head. He looked at his assailant from disbelieving eyes, groaned out "Don't 'ee tell ..." And then lost consciousness. The Apothecary scooped the child up in his arms.

"Did he touch you?" he asked.

She shook her head. "No, just looked. Then he got his thing out."

"Who is he? Do you know?"

"No, but he's sort of local. He sleeps in the hay because he always has straw in his clothes. I don't think he has a place to live."

"Come on Lucinda. I'll take you home."

When he came out of the straggle of trees he saw that the children had gathered in a body and the largest boy was clutching a hammer.

"Is he in there, mister?"

"Yes, but for heaven's sake don't use that on him. You'll kill him."

"I wouldn't mind," the boy answered with much bravado.

"I want to talk to him first," John answered, looking severe.

But despite the fact that the child's aunt snatched Lucinda into her capacious bosom—the aunt sobbing loudly all the while—and that John hurried back to the copse, the Straw Man had gone. His trail was clear until it reached the river but then it vanished. Wearily, the Apothecary made his way home, thinking that the creature must have dived into the water to shake off any pursuers. Not as stupid as he looked obviously.

The candles were lit in Zoffany's house and John could not resist knocking on the door. Once inside, seated comfortably, a glass of batavia arrack in his hand, he proceeded to tell the painter of his day, particularly with regard to the Straw Man. Zoffany pursed his lips.

"Of course the creature must be caught before he rapes some child—that is if he hasn't already done so."

John looked solemn. "He said 'don't 'ee tell' before he passed out. What did that mean? Tell who?"

The painter shrugged. "The world in general perhaps?"

"You don't think, do you, that he meant somebody specific? That it is possible that someone else was involved?"

"How could they be?"

"The child concerned was the same as the one who said she was pushed in the river outside this house. She also happens to have been fathered by the son of some big family living in Chiswick."

"Do you know who?"

"No, that's the devil of it, I don't."

"But why would anybody want to harm her? Poor little thing has never done anything wrong."

"It is quite inexplicable."

They sat in silence for a long while and, even later when the Apothecary had retired to his bedroom he lay sleepless, thinking about the strangeness of the situation.

Next morning saw him rise early, put on the clothes he wore when attending a patient—something he had never given up—and heading purposefully for the cottage in Sutton Lane. He was carrying a bag with some basic medicaments and his purpose was to call in on the child Lucinda and—much more importantly—to talk to her aunt. If anyone would know the name of her niece's father it would be her.

She was a sweet baked-apple of a woman, round of cheek and eye, very much—as those sharp-wits who caroused in London society—thought of as a country person. After John had seen Lucinda, who was remarkably resilient and greeted him cheerfully, he asked Mrs. Robyns if he could have a private word with her. And so it was, sitting opposite her on a hard-backed wooden chair, that he looked at her very seriously.

"You know that I have spoken to your brother Thomas." She nodded and he continued, "I asked him if he knew the name of Lucinda's father. He said no but he thought he had some connection with a big local family. Would that be correct?"

She turned from being an apple to sour fruit indeed. Her lips drew back in a snarl as she hissed, "Yes, the devil. I can see him now standing laughing at her when she told him that she carried his child. Despite his ugly nature he was beautiful to look at, with his black curling hair—he never wore a wig—and his height and his polished riding boots and all. If I had had a gun at that moment I would have shot him dead. She begged him to help her and do you know what he did?"

"No."

"He grabbed her by the chin, looked in her face with his great jade eyes all creasing up at the corners with merriment, then he pinched her face hard and walked away."

"What a brutal thing to do."

"Aye, and that was what he was—brutish. Oh, we all heard tales of what he was like. Even as a small child nobody could control him. His father died when he was three and his baby brother died in infancy. That left his sister, a year older than he was. Tales would come via the servants that he used to have relations with her, force her to let him into her bedroom, take her outdoors in the moonlight and there know her carnally. It was no surprise to me or anyone else that one night she climbed up to the roof and jumped to her death. She was eighteen years old and he had frightened her so much that she ended her life."

"He sounds like a monster, an uncontrollable beast."

"Oh, he was. The decease of his sister caused a stir locally and he upped sticks and moved abroad before too many questions could be asked. Nobody ever heard of him after that. I just thank God that Lucinda is sweet and kind like her dear mother and does not take after him at all."

"But was he one of the Redwoods? It sounds to me as if he came from some other family."

"That is something we all would like to know. He let it be put about that one of their boys was responsible. But it was him all along, the rotten bastard. Yet, do you know, some said that he was really one of them. That Mrs. Redwood was no better than she should be and had lovers. But told old man Ainsley—who also sought her favours—that the child was his."

"So do you think these two incidents regarding the child are related or just a hideous coincidence? I mean, is he trying to kill her? He sounds evil enough. But where is he now?"

"Gone abroad. Changed his name, no doubt. Somehow I doubt he would be interested enough to want to harm her." The wretched woman shook her head. "But it is impossible to know what to think. Except that no harm seems to befall her in London. I feel I should send her back immediately."

The Apothecary nodded. "I think you are right. It is as if he has some agent here in Chiswick who still carries out his orders."

The poor creature wept bitterly. "And I love her so much. I thought to give her a break from the crowded conditions of Mr. Buffitt's house."

"Small it might be," John answered wisely, "but it is full of a good man's kindness. Send her back tomorrow if you can."

"I shall take her on the stage myself. She'll come to no harm while I am by her side."

He was quite glad that his offspring remained in town, presumably enjoying the sights and shows, dutifully chaperoned by servants living at his old address in Nassau Street. How far the chaperoning went with regard to James and Jasper he did not know, nor was he going to attempt to find out. He must just put his trust in their basic good sense and hope that this would bring them through relatively unscathed. Meanwhile he preferred the silence of the house, giving him time to ponder the problem of the mysterious occurrences that had taken place recently. He was annoyed therefore when his morning was shattered by a ring at the front door and a few moments later his servant appeared enquiring as to whether he was ready to receive a visitor. Glancing at the card, John saw that Mr. Robert Rotmuller was calling. Intrigued by the fact that the young man had bought the monoculars from the fence but had not returned them—as far as he knew—to Miss Feathering, the Apothecary nodded.

"Yes, please to show him in."

He had risen from his desk and was sitting on the window seat, the playful river gurgling behind him, throwing him into contrast against the sharp light outside. Robert Rotmuller entered the room and stood bowing several times, he ended this display with a resounding click of his heels, then bounded forward to where John sat.

"Please," said his host, indicating a chair.

"I have come to ask your permission, sir, so will remain standing until I have done so."

"Good gracious. My dear chap whatever for?"

"To pay court to Miss Rose, sir. I met her in London recently and wish to extend my addresses."

A grin—which was most unsuitable considering the serious expression on Robert's face—twitched the Apothecary's mouth.

"Well, it's very polite of you I must say. Did she give you any indication of how she felt?"

"No, sir, she did not. I realise that I am only a junior actor at the moment but I aim to get to the top of the tree."

"That's very commendable. And how precisely are you going to achieve this?"

"I intend to audition for every part that is on offer, sir. And to persist until somebody appreciates that I have great talent."

"And supposing that they don't?" asked John, slightly unkindly.

"I have certain family money, sir. I could support your daughter in basic style."

"And you are now finished with elderly admirers I take it?"

Robert went crimson. "Miss Feathering and I were just good friends."

John shook his head. "Don't worry, my boy. We have all done foolish things in our youth. But I think you ought to return her monoculars to her, don't you?"

The young man went ashen. "How did you know about them?"

The Apothecary looked mysterious. "That I cannot tell you. Just take it from me that I know a great deal about what goes on in the— how shall I put it?—darker side of London life."

"May I sit? I suddenly feel rather faint."

"My dear boy, do. Let me fetch you some brandy."

Half an hour—and several brandies—later, harmony was restored. John, feeling mellow, decided that the banking family of Rotmuller were not too bad a lot, while young Robert was hoping sincerely that one day he could have a father-in-law as jovial as the Apothecary. The meeting ended with the two men going for a riverside stroll, admiring the scenery and the lovely houses as they passed whimsically by.

It was as they were nearing the end of the parade of dwellings that John wondered whether his eyes were deceiving him, for he thought he saw something move behind a clump of rushes that had grown up on the riverbank. Motioning the younger man to keep silent he walked quietly forward and poked the leaves with his walking cane. There was a yelp from within, then suddenly a person reared up and hurled themselves at the Apothecary, growling deep like a savage dog. Taken by surprise, John Rawlings fell flat, gasping for breath as the wind was savagely knocked clean out of him. Robert paused momentarily, gazing at the scene, then flung himself on the older man's assailant.

"Stand off, you bastard, or I'll crack your head open. Stand off, I say."

The other just grunted, too busy with raining blows on his victim, who was choking alarmingly. Robert, without hesitation, leapt on his back, bringing the youth down onto the ground and thus giving the Apothecary a chance to get his gasping breath back. And then the actor did something that had never been taught in fencing lessons or anywhere else for that matter. He kicked the man so hard that his victim started to roll down the small incline and went straight into the River Thames. The waters gave a plopping sound and promptly closed over his head. The Apothecary dragged himself up and stood looking to where his assailant was thrashing madly, clearly unable to swim.

"We'd better fish him out, you know."

"Yes," Robert answered, "I do know. But he looks such a ruffian it seems a pity."

"It's the Straw Man."

"Who?"

"I'll explain later. I think you'd better get him, my friend. I simply haven't the breath."

"Very well." Robert suddenly gave a sudden grin. "Speak well of me to your daughter, won't you."

He dived in immaculately and pulled the Straw Man roughly to the bank where John stooped to help them out. Seeing him closely, the Apothecary thought that the youth was one of the ugliest people on the face of the planet. His hair was fetid mould and his complexion was as ghastly as someone who dwelt permanently in a cave. The thought of his underwear was enough to make mortal man shiver. John extended his cane to pull the wretched creature in.

"I've a mind to set you before the magistrate," he said, when the Straw Man eventually stood shivering on the riverbank. "You'd go to gaol for years for exposing yourself to little girls."

The ugly creature shook violently. "I'm sorry, sir. I never done it before. Honest, I never."

John looked at him through his quizzing glass, then wished he hadn't. "What did you mean when you said 'Don't 'ee tell' to me?' The magistrate—or somebody else?"

The Straw Man gazed at his feet which were covered in a pair of work boots, obviously stolen because they were a couple of sizes too big. As they now had water squelching through them the sound was grim when he shuffled his feet.

"Come on," John ordered, looking merciless.

"I was 'ired to frighten that gal, I was. Honest."

"How interesting. And who hired you?"

The Straw Man's face turned green with fear. "No, no, can't tell," he mumbled.

Robert spoke up. "He looks fit to faint. My God, he's going to."

And they watched in horror as the unsightly youth went from verdant to lily and lost consciousness.

"I've a mind to leave him be," said the Apothecary.

Robert looked at him in astonishment. "I thought you were trained to tend the sick."

"I am, but there come moments …"

The Straw Man suddenly opened one eye and sat up, all in one great movement. Then, slippery as a snake, he was off. Running down the embankment, kicking his big boots to one side, going barefoot into the river and swimming like a dog—paddling with his arms and legs downstream until he became nothing but a distant blur. Robert and the Apothecary stared at one another in blank astonishment.

"Shall I go after him, Mr. Rawlings?"

John shook his head slowly, sighed a deep sigh, and said, "I don't think it is worth it, my friend. He will probably either drown or land up somewhere like Wapping—not a fate I would wish on anyone in their right senses."

"Why? Is it rough?"

"My dear Mr. Rotmuller, I do not dare speak of it except to say it is rougher and tougher than the darker side of hell. Come, let us away and leave the Straw Man to his own particular fate."

And so saying they marched off down the tow path in the direction of a tavern.

Chapter Sixteen

Two days later John set off for London to fetch his brood. Arriving by chair from Whitehall Stairs he stood a moment outside the front door and listened to the tumult within. A lovely smile crossed his features as he thought with pleasure as to how much his father, the late Sir Gabriel Kent, would approve. The house seemed to be laughing—as did the footman who answered the door—glad that its quiet days were gone and it was once more full of lively young people. John motioned the servant not to announce him and crept into the hall to observe goings on. It would appear that the company was mixed and included several people that he did not know at all, because, as he watched, a young girl dressed in pink came shrieking out of one room and into another, hotly pursued by a young man with a handkerchief tied over his eyes and his arms outstretched in front of him. So it would seem that Blind Man's Buff was being played. Next to follow was Rose, as fresh as a beautiful flower that could make one weep if you damaged its petals. Tumbling after her, looking years younger and on fire with passion, came Julian Merrett, the young apothecary in charge of John's shop in Shug Lane.

"My, my," the Apothecary muttered, "the things that happen when my back is turned."

Out of the corner of her eye his daughter saw him and let out a shriek of amusement.

"Papa! What are you doing here?"

"I've come to play, my dearest. That is if you will let an old man like myself join your merry throng."

"Stop, Mr. Rawlings," she answered, giving him the smile he could never resist. "This is your house after all. Now come and have some summer punch. Miller mixed it and it certainly has an effect."

"So I observe," John answered drily. "Ah, Merrett, surely you haven't closed the shop?"

The poor chap went scarlet and stuttered out, "No, sir. I asked one of the others to deputise in my absence. Should there be any crisis he will send an errand boy here to fetch me."

"I see."

"Don't be unkind Papa. Mr. Merrett is allowed a day off occasionally and I stopped by the shop and invited him to join us. And I am so glad I did."

And she twinkled at the susceptible widower who blushed even deeper.

John cleared his throat. "Let me not spoil a moment of your festivities. Lead me to the punch bowl."

The party finally broke up when darkness fell. A goodly proportion of youngsters headed off purposefully in the direction of Drury Lane Theatre—including Rose and Mr. Merrett – leaving John alone with one of the twins. It was Jasper, James having gone to the theatre with the rest of the merry crowd. Instead of taking a chair opposite his—as John had done so often with Sir Gabriel Kent—the young man sat on the floor, resting against John's knees.

"I like sitting like this," he said quietly.

"I am pleased that you do. I used to sit in here with Sir Gabriel and discuss matters of importance."

"I can remember him. He was tall and elegant and wore a great powdered wig."

"But Jasper you were only just over two."

"He comes to me sometimes in my dreams. I tell you, Father, that I have a memory of calling him Grandpa. He was the sort of man that one could never forget."

"That," John answered thoughtfully, "is very true."

There was a comfortable silence then Jasper said, "Can I help you in any way?"

The Apothecary gave a deep sigh. "Yes, if you can unravel all the mysteries surrounding this extraordinary problem."

"You mean about that poor child Lucinda being in danger twice?"

"Yes. How did you know?"

Jasper turned his head and a wonderful smile flashed over his face. "I am Elizabeth's son," he said.

John put his arms round him and kissed the top of that dark head. "So you are," he answered.

Half an hour later and the entire set of circumstances had been laid out. Japer had taken a seat opposite and had absorbed every word his father said.

"Circumstantial evidence points to one of the Jacquard boys, Hyacinth's brothers, fathering Lucinda Buffitt," he said.

"Which do you think?"

"The one I have never seen. Giles. Do you know him?"

"I met him once," Jasper answered. "He's terribly short sighted."

"Do you think he is capable of organising such a cruel plot?"

"I don't see why not," his son replied thoughtfully, taking the glass of port that John handed him. "He's as likely as anyone and now suffers from guilt and wants to snuff the poor child out of existence."

"A little harsh that, my dear. And why attack poor Miss Feathering who has done no harm in this world except fall in love with a much younger man? How do you explain that?"

"I can't," Jasper answered, "but I can find out."

John laughed. "You sound a useful chap to have around. May I give you a task?"

"Please do. I am all eagerness."

"When you are next calling on Miss Hyacinth…"

"I thought that was your prerogative, Papa."

John kept his face straight.

"As I was saying, when next you call on that particular family try and engage Giles in earnest conversation. If he is acting a part endeavour to see through it. Ask him a few questions about the past. You know the sort of thing."

"Unfortunately I don't—but I am rapidly learning."

"And now let us change the subject, instead tell me who you think your beautiful sister is going to marry."

Jasper shook his head. "I have no idea. She has a mass of suitors. It could be any one of them. And there again it could still be someone she has yet to meet."

John nodded. "You are very wise. Tell me, have you come across Baron Rotmuller?"

"Not yet but the gossip goes that he is immensely rich."

"I believe that the Rotmullers are very well known on the continent."

"They are and now they have their beady eyes on Britain."

"Ah well. I will introduce you when the opportune moment arises. I will be interested to know your reaction."

They were still talking when the theatregoers—some of whom appeared to be staying the night—arrived home, creeping in on tiptoe to find Rose's father and brother chatting with animation.

John thought—having wished them all good night and blown out the candles—that somewhere Sir Gabriel Kent would be smiling benignly as all the laughter died away.

An invitation was awaiting him at his house at Strand-on-the-Green. It was surprisingly—and yet not in a way—from Baron Rotmuller. It invited John and all his children to attend a gala ball to be given at Oakridge House. By the same post there was a letter from Sam saying that he had received a bidding and was John going? It was with much pleasure that the Apothecary sat down and replied to both in the affirmative. Rose was particularly overjoyed.

"Do you realise, Papa, that this will be my very first appearance amongst the *bon ton.*"

"I didn't know that you cared about that sort of thing."

She smiled and said, "I don't. It is just the thought of having a new gown that I am looking forward to."

"Oh, I see. Well, I'm delighted to hear it. I wouldn't like to think that any of my children were snobbish."

"I'm snobbish," called James from the doorway. "And me," shouted his brother, right behind him.

"Out with you both instantly," and the Apothecary rose in mock anger and chased them halfway down Strand-on-the-Green, at which point he ran out of breath and turned back to the house, grinning. But they did not disgrace him when they tried on their clothes for the Grand Ball. James wore starkest black silk trimmed with silver facings, while Jasper wore blue trimmed with pale gold. Cut in the very latest fashion, both had stand up collars and coats that were perfectly aligned to the join between their trousers and their silken hose. Seeing them standing there, so young and so handsome, poised on the brink of life and somehow so vulnerable, the Apothecary felt his heart sing with joy and just wished that Elizabeth had lived to admire them.

Because Oakridge House was a goodly distance from Chiswick, John had joined forces with Zoffany and the Redwood family and they all made their way to The King's Arms in Berkhamsted the day before. The landlord himself came out to greet the four coaches, thrilled to see such a large and happy crowd of excitable people who would be occupying his inn for two nights. The younger persons poured out in a jolly torrent, John delighted to see that his two sons were acting with great gallantry and offering their arm to the ladies as they dismounted. He was not so pleased to observe that that nasty old dame—Cecily Redwood, mother of the viscount—was puffing in the doorway of her cumbersome coach, looking round for someone to assist her. In the end the landlord stepped forward genially which annoyed her as she considered him one of the 'savants'.

Despite the general atmosphere of good humour—Cecily Redwood excepted—John could not shake off the feeling of something stepping out of kilter. As always, he could not describe what it was that was bothering him but knew by the very air that trouble was out hunting. Therefore, nobody could have been more delighted than he was when Samuel's comfortable coach trundled into the courtyard and a second or so later his friend's shining face appeared on the step and handed out an unsmiling Jocasta.

Why does she dislike me? thought John, as he bent double in an elegant bow and kissed her reluctant hand, every inch the welcoming gentleman. He looked up and saw Samuel gazing at him, grinning and winking, and felt somewhat restored.

That night the Apothecary had the most terrifying dream. He dreamt that he was sitting in the great hall of the Jacobean mansion and saw that ghastly face again. This time the hall was in semi darkness, the only illumination coming from some weak shards of light which were piercing through the huge window. He stared over his shoulder and saw the face, contorted and terrible, gazing at him from outside. It was fearful and yet somehow pathetic and desperate. In the dream John stood up and went to the window and the woman leaned her ravaged features towards him. He could not help it, he recoiled, wanting to help her but unable to approach so fearful a creature. She opened her mouth and a silent scream came out. John could not help himself, he gave a cry and sat bolt upright in bed, awakening Jasper and James who were sharing a room with him.

"Papa, whatever frightened you?"

"I had a bad dream, t'is all."

"What happened?" asked Jasper, yawning himself awake.

"Nothing really. I saw a terrible face that scared me witless."

"What sort of face?"

"Scarred and awful."

"Why did you dream that?"

"I have no idea," John answered with asperity. "Now go back to sleep the pair of you. There's a great deal of partying to be done tomorrow."

But despite his instructions the Apothecary lay awake for hours and the sun was coming up before he finally drifted into unconsciousness.

The next morning the group set off on the journey to the former home of the Blue Friars—the Bonhommes—an order founded by the Earl of Cornwall, nephew of Henry III, in 1283. It had remained as a holy order until the dissolution of the monasteries, when the estate passed into the greedy hands of Henry VIII. On the monarch's death, however, it had been left to Elizabeth and for a while she had made her home there, until her arrest by her half-sister, Mary. In 1604 it had been bought by Thomas Egerton, a loyal servant of the crown, then in 1760 the great landscape artist Capability Brown had created its glorious parkland. But the most interesting part of the estate's history—or so John had thought—was when it passed into the hands of Baron Rotmuller on the turn of a single dice. And now the carriages were rolling up his drive to attend the evening's grand ball and he was standing on the steps to greet them, all smiles and good humour, obviously one of the coming men in England's social history. Behind him, handsome as hell in claret faced with deep blue, stood his younger brother Robert.

John vividly recalled the night when he had first seen the place, plunged in darkness, a groaning Sir Humphrey Warburton threshing in a carriage, screaming for help, as he had begged for admittance. Then, it had seemed to him that it was smaller, closely confined, but now in the vivid sunshine he saw how wrong he had been. Elizabeth had sent for master builders to restructure the house to her designs. And now it was obvious that a team of workmen had recently been smartening up the baron's mansion to a state of magnificence worthy of a great family of European bankers. As if to emphasise the point, as the first carriages appeared in the driveway the baron's servants appeared in a body and stood in a reception committee, while young Robert joined the footmen waiting to hand the ladies down to the safety of the ground. At the same moment a hidden orchestra burst forth with an anthem of joyous welcome that filled the air with a tremendous heart-lifting sound. It was memorable indeed.

The first person to get out was Sir Humphrey Warburton who had travelled from London on the previous evening but not stayed with the jocund crowd at The Kings Arms. He was escorted from his conveyance by young Robert and after that limped up the steps to greet the baron, who was coming down to meet him. This done and with the orchestra now playing a festive air, the rest of the crowd disgorged and John—standing back a little—was able to observe the elegant gentlemen, James and Jasper included, helping the pretty young things out of their carriages. The ghastly Mrs. Redwood senior was handed down by the baron's brother, Robert. But then John observed him going very pale as a newcomer appeared on the scene and put a large and unyielding foot on the step—it was Miss Phoebe Feathering, got up like a small-part soprano in a second-rate opera company and clearly employed by Mrs. Redwood as some sort of companion, the London employer presumably having gone, either to her Maker or some other aged crony.

"Robert," she breathed in ecstasy.

The young fellow literally rocked where he stood and a nearby footman came to the rescue and offered Miss Feathering his hand as she stepped down from the carriage.

"Feathering," ordered Mrs. Redwood in stentorian tones. "See me indoors if you please."

"Certainly, my dear. Just coming."

Phoebe turned to Robert, who had gone the shade of a crimson cyclamen, and tapped him with a huge, feathered fan which she had attached to her wrist. "You naughty puppy," she cooed playfully, then strode as best she could to the glowering Cecily's side.

John did not know whether to laugh or cry. The scene he had just witnessed had expressed everything that was pathetic in humanity and yet, he thought, Phoebe Feathering was happy enough. If he should feel sorry for anyone it should be naughty Robert. The young man had just had the shock of his life and was now wandering about, blanched white, trying to fulfil the wishes of his elder brother who was shouting instructions at him in a non-stop staccato. Meanwhile, more and more carriages were coming up the drive and nobody was going into the house, anxious to see who was going to join them at the ball. The servants had brought out trays of drinks and the guests were peering over the balustrade and passing whispered comments about the new arrivals.

A very delightful carriage came up the drive and there was a low murmur as the Viscount Lovell appeared and handed down his wife, ravishing in blue and white and clearly pregnant. John thought to himself that any trouble from his two lads and he would put them both under that creaky old pump which obviously had some secret magic in its splashing water. It became obvious that the old harridan Cecily had reappeared—plus her escort Miss Feathering—because a commanding voice shouted, "Michael, come here," and at the same moment Robert ducked down behind a tall and stately young woman carrying a parasol, concealing himself from view. John chuckled audibly. It was like something from one of Mr. Foote's theatrical farces.

A voice spoke beside him. "I see you are enjoying yourself, Mr. Rawlings."

He turned and saw that it was pretty Hyacinth and still—despite the fact he was old enough to be her father—his heart skipped a beat. But further conversation was impossible. The hidden orchestra which had merrily been playing a selection of tunes from *The Beggar's Opera* suddenly went silent for a minute or two then burst forth with Handel's *Hallelujah Chorus*. Those who were seated immediately rose to their feet as this had become the definite custom following the action of George II, who had stood up in admiration on first hearing the mighty sound ring out.

Meanwhile a dark coach had appeared at the far end of the drive and a silent signal went up that someone of importance was arriving. People jostled as they crowded towards the stone balustrade to get a better look. Hyacinth stepped in front of the Apothecary and over the ostrich feather of her hat he saw the equipage come to a halt at the foot of the steps. The servants positively rushed headlong to be the first to open the door but too late, a flunky leapt down from the coachman's box and did so, bowing low immediately. John, half expecting royalty after this grand entrance, was almost disappointed when the looming figure of the Duke of Derwent appeared in the coach's doorway. Seeing the peering crowd he grimaced and waved, his mighty arm sweeping upward and a hand the size of a cured ham shaking its fingers.

"That old creature," snorted Hyacinth *sotto voce.*

"Not the most pleasant of characters," John whispered in reply.

But the Duke was turning to extend his hand to his wife who stood lingering in the doorframe. Today she looked lovely, exactly like her twin sister. She was tricked out in violet velvet and had on a great sweeping hat with a feather that almost met the ground. John had a sudden mental picture of that gorgeous face being bruised and blackened by one of the duke's mighty fists and shudderingly hoped that it was all his imagination. He must have made a small sound because Hyacinth looked up at him and smiled.

"Shall we go inside, Mr. Rawlings?"

He nodded. "It will be my pleasure, Miss Jacquard."

By now many people had drifted into the house and were looking around them with much obvious interest. The Apothecary, however, preferred to examine the Redwood family who had gathered *en masse* round the old wretch Cecily, pretending to hang on her every word. The viscount sat at a distance, his wife very close to him, idly playing with a satin ribbon at the neckline of her frock and not listening to a word his mother said. Next to them, not even pretending to pay attention, were her two naughty boys, as she had lovingly described them, Roderick and Percival. They were both handsome in an ugly sort of way, with thick dark hair tied back and a set of regular reasonably attractive features. However, their eyes were on the small side, dark brown and vicious looking, as they clearly darted after every female in the room. John imagined that there was probably only a year between them and that they egged each other on unpleasantly.

Next came three grim faced women, ranging from extremely vast to skeletal in size. One of them had a husband, for a small miserable man sat amongst them, though which of the three had dragged him to the altar it was difficult to tell. The large one—large indeed—had fat hands which were surreptitiously sliding into a bag of sweetmeats and popping one into her mouth as soon as she had swallowed the last. The other two women ranked each other in the matter of dreary expressions and lacklustre postures. The Apothecary wondered when he had last seen a more uninspiring crowd and puzzled how Mrs. Redwood had managed to produce anyone as interesting as the viscount.

Humming to herself with pleasure at being in such palatial surroundings, Miss Phoebe Feathering wandered happily around, hoping to engage Robert in conversation. John, looking in the young man's direction, saw that he was speaking to all three of the Rawlings children and obviously enjoying himself. It was at that moment that Baron Rotmuller's voice rang out.

"Honoured guests, a cold collation has been laid out in the Blue and Red rooms. I hope you will make your way there and enjoy yourselves. For those of you who are staying here tonight you will find your things have been unpacked and after the repast you will be guided to your rooms by my staff. For others of you who wish to change into formal wear for tonight, adequate arrangements have been made. The ball will begin at 7.30 this evening. Thank you all for attending this joyful day."

The hidden orchestra played a final chord, then stood up and took a bow before disappearing from the Musician's Gallery where they had been concealed. The afternoon wore on splendidly. The older people slept, some in comfortable chairs, those that were staying, in their rooms. The younger, heartier set, strode forth in the summer afternoon and gazed upon the estate and the genius of Capability Brown, walked to the nearby fields and looked at the sheep and cows, others again crept off into the woods to hide from prying eyes and investigate each other's anatomy. John Rawlings going on a navigation of the great house and heading for the ruined abbey was waylaid by a panting Miss Feathering.

"Oh Mr. Rawlings, have you seen Robert Rotmuller anywhere? I do so want a private word with him."

John truthfully replied, "No, I haven't. I imagine he is with his brother and they are discussing the arrangements for tonight."

"Oh, I hadn't thought of that. What a nuisance."

"To be sure." The Apothecary changed the subject. "The Redwood family are quite a mixed bag, aren't they? I don't think I have ever met such a dissimilar group of people."

She fell into step beside him. "Yes, they are rather, though I mustn't speak ill of them. I didn't own the house in London, you know. I was a companion to the lady who did—but she has recently died. Cecily offered me a post and, to be honest, I accepted it with gratitude. Of course it is Cecily that I know really well. A very long-suffering woman that. She has had much to bear."

"Really? What?"

"Well, I know I am talking out of turn, but her husband was a cruel beast. For ever at the gaming tables and never by her side. He was related to the Earl of Cumbria, you know, and thought very highly of himself. Then of course he died, followed by two cousins—most sadly of fever I might add—and Michael became the heir. I think he has improved a great deal recently. Seems very much in love with his wife all of a sudden."

"I think he is," John answered—and meant it.

By six o'clock that evening a great quiet had descended on the upper part of the house with the guests bathing or flirting or being dressed by their personal servants for the forthcoming ball. Below stairs, however, all hell had broken loose as Baron Rotmuller's army of minions scurried about the million and one final tasks preparing the great house for the evening's festivities. At exactly quarter past seven the baron strode out of his bedroom and took up position beside his younger brother at the top of the staircase leading up from the hall. They both dazzled in dress uniforms of the German Navy, each with a brilliant star pinned to their chest. They had presumably been in the service and won a medal and, remembering Robert's performance during his scuffle with the Straw Man, John's estimation of the young man went a step higher. At half-past seven carriages could be heard arriving and those guests already present formed into a long queue ready to climb the staircase and be greeted by their hosts. One of the first to go up was the Duke of Derwent accompanied by his Duchess, followed by various other members of the nobility—some from Germany, bristling with importance. The Earl of Cumbria was not present but his second cousin, the Viscount Lovell and his wife were, and they proceeded up the stairs in a charming and relaxed manner. John, remembering the young man dripping under the pump, smiled into his sleeve.

As soon as the titled people had been greeted the rest of the guests followed. First, very charmingly John thought, was Sir Humphrey Warburton, limping slowly but surely, accompanied by his sister Cecily Redwood. She was crowing with self-importance, covered with every jewel she possessed, head held as high as she could get it, weighed down as it was by an old-fashioned tiara. Behind her the two favourite sons lounged up the stairs nonchalantly as if they didn't give a tuppeny damn about German aristocracy and were cursed if they were giving anything but the briefest of bows. The baron must have guessed because he gave the minutest of nudges to his brother and they both clicked their heels as Roderick and Percival arrived before them, meanwhile remaining stony faced. The Apothecary, observing all, mentally raised his hat to the pair of hosts.

The ballroom was transformed. When John had visited before he had passed through the large space and thought nothing of it. But now he drew breath as he entered fairyland. Two mighty chandeliers glowing with lights were suspended above, while on the walls hung chains of illuminations. There were elegant plush chairs set in a semi-circle round the dance floor in which the elderly and infirm could sit, while at the very back a huge trestle table was covered with refreshments of a liquid variety. This table was currently surrounded by the guests anxious to refresh themselves before the serious dancing began.

John turned to the twins who had climbed the staircase just behind him.

"Have you seen anything of Rose? I would have thought she might have joined us."

"I know she wanted to but Hyacinth called for her help at the last minute. A missing button or something of that sort."

"Ah well at least I know where I stand in the order of things. Who could compete with a button?"

"I never realised you had a crotchety streak, Papa."

"My dear boy, you wait till you get to my age."

"Would you like us to carry you to a chair?"

But the banter was interrupted by the entry of the Master of Ceremonies who came onto the dance floor clapping his gloved hands together.

"Ladies and Gentlemen, good evening. Will you please join me for a cotillion? We shall dance The Duchess of Marlborough. But first a line of ladies and a line of gentleman also."

There was a general rush onto the ballroom floor and John found himself with the rest of the men present standing opposite the ladies, who smiled and curtsied in return. The orchestra struck up a country air and John felt the usual lift of his spirits as the crowd whirled away, all troubles temporarily forgotten. He had not fully realised how very much he enjoyed dancing. It was an extraordinary experience, any worries he had completely put away. He saw Baron Rotmuller circling round to meet Cecily Redwood, who was obviously labouring somewhat as she panted her way through the steps. But panting or no, the dancers were to be given no rest. Following the Duchess of Marlborough the orchestra immediately struck up Gang No More To Yon Town and once more couples whirled away in figures of eight, the top two proceeding under the arched arms and clasped hands of the others. John changed partners several times, one dance being with the viscountess herself, who took the steps slowly but smiled throughout.

"You look in good spirits, madam, if I may say so. Is all well at home?"

"It is indeed. I am so happy. Long may it last."

"The viscount is being more—attentive?"

"Very much so. I think you are a bit of a magician, Mr. Rawlings. Did you practice a bit of wizardry on him by any chance?"

The Apothecary winked an eye, thinking of the pump. "We study a multitude of disciplines, madam. Tell me, do you grow jessamine in your garden?"

Miranda's eyebrows shot up. "No, I don't believe so."

"Then I would get some if I were you. The leaves can be boiled up and the juices mixed with wine. It can be most conducive to a sleepless night."

"Did I hear you correctly? You meant sleeping night surely."

"No, my lady. I meant exactly what I said."

And with that John kissed her hand and made his way to the bar.

There were several gentlemen already there, in fact most of the younger members of the Redwood clan together with two of the Jacquard boys and a guest of the baron's. They all bowed as the Apothecary approached. He returned the compliment. The viscount stepped forward.

"My dear Mr. Rawlings, may I present my brothers and my cousin. Roderick and Percival Redwood and the Comte d'Etoile."

The two loutish young men made a great deal of hand whirling while they bowed whereas the Frenchman was almost abrupt, bowing in an off-hand manner, his face regarding John expressionlessly while he did so. The Apothecary decided that he was considered as not worth knowing by any of them.

"Percival Redwood," said one of the oafs by way of introduction. "Damn fine evening, what?"

So this was to be the level of conversation. "Yes," replied John, applying a lacey handkerchief to his nostrils, "very fine orchestra in my opinion, don't you know."

The Frenchman let out a sudden guffaw and said, "Well, well, is this all you English can talk about?"

"No. I can debate anything you wish to suggest. What would you like to discuss?" John answered.

A pair of dark jade eyes regarded him with some amusement. "I spoke in jest only, monsieur. It is, as you say, an evening most elegant."

What was it about the man that was so enormously irritating, the Apothecary wondered? Nonetheless it was a splendid party and he must be polite. He smiled and said, "But you as a Frenchman, sir, would be very used to this kind of occasion surely."

178

Behind him he heard a ripple of laughter come from the Redwood layabouts and wondered why.

Charles Jacquard spoke. "I don't think you have met my brother Giles, Mr. Rawlings. He was out when you came to dine with us. May I present him to you?"

"Certainly," John answered.

A plain but pleasant young man was bowing before him, his face dominated by a powerful pair of spectacles behind which blinked a greatly magnified set of light blue eyes. The Apothecary realised immediately that the fellow was practically blind but determined to enjoy life as best he could.

"How do you do, sir?" he said. "John Rawlings of Nassau Street and Chiswick. I am delighted to make your acquaintance."

On closer inspection he realised that his new arrival was not as young as he had first thought, probably about thirty-five, but other than for his terrible sight a reasonably handsome being and quite definitely nothing like the evil monster that Jasper had imagined. Then he witnessed something extremely odd. The Comte d'Etoile was drawling out some remark about the dancers when suddenly Giles Jacquard looked at him, a look—even from those eyes that could see so faintly—of pure hatred. There was no other way to describe it; it was complete and utter raw loathing. The Apothecary wondered what ancient feud could have sparked off such a feeling. But his attention was drawn elsewhere. The Master of Ceremonies was calling them for the last dance before the supper break and every man in the group hurried to finish his drink and take his place. Even the short-sighted Giles joining them. Then it was time to eat.

The meal was utterly delicious. Two vast tables had been set up, one in the conservatory, the other in the damask room and the occasion began with a choice of soups and went on to every delicacy that

179

one could imagine. There was fish in champagne, pigeons in almond butter, beef en croute, to name but a few of the items of the main course. This then went on to ices, jellies, puddings and fruit, and all kinds of confection to delight the eyes and appetites of the various guests. The Apothecary found himself sitting between two women, neither of whom he knew but who gossiped about everyone else, particularly Miranda Redwood.

"I've heard it said that her husband will soon become the Earl of Cumbria, the old man being very poorly, so it's rumoured."

"She is perfectly beautiful, lucky creature. What an odd business though."

"What?"

"About her sister."

"Best not to talk about it, dear. Least said and all that."

"They never did catch the man though, did they?"

"No, I don't think they did."

To say John was startled would have been to understate the case. That there had been a scandal surrounding Lady Derwent was astonishing. And then a faint memory bell rang in his brain. One night, perhaps over drinks in Zoffany's house, hadn't the painter said something about a third sister being injured in some way. Presently John had had too many glasses of wine to be able to recall all the details but now he made a mental note to talk to the painter as soon as he got back. The tables were being cleared and people were given half an hour to prepare themselves for the second half and dancing the night away. The ladies rushed to the water closets, the gentlemen to a latrine erected in the grounds. It was in there that Samuel finally caught John up.

"I say, what a splendid feast—and what perfectly grand company. Everybody who is anybody is here—and a few old wastrels as well, including me."

"Sam, dearest fellow, how can you say that? I am just sorry I haven't had a chance to speak to you yet. But there's a massive crowd here and I didn't see you at the refreshment table."

"No, Jocasta decided she needed a little fresh air and I could not let her walk out on her own."

"No, I suppose not."

The Apothecary considered telling his oldest friend that he should have let the selfish woman go by herself but remembering all their years of comradeship, decided against. In any case the Master of Ceremonies could be heard calling people to return to the ballroom. He and Samuel jostled their way back in to be joined by Jasper and James, who had been seated elsewhere during the meal. However, there was no sign of Rose.

"Where's your sister? Do you know?"

"No, sorry, Papa. We saw her earlier, very much in the care of the younger Rotmuller. He treats her as if she is a precious piece of glass."

"So I noticed," John answered drily.

"Pray silence for your host if you please."

There was an enormous cheer as the baron made his way to the front.

"Ladies and gentlemen, before we begin the second half of dancing there is something I want you to see. We have had in Europe for a long while now a form of dance that is quite revolutionary and it is yet to visit these shores. You may have heard the music. It is in triple time. Tonight, for the very first time in England, I would like you to look at der Waltzer or the Waltz."

There was a smattering of applause and the orchestra began to play, a tuneful melody which people tapped their feet to. Then out of the shadows appeared a couple dancing—but not facing one another as was the English tradition. This pair were holding one another tightly, body to body, he with an arm round her waist, she with her hand on his shoulder. It was quite, quite shocking and yet at the same time it was beautiful to behold. With a start John realised that the girl was his own daughter, her partner who else but the young Rotmuller.

There was a very loud scream from Mrs. Redwood. "It's obscene," she shouted. "It's public fornication."

"They're *touching* one another," quavered an elderly cleric. "It's against the laws of the church."

Several older women shouted. "Repulsive." "Disgusting." "Tell them to stop at once." "We are British and proud of it." "You should be ashamed of yourselves." One voice echoed round the hall. "We don't want any European rubbish in England thank you."

Typical, thought John.

Rose and Robert waltzed into the darkness as there was a stampede of elderly feet making their way out. Undaunted, the Master of Ceremonies clapped his gloved hands.

"Ladies and gentlemen, by way of contrast we will now do Miss Pringle's Minuet."

There was a subdued laugh from the young people and the couples formed up. John excused himself and went to find Samuel but could not do so. He thought that his friend had, in all probability, been captured by Jocasta and was currently engaged in a boring conversation somewhere.

No-one was about that the Apothecary wished to exchange civilities with so he took the opportunity of exploring the house on his own. The damask room still had some greedy hogs sitting at table and stuffing food down themselves but the conservatory had been restored to its usual state, the great trestle taken down and the fine cloth removed. Chairs had been set out by exotic plants and in one of these sat Cecily Redwood, very upright and with not one member of her family in sight. John glanced at her, thinking it strange that above her plum-coloured dress she had tied a band of scarlet ribbon. And then he let out a great cry and literally jumped forward as he saw that it wasn't a scarlet ribbon at all, for someone had slashed the woman's throat and what he was looking at was a gaping, bloody, wound. He felt for her pulse but knew it was hopeless. She had been done to death and sat with her eyes staring and wide in shock. She had clearly looked up as she had felt that first touch of someone standing behind her chair and cutting her open. John heard a person come up and knew by the very tread that it was Samuel.

"Where have you been …" his friend started, then drew in a sharp breath. "My God, oh merciful heavens, her throat's been slashed."

John stood up, wiping the blood from his fingers. "Sam, go and fetch the baron. He must be informed immediately. I'll guard the body. If anyone approaches tell them there has been an accident and to keep away."

His friend had gone pale as snow but—nodding silently—spun on his heel and ran. John turned and spread out the tails of his coat as if warming himself at a fire, hoping, at the very least, to protect the poor woman from prying eyes. Fortunately, as most of the other guests were still dancing the traditional dances and trying to forget the impact the waltz had had on them, nobody came by. A few minutes later, however, John saw the baron with several sturdy-looking footmen arrive with an aged man carrying a medical bag who had been fetched from the damask room.

"So what have we here?" the doctor asked, his voice rather fragile and fluting.

John answered firmly. "John Rawlings, Apothecary, Shug Lane, Piccadilly. I'm afraid this poor woman has been murdered, sir."

The elderly man looked startled. "Murdered you say? How can you tell?"

"Because her throat has been cut open. The attack was made from behind. A person unknown lent over the back of the chair and slit her under the chin."

"Good gracious—and at such a lovely gathering. Let me see."

The Apothecary stood to one side and the medical man opened his ancient leather bag and took out a pair of spectacles before bending over the body of Mrs. Redwood. He recoiled in horror.

"You're quite right, Mr. Rawlings, she has been done to death." He closed the staring eyes. "What a terrible thing. I suppose, Baron Rotmuller, that we had better send for the constable."

The baron, looking exceedingly glum, said, "I suppose you are correct."

"Palmer is quite a nice chap actually. Paid to do it by a consortium who don't want the job themselves."

"Then at least he'll have some experience," said John, with a certain amount of relief.

The doctor smiled thinly. "Actually we don't have many murders round here so I don't know about that."

A fact which Constable Richard Palmer, when he finally arrived, was pleased to confirm. By this time John and the doctor had covered the body with a cloth and Baron Rotmuller in stentorian tones had ordered everyone in the conservatory to remove themselves promptly.

The assembly had at last ground to a halt. Somehow news of what had happened had filtered through to the Master of Ceremonies who had called a halt to the dancing, explaining that there had been an unfortunate death. The entire Redwood family had gone in a rush to the conservatory when they had heard the identity of the deceased, only to be told in no uncertain terms that they were not allowed to enter. Roderick and Percival had immediately put up their fists, to be warned that they must behave like gentlemen by their older brother,

184

the viscount. But there was worse to come. The constable informed the remaining guests that no-one was allowed to leave until he had spoken to them individually. The rapturous evening had turned into a nightmare.

The ladies all stayed together in a manner which John in other circumstances would have found amusing. The men did likewise, grouped round the long table at which alcoholic beverages were going at a rate of knots. None of Cecily's sons had wept a tear, John noticed, whereas the three unlovely daughters had indulged in loud and prolonged bouts of hysteria, comforted by poor Miss Feathering, who had cried a little into a muslin handkerchief. However, despite the baron's best attempts several people had left before Constable Palmer had arrived and taken control, these included the Duke and Duchess of Derwent and that peculiar Frenchman d'Etoile.

Samuel whispered to John, "Poor old Sir Humphrey Warburton. To lose a leg and a sister all within a year is terribly bad luck."

The Apothecary gave a humourless smile and said, "I agree with you." But on second thoughts there was something about the remark that would not go away. It was bad luck indeed that such evil should have fallen on one person. Something in his brain was trying to tell him something but as yet he could not grasp what it was.

At about two o'clock in the morning something like order had been finally restored. Two burly men had removed the body, Constable Palmer had seen every one of the guests and knew where to contact them, sleepy coachmen were woken up and brought carriages round to the front door to collect the remnants of what had been a marvellous assembly. Robert Rotmuller, pale but determined, had arrived to give his brother support. John, standing quietly in the background with Samuel, saw the look on Rose's face as she said goodnight to him—and knew at that moment that Robert must join the flock of the other admirers. He anxiously turned to Samuel.

"If you can manage to stay an extra day there is much that I would like to discuss."

"I will do what I can. It has been a very eventful night, hasn't it."

"Extremely thought provoking."

Both men watched the retreating figures of the Redwood family as they made their way out, the three women still sobbing loudly, poor Miss Feathering staggering beneath the weight of discarded shawls, gloves and fans.

"Interesting," murmured John, regarding her.

"Very," answered Samuel, nodding his head.

Chapter Seventeen

Jasper, good as his recent promise to keep a look-out, lingered on after breakfast, served late the next morning as none of the Rawlings family had slept much before dawn.

"May I speak to you, Papa?" he asked as his brother and sister left the room.

"Certainly you may. Did you observe anything at the great Assembly last night?"

"Several things. First of all, I don't think the Comte d'Etoile is French. I think it is all assumed."

"Why?"

"He was out in the garden—relieving himself—with one of those ghastly Redwood fellows and I overheard him speaking English with not a trace of an accent. Quite a harsh, cruel voice indeed."

"Interesting. I met him briefly and didn't like him at all."

"The other thing that I noticed was how very little Giles Jacquard can see. He was dancing and several times went off in the wrong direction. Fortunately his partner—a big, blonde, giggling girl—caught him in time and steered him in the right path. But he's a nice chap. I liked him. I spoke to him quite a lot and thought him very good hearted."

"Anything else?"

"No, but I wanted to ask you about Miss Feathering. The poor soul spent most of the evening waiting upon the Redwood ladies. That is when she wasn't looking for Robert Rotmuller. I find her a sad case."

"I think I'll go and talk to her again."

"Papa, you won't be able to winkle her out from all those wailing women."

"If she has any sense she will get the next stage to London. I'll try her there in a couple of days. Meanwhile I might call on the Redwoods. To offer my condolences and so on."

"Do you mind if I come with you?"

"Not in the least. See if you can find anything out about those two charmers Roderick and Percival, or best of all, their friend the phoney Frenchman."

"They all think I'm an ass."

"Then play the part, Jasper." Rawlings raised an eyebrow. "It shouldn't be too difficult."

"Really, Papa," said James—and looked fractionally hurt.

Sometime later, clad in dark mournful clothes, they set out in ghastly damp weather for the Jacobean mansion, which today had the chilling atmosphere of a haunted house. It loomed through the rain-sodden landscape as if it knew it was condemned to die, that a powerful duke wanted it done to death in order to make way for the bright new wings he was going to attach to his villa. John, his hat dripping raindrops, felt that he was approaching a house of doom and was almost glad when he and Jasper at last stood within the shelter of the porch. He pulled the rope and the sound of the bell boomed and echoed down the corridors of time—or so it seemed to him. It was answered by a footman wearing a black armband and looking mournful. And when they were ushered into the huge receiving room they found that it was candlelit and all the curtains had been pulled closed. Very distantly there could be heard sobbing and a woman's voice making a mooing sound as if in pain.

John was relieved when Miranda, the viscountess, walked towards them, smiling radiantly despite the general gloomy atmosphere. John and Jasper simultaneously swept off their dripping hats and bowed low.

"How pleasant," she said, "to be visited by two such charming gentlemen."

John answered, "Your Grace, may I present my son, Jasper Rawlings?"

"My goodness, of course you may. He is very attractive to behold."

"His mother was a beautiful woman."

"And you are not ugly, Mr. Rawlings."

He answered, smiling, "Is this a suitable discussion for a house of mourning?"

The viscountess laughed and said, "No, of course it isn't. But then I do not mourn my mother-in-law's loss. She was perfectly beastly to me at first because my sisters and I were much loved by society and she was jealous. She tolerated me only after my husband became a member of the peerage."

John moved his head slightly. "Excuse me, my lady, but did you say sisters, in the plural?"

"Yes, I did. There were three of us, the Beautiful Misses Winterlight we were known as. The loveliest, my elder sister, retired from public life some years ago—and then she died."

"Oh dear. How terribly sad."

The viscountess turned away and stared at the drawn curtains. "Yes. She just grew tired of living."

"What a pity," Jasper said.

Miranda looked at him, a strange expression on her face.

"The truth is that she was injured in an accident and as a result withdrew from prying eyes. But she is, in fact, still alive."

There was a moment's silence, then John asked, "Was she badly hurt?"

"Very badly." Miranda said these words with such finality that neither father nor son dared ask another thing. She smiled. "It was so kind of you to call. I will pass on your good wishes to the rest of the family. I am afraid that my sisters-in-law are unable to receive anyone at the moment."

"I quite understand," John answered pleasantly. "Come Jasper. Let us be on our way."

His son suddenly seized Miranda's hand and kissed it, a movement which pleased both her and his father, who felt a certain pride that the twins were growing up so pleasantly.

"Thank you for receiving us at such a wretched time," Jasper said hurriedly, then without another word made his way out and into the blinding rain.

Miranda stared after him. "You have wonderful children, Mr. Rawlings."

"Thank you, my lady," he answered and followed his son outside.

Jasper was sheltering beneath a slightly overhanging roof but was staring intently at the spinney of trees opposite. As John joined him, he motioned him to be quiet.

"What's up?"

"It's that odd fellow I met at the ball last night. The one I told you about who is so very short-sighted. He's over there and he seems to be waiting for someone."

John followed the line of Jasper's pointing finger and there, sure enough, standing silently amongst the trees, his cloak so wet that it clung to him like a shroud, his hat a shapeless pudding on his head, was the wretched figure of Giles. Fortunately his back was turned though John doubted with his poor eyesight whether the fellow would have been able to see the two who stood watching. Then Jasper drew his father tighter still into the place where they stood. Another figure, heavily cloaked and fully masked, was making its way through the downpour, this one coming from behind where Giles waited. Both the observers tensed, wondering what was going to happen next and Jasper flexed himself, ready to intervene if it was going to be an attack. But on the contrary, the approaching figure hurried through the ground—sticky with rainfall—and tugged at Giles's sleeve. He turned his head to see who it was and then, surprisingly, gave the intruder a hug before hurrying them off and out of sight.

"Do we follow?" Jasper whispered.

"Yes, at a discreet distance. They're going in our direction anyhow."

But in that wish John and Jasper were thwarted. There was a small cottage near the duke's estate, standing amongst other similar dwellings, probably all owned by his Grace and lived in by his workers. Into this Giles and his human bundle of cloaks suddenly vanished and father and son were left staring.

"What do we do now?" asked Jasper, just beginning to enjoy his detective work.

John laughed. "We either wait here for hours on end to see what happens next. Or we go to a hostelry on the riverbank. Your choice."

"The inn," Jasper said without hesitation, and seizing the Apothecary by the elbow led him off with determination.

They walked home two hours later, John taking Jasper's arm and feeling comfortable. They had discussed the mystery of Giles's friend, though neither of them could be certain whether it was a short man or a tallish woman, so wrapped up had the creature been in coats and capes, and with a great hood set upon its head.

"I reckon it was his light-o'-love," said Jasper.

"Male or female?" queried John.

"The poor devil is so short-sighted that I don't think it would make much difference to him."

The Apothecary tried to look severe, failed utterly and laughed with amusement.

Rose had arrived home, somewhat pink of the cheek John noticed. She was clearly thinking herself to be in love and was talking excitedly about the ball and how tragic had been the ending.

"Did you not get a chance to say farewell to Mr. Rotmuller?" asked James innocently.

"No, I'm afraid not."

"You mean that there were too many other people around?"

"Oh really!" she said and threw a spoon at him, it being the first thing she could lay her hand on.

John listened to them arguing and felt his heart lift with the sheer pride of having such a beautiful, boisterous brood. He thought then about the two women who had given him those wonderful gifts. Rose's mother, the vivacious Emilia, doomed to such a cruel ending, and the magnificent, scarred Elizabeth, who had given birth to the twin boys in her mature years. He thought finally of the great Coralie Clive, still very much alive and a woman who could control an audience in Drury Lane just by raising her glorious voice. How lucky he had been to have been loved by three so very different and unusual females. Of course, there had been the odd peccadillo here and there but no-one had ever touched his heart like that amazing trio and the thought of them would be with him for ever.

Rose had marched out of the room in very high stirrup and James said, "I think you had better go after her, Papa. I believe she has had enough teasing. I'm sorry, I didn't mean anything by it."

"You will learn, my dear child, that women can be very huffy about that kind of thing when they think they are in love. Don't worry. Leave your sister to me."

But Rose was not so easy to talk round. She was in the kitchen mixing something with great zeal and a thunderous look on her face. She glanced up as John came in and managed a grimace that passed for a smile.

"My sweet girl, don't let the boys upset you. You know that they love you dearly."

She put down the wooden spoon and said, "I am glad you have come, Papa, because I want to talk to you."

"Then talk away, my dear, talk away."

"I will. Robert Rotmuller has asked me to marry him, unofficially of course. He would not do anything so forward as propose until he had your permission to do so. But he is going to visit you as soon as that horrible business which happened the other night has been resolved. Tell me, what will your answer be?"

John was temporarily flummoxed. Firstly, he had never known his daughter to be quite so direct. Secondly, he could see she meant every word she said.

"Well, I should ask him what his prospects are but I imagine they would be very healthy considering he is a member of that great banking family."

"And there you would be wrong, sir. The family originated in Germany, and it is a tradition that each member has to earn his personal rewards within the company. Baron Rotmuller will not help him till he joins the firm."

"I see. Well Robert will just have to make his mind up, won't he? Is the roar of the greasepaint better than the clink of gold coins?"

"He may be a little foolish," Rose answered. "But he is one of the nicest, kindest men I have ever met."

It was time—and John knew it—to draw this particular conversation to a close. "I am sure he is, my darling. Now stop making whatever it is you are beating into such an angry pulp—what would cook say if he saw you taking charge of his little kingdom?—and make friends again with your brothers and, hopefully, your old Papa."

She smiled. She had loved him all her life and possibly longer, if one believed such things. So Rose gave him a kiss on the cheek and allowed him to lead her back into the salon. But John's hopes of a quiet family evening were dashed once more when James plucked him by the sleeve and asked if he could have a word in confidence. So it was that after supper—which was a small cold collation—and when Rose and Jasper had gone for a short walk before bedtime, that James said, "I know I am far too young for all this but I feel that I have fallen in love, Papa."

With an amused but sinking heart John asked, "Who with? Do I know the lady?"

"Of course you do. It's Hyacinth Jacquard. It was that night on Oliver's Island when she played the flute so divinely and I sang, that's when I knew that I truly loved her."

John stared into the abyss of middle age. Hyacinth, the girl for whom he had felt feelings of deep attraction, was set fair to become his daughter-in-law. What the devil, he thought. Do other men of forty-nine get similar kicks in the teeth? But he put on a brave smile and said, "Good luck to you, my boy. There are several years that must pass before you can take this any further."

"I do realise that, Papa. But I just thought I ought to tell you because you are so terribly wise."

In the shadows at the far end of the room John could have sworn he briefly saw Sir Gabriel Kent sitting nonchalantly, one leg crossed over the knee of the other, with a highly amused grin on his face. Inwardly John shook his head at the entire ludicrousness of life's little twists and turns and went to pour himself a glass of claret wine.

Chapter Eighteen

The next morning he was awoken—having decided to lie in and dwell upon his middle-aged sorrows—by a thunderous knocking on the front door. Cautiously putting his nose out of the window it was to see Samuel standing below, portmanteau at his feet.

"John, you rogue, I can see you twitching your curtains. Come down and let me in. I have arrived to stay."

By the time he had slipped a robe over his underwear, the door had been opened by a serving man and Samuel was filling the hallway with his cheery personality.

"My dear boy," he said, giving John a hearty slap on the back which was the last thing he wanted in his fit of mid-life crisis. "I have managed to persuade Jocasta to journey home to see that the house is being well run in her absence. Because I knew that after the terrible happenings at the Rotmuller ball you would want me to help you peel the layers off this particular mystery."

Momentarily, John did not know whether to laugh or weep but decided on the former. "Thank you, old friend," he said. "It is all a great puzzle."

"But we shall solve it together."

"I think I could do with a hearty breakfast."

An hour later after eating a particularly large repast, the two friends repaired to John's snug to discuss the terrible happenings and try to make sense of them.

"Repeat to me," Samuel said, "the order of events that have happened. Right from the start."

"Well, first of all that unfortunate child Lucinda was pushed into the Thames and if she had not been dragged out by one of Rose's many suitors …" John gave a slightly hollow laugh. "… would have drowned. Second thing which I would have counted as a mere coincidence was the shaming of Miss Feathering at Drury Lane Theatre. Who, as I am sure you are aware, has a passion for young Robert Rotmuller, who has also asked my daughter to marry him."

"Eh?" said Samuel.

"Yes, you heard correctly." John gave a deep sigh. "It is all quite confusing, my dear friend. Anyway, the next thing that happened is that I met with the father of the afore mentioned child, Lucinda. He is a charming man who works in a bookshop near St. Paul's. He told me that she in actuality was the bastard child of a no-good fellow from one of the great houses in Chiswick."

"Good God! Does that mean one of the Jacquard family?"

"Not necessarily. The Redwoods also dwelt in this area. When I pressed the poor fellow for more information he simply couldn't help me. His wife—the mother of Lucinda—died without ever telling him the identity of the man."

"Oh dear."

"Oh dear indeed. The next thing that happened is that poor little Lucinda was attacked again, this time by a local lunatic known as the Straw Man. It is a good thing that the child is what they would refer to as a 'tough customer' because she has not been affected by these awful assaults. Following that I heard a ghastly tale of a man who once lived in this same area, had sexual relations with his own sister, driving her to suicide, and then had to escape from the place and assume a new identity."

"But how does he fit into the picture?"

"I have no idea except that he is a possible candidate for Lucinda's father."

Samuel clapped his hand to his head in a somewhat theatrical gesture. "My God, it would seem that the whole of Chiswick is populated by licentious villains."

"Indeed," John replied, nodding his head. "So it would appear. Anyway, the next thing I saw—though it may not be related—is that poor Giles Jacquard, who is very badly sighted, has a mysterious lover and was seen disappearing into a worker's cottage on the Duke of Devonshire's estate presumably for a sexual encounter."

Samuel silently mopped his brow.

"And then to top it all, that nasty woman Cecily Redwood gets her throat cut at the Baron Rotmuller's ball."

There was silence as both men sat mournfully gazing at one another.

Finally John said, "Do you think it is too early for a glass of canary?"

"No, I don't," Samuel replied with much feeling. They sat in silence for several minutes then he asked, "So are you saying to me that there is one terrible thread in all this?"

"It would appear so, yes."

"Not the Viscount, surely?"

"Could be. Apparently he was a hell of a rip at one time and is still in debt up to his oxters. But the point is why is this mysterious someone getting at that particular family?"

There was silence for a few minutes then Samuel said, "But not just the Redwoods. Think of Miss Feathering."

"I believe that whoever is behind this—and there must be somebody if all these incidents are connected—is targeting anyone who is associated with past events. Lord help me, but it must be a devious mind."

"Well, in that case we must trap them quickly."

"Easier said than done, my friend."

"Could we not make a start with your neighbour Zoffany? He must surely have picked up a few tit-bits in all his wanderings around with his canvasses."

"He was not at the ball, however."

"No, I believe he had a prior engagement at the royal palace. But I know he is doing a painting of Baron Rotmuller so he might have some information."

"True. Let us have another glass of canary then call on him forthwith."

Looking out of the window they saw that this morning the Thames was sparkling with a recent shower, cascading a thousand gleaming droplets into the air. Beneath this playful mood the power of the mighty river was pulling with a strong current, whipping fishing boats and other craft at a fair pace along its glittering surface.

"It's a beautiful sight," said Samuel.

"I love the river's various moods," John answered. "You know Sam when you live by its side you can almost believe that it is alive sometimes. Like this, it is playful. But you get it on a cold night when the wind is howling along like a beast pursuing food and the river becomes as cruel as can be."

"I can picture it." And Samuel gave a deep shiver as he momentarily felt the fear that somebody drowning must suffer.

Leaving the house they stepped next door and knocked. The door opened and Zoffany, in a paint bespattered smock and slouch hat, appeared.

"Good morning, my friends. How very pleasant to see you. I believe I missed something by not attending the ball the other night."

"You most certainly did, sir."

"I know. The Baron has just left. A few minutes ago. I am painting his portrait and just needed to put in some final detail."

"Do you think he would mind if I called him back?"

"Not in the least. You'll have to hurry though."

John caught up with the banker on the river path, strolling along, twirling his cane and humming a tune under his breath. Considering that there had been a murder in his house just a few days earlier he seemed to be in remarkably good spirits.

"Herr Baron," called the Apothecary.

He turned, looking every inch the European aristocrat. His grey hair had been cut short, so that little of it showed beneath his hat, and he also had an unfashionable moustache. Yet despite this somewhat formidable appearance he had a twinkle in his steely blue eye and his grin, when he smiled in greeting, was full of glinting white teeth.

John bowed from the waist. "Excuse me running after you, sir. Samuel Swann and I have just arrived at Zoffany's house and he wonders if he might draw you back to speak about the other night. That—and other things."

The baron hesitated, drew out an ornate fob watch, looked at it then said, "I have to go and see the constable but I can certainly give you a little time."

"The constable. Is he here?"

The baron laughed. "No, no. He is coming to Oakridge to see me. He will want to see you as well. Why don't you come and stay with me for the next few days?"

"Samuel arrived this morning. I wouldn't impose."

"No imposition, my friend. It will be good to have some company. It's a big old house to live in on your own."

"Thank you, that is most kind. We will travel down tonight."

"No, no. You must come with me. I am returning this afternoon."

"You are extremely generous, baron. But tell me more about the constable. I only gave him my name and address the other night."

"He is a very thorough man and knows what he is doing. Apparently he has taken the job for the last four years."

The role of constable—a much dreaded and non-paid position—was handed out annually amongst the citizens of small towns. But many of them rebelled and frequently appointed one man to do the work in return for a small fee which they rustled up between them. Such was the position locally. The burghers of Berkhamsted had considered it too dangerous a job to take on and had subsequently each given an amount of money to one Gilbert Palmer to do it for them. It was said that he could not have been a better choice. He was young, strong, and extremely tough. Moreover, he had a brain and used it.

"This is my second interview with him," the baron continued. "During the first he took copious notes and filed them away."

"He sounds extremely efficient. What did he want you to tell him – or is that confidential?"

"It was mainly about the victim. Did I know her well and so forth."

"And did you?"

"Hardly at all. I had met her once, I think. Unlike the viscount, her son, who is a regular at the gaming tables."

"Yes, so I have heard," John answered—and there the matter was dropped.

Though the four men talked about the killing of Cecily Redwood in detail none of them could come up with any further theories and after half an hour parted company. As soon as John arrived home he packed a small portmanteau. Samuel had not even unpacked his. Then they went to join the baron's coach which awaited them at Kew.

* * *

"I believe," stated John after breakfast the next day, "that we should walk into Berkhamsted and see if we can find the constable's office."

"Fine by me," answered Samuel.

It was a lovely morning, though the early September sunshine had that first hint of chillier weather yet to come. Soon the two walkers picked up the traces of the old Roman road and followed its trail into the heart of what had been a bustling town ever since the mighty hordes of the marching soldiers of Rome had founded it. Here—or so legend had it—Duke William had been offered the crown of England by his half-brother Count Robert de Mortain following the battle of 1066. John had always doubted this, feeling it far more likely that William would have been given it as soon after that awful bloody fight as possible. Whatever the truth, the ruins of Robert's castle—once a splendid building with motte and bailey and two moats—were still clearly visible. It was here that Edward, the Black Prince, had honeymooned with Joan, the Fair Maid of Kent. Other figures from history had visited—Becket, Chaucer—but today the two men were heading for a tiny winding street wherein Gilbert Palmer had a small office. Eventually they found it, an ancient ill-painted door. John looked at Sam.

"You knock," he whispered.

His friend did so, with the butt of his walking cane.

"Come in," called a voice, and John pushed the door open and went inside.

Just for a second he had the vivid impression that a raven flew down from above, beating its wings and looking at them with a flashing beady eye. But then he realised that it was just a man who had seated himself at the desk and who had been standing, gazing at a book. Yet he could be forgiven for the mistake, for the creature he was staring at was dark, with great topaz eyes and slicked down black hair, and a way of putting his head on one side, that suggested a creature avine.

John could not recall noticing these features when they had briefly met on the night of the murder.

"Gentlemen," he said, "how can I assist you?"

Samuel cleared his throat but remained silent. John spoke up. "We've come about the murder at Oakridge House. Baron Rotmuller's place."

The man turned his head sharply, and John's impression of a dark bird came back strongly.

He had a cultured voice not like the uncompromising growl that John usually associated with people who earned their living by acting as a constable. This bird-like creature was fascinating indeed. Samuel Swann spoke up.

"Mr. Rawlings discovered the body you know."

"Ah, so you are he. I was going to ask you to come and visit me. In fact I was going to take a letter to you this very afternoon."

"And what if I had been in to receive it?"

"I would have interviewed you then and there, sir."

"And what if I had refused?"

"I would have put you down in my book of suspects."

The raven's plumage had been ruffled very slightly by the question. John laughed.

"I was speaking in jest I assure you. I would never do anything so foolish as to refuse to speak to an officer of the law."

"No he jolly well wouldn't," added Samuel heartily.

"I believe, sir, that you are an apothecary."

"How did you find that out? But it is true enough. I have a practice in Shug Lane, Piccadilly."

"Then I am going to rely on your expertise, if I may. Tell me, sir, had the throat of Mrs. Redwood been freshly cut?"

"Very much so. It was still bleeding."

The raven extended a beautiful hand, wonderfully sinuous with long sensitive fingers. John stared, feeling more and more puzzled by Mr. Palmer, who had seized a small notebook and was busily writing in it.

"So how long before your finding her would you say the murder had been committed?"

John paused momentarily, thinking. "About fifteen minutes. The blood had spurted on death which must have been almost instantaneous. Incidentally, I think it was done by somebody right-handed."

"Could have been a woman?"

"Easily."

All this was being noted down and Samuel commented, "I say you write awfully quickly. Do you use a kind of shorthand?"

The vivid eyes, the colour of night, looked up. "Yes. It's personal to me. But it is extremely useful."

"I can see that. Well done."

It was quite obvious, John thought, that his great friend admired Constable Gilbert Palmer—and he had to admit that he was growing more and more interested, not only in his methods but also in his extraordinarily dark and avine appearance.

"Now, Mr. Rawlings, can you recall who went into the conservatory—or indeed who was leaving it—as you went in?"

"Much as I would like to help you, constable, you must remember that it was a very crowded occasion. I can remember Mrs. Redwood flouncing out of the ballroom with a crowd of elderly protestors because the baron had dared to show us a waltz, which is apparently being danced in Europe but not in Britain. She left on the grounds of it being foreign, no doubt."

A smile flitted across Gilbert's mouth but disappeared rapidly. "It is the opinion of many born in Britain that we are the dominant race."

John nodded. "I have met many of that persuasion. But as to your earlier question, I recall that there were several groups of people sitting in the conservatory, well away from the dead woman. It is my belief that she probably dozed off, awoke and saw her killer who then stepped behind her chair and cut her throat before she had time to cry out a greeting."

"And all done in comparative silence."

John jumped on the word. "Do you mean that some noise was made?"

"I have interviewed the Reverend and Mrs. Arbuthnot who were sitting several feet away from her but behind a large palm tree. The vicar says that he heard her say, 'Gracious' followed by total silence."

"Surprised to see her visitor?"

"The exclamation could be open to other interpretations but I imagine yours to be the correct one."

John was lost in admiration. The burghers of Berkhamsted had got themselves a bargain indeed when they had decided to hire Gilbert Palmer to be their constable.

"Is there anything else you want to know?"

"A very great deal but would you and your companion be more at ease in a hostelry?"

This was without doubt the most unusual officer of the law that John had ever met.

Samuel answered for him. "I say. What a splendid notion."

The Kings Arms was a coaching inn and, as such, had a goodly selection of visitors but Gilbert Palmer led them to a quiet corner where they were more or less private. Having bought them both a pint of home-brewed ale while he sipped some blameless substance, he leant back in his chair and began to give them a history lesson on the ancient town in which he lived. But all the time he spoke, John noticed, his clever eyes were studying their faces, and though he wrote no notes the Apothecary felt certain that he was mentally making them.

"… it was built by John de Mortain—the half-brother of William, of course—but it was bombarded in the reign of King John when the Barons of England required a young French prince to join forces with them."

"Who won?" asked Samuel.

"The Frenchmen. Henry III, who was only nine when he came to the throne, interceded in some way."

"Was he a good king?" Samuel again.

"One of the best. His father—the nasty John—had signed the Magna Carta but it was the boy king who saw it through. He loved his wife, Eleanor of Provence, and she loved him back. And do you know the last thing he did on his death bed?"

"No."

"He settled his wine bill with his wine merchant. Now that is what I call a true gentleman."

They all laughed and John did the unusual thing of asking the young man to dine with him at Strand-on-the-Green.

"I would request you to call sooner but am staying with the baron at the moment and can hardly invite you to his palatial mansion."

"That is quite understood. But I have to call on him this very afternoon so if you gentlemen would like a lift back to his house in my little chaise—it is a two-seater but has a pull-out chair for a third passenger—I would be delighted."

"Did the good burghers of the town buy you this?" asked John, astonished.

"No, it is on loan from one of them. He got a bigger, better conveyance and decided to lend me his old one."

They clambered in as best they could. The chaise was kept in a stabling yard near The Kings Arms and Gilbert drove the horse, a coachman definitely not being provided. Samuel, who had grown rather weighty, sat on the seat and John took the pull-out and felt a surge of excitement as Gilbert cracked the reins on the animal's back and they lurched forwards. Boyhood came back in a vivid memory, so much so that John whistled, a sure sign of being happy. It seemed to him at that moment that being an apothecary and solving mysteries had a great deal in common. With plants one probed the depths as to what they could provide in the way of healing for mankind, solving mysteries was so similar. One picked and picked at the evidence until finally one tantalising piece was revealed—and then you knew that you had reached the correct conclusion. And now he believed he was on the trail again with that most extraordinary being, the constable who closely resembled a raven.

Seen in the full beam of daylight, Oakridge Place was quite stunning. To Elizabeth's fairly modest home, the family from whom the baron had won the entire acreage had made some significant and beautiful additions. An imposing entrance with a balcony at the top of the outside steps, on which the Apothecary had sat just a short time ago; the ballroom in which had been danced that ultra-shocking waltz; the conservatory where that most cruel of murders had taken place. Looking at the glass house in the full gleam of high afternoon John saw that it ran the length of the downstairs wing and was full of rare and strange plants, to say nothing of trees bursting with vivid green branches. An easy place in which to conceal oneself, he thought.

The baron was standing at the top of the stone stairs. He had on some kind of military uniform—presumably to lend authority to whatever statement he was about to make to the serving staff. Everything about him seemed highly polished—including his moustache—and he looked austere and formidable.

"He is not as frightening as he seems," John said to Gilbert, speaking barely above a whisper.

The raven fluttered its wings as the constable pulled the horse to a stop at the foot of the steps and the three men got out. Leading the way, he bowed low and said, "Herr Baron, I am here on behalf of the county law officials, acting in the role of constable, as you already know. I do hope I will not be inconveniencing your lordship but if you could grant me a short interview I would be delighted." Smooth-tongued flatterer, thought the Apothecary, smiling. "These two gentlemen, who I believe are your house guests, took the opportunity of walking into Berkhamsted and calling on me in my office. I offered to give them a lift back to your place and that, I hope, explains my unexpected appearance."

Gilbert gave another short bow and put his foot on the bottom step. The baron, who had looked somewhat put out, decided that this polite young man was better than he could have hoped for, rubbed his hands together and said, "So you wish to talk, well talk you shall. Come in, come in. I will give you all the help I can. As for you two reprobates, I thought you might be under arrest." He laughed extremely heartily at his own joke.

As it turned out he could help Gilbert Palmer hardly at all. He had not been near the conservatory that evening and had noticed Mrs. Redwood only twice. Once, when she entered, full of pride and puffed up as a partridge, as he put it, the other time when she had led a posse of horrified dancers out of the ballroom in protest at being shown the waltz, which they had classified as foreign filth.

"Other than that I did not notice her until I was called in to see her with her throat cut, which was not at all an attractive sight."

"I can imagine," said Gilbert sympathetically.

A half hour later he looked at his fob watch, drank a very small, very weak, beer, pressed on him by the baron, then mounted the box of his little chaise and trotted off into the early evening.

"Remarkable," said Rotmuller, watching as the conveyance became a speck in the distance. "Quite an educated fellow, I think. What do you feel, John?"

"He makes me think of a raven, quick and light but having a dark brooding within."

"That's a damned good description of him," added Samuel.

"Very apt," added the baron, and smiled jovially into his moustache.

Later that evening, while Mr. Swann had withdrawn to write a letter to his wife, John approached him on another subject.

"If I might have a word, my dear sir, it is about your brother Robert."

The baron looked alarmed. "He is not in any trouble, is he?"

The Apothecary shook his head. "None that I know of. The fact is that he wants to marry my daughter, Rose. And I am sure it would be a delightful union but for one thing."

"What?" asked Rotmuller, alarmed.

"He intends to continue his career as an actor and, to be perfectly frank, he isn't any good."

The baron's face was a study. "You do not think so? I find that disappointing. I thought he might have a great career in theatre. Which would make a change from all us banking people."

"And you would not be able to help him?"

"Definitely not. The legal instructions were given to all of us on my late father's death. No brother is to help another. Each individual was to act as a spearhead until the name of Rotmuller was firmly established throughout the world."

"Very ambitious."

"And very far seeing."

John sighed. "Perhaps I am wrong, listening to other people too much. Perhaps Robert will become famous after all."

"It is always a possibility," answered the baron drily.

Chapter Nineteen

The funeral of Cecily Redwood was a sight to behold. Setting out from the Jacobean mansion—the property of the Duke of Devonshire but let out as a grace-and-favour to his friends and relatives—it had all the trappings of a royal event. First came a small band of twelve musicians, marching with great solemnity and playing a set of mournful airs—rather badly, John thought. This was followed by a host of family mourners, all clad in deepest black, led by the viscount and the viscountess, being carried aloft in a small chair hefted by a beefy servant, this no doubt because of her precious pregnancy. Alongside his nephew, limping but game, came Sir Humphrey Warburton, sweating slightly. These three were followed by the rest of the family, namely the two surly brothers, Roderick and Percival, and then the three grim women, one huge, one middling and one minute, together with the man who was clearly husband of one of them, though which one John could never fathom. Behind them came a stream of ordinary mourners, including one who fainted on every possible occasion and was doing so now, screaming as she went down amidst the plodding feet. To cap it all it was raining, not a gentle dew but fairly bucketing it down. John and his family exchanged a glance and trudged with the rest. Bringing up the rear and carried shoulder high by six professional funeral attendants came the coffin, resplendent in velvet drapery and ermine trim. Behind it walked one small boy doing his best to play the bagpipes, which were heartily resisting his efforts.

On arrival at the church of St. Egbert there was a rush to get out of the wet and the fainting woman went down again shrieking, "Oh mercy, mercy, dear Lord." Rose flickered a glance at her brothers but said nothing, Jasper and James stared fixedly at the floor. John, trying to look deadly serious but failing, ushered them to the back pew, his favourite spot at funerals. The band of black-clad men playing doleful airs had been disposed of but as the church organ thundered out some vastly depressing chords the coffin was borne in, in state, by the professionals, still with the small boy attached, blowing gamely but uselessly on his bagpipes. This was as well because the invisible organist was crashing out some terrible anthem unaware of the child's existence. Added to this was the noisy sobbing of the three sisters and the high-pitched screech of someone who had set up in competition to the screaming woman. John did not know where to put himself.

To crown all this the vicar was young and inexperienced and not good at dealing with crowds, together with the fact that he knew nothing about voice projection. The congregation, wet and restive, began to whisper amongst themselves, and this undercurrent of syllables accompanied the entire service. Finally, it was over and the band of musicians, who had been sheltering in the porch whistling and laughing noiselessly, led the solemn procession to the graveside. John followed, observing, leaving his children to their own devices. Sir Humphrey started to slip and was held firmly by his nephew, the viscount. His Lordship's brothers—the other two Redwood males— were, in John's opinion, unbelievably ghastly. Whereas the viscount had a somewhat feminine cast of features these other two were quite definitely déclassé. John could imagine a young and eager Cecily taking a liking to a brewer's drayman or a roughneck and allowing a quick bit of fumbling in a darkened doorway with nine months reward for it!

John stopped short of going to the actual graveside as Viscountess Lovell was sitting a little to the right in the shelter of some trees. She was still perched on her little portable chair and smiled at him as she saw him approaching. He bowed low and kissed her outstretched hand.

"An apt day for a funeral, my lady." He glanced with a wry grin at the lowering skies.

"Serves the old witch right."

"It does not worry you that all your relatives might get wet?"

"As I have already told you, I was never particularly liked by any of them. It was just by chance that Michael came to my father's studio to see a portrait that Papa was painting of his cousin. He was supposed to marry her—the cousin—and his mother could not stand it when he chose me instead. I do not mourn her in the slightest."

"Can you possibly tell me about her three daughters?"

"The weird sisters. I can never work out which is which, though I believe the eldest is called Maud."

"Do you think any of them are capable of murdering their mother?"

"No, I don't. And besides they were all in the ballroom taking it in turns to dance with their husband."

John laughed, though quietly, and received several dirty looks from people plodding to the graveside.

"So they didn't follow her when she rallied her troops and swept from the ballroom?"

"Only Maud, the big fat one. But she lost heart and sat down at the refreshment table reminding herself that it had been a quarter of an hour since she had last eaten and she must keep her strength up."

John laughed once more. "You have a very dry wit, madam."

Miranda nodded. "So I have been told. Seriously, though, I think you can rule my sisters-in-law out. They are not the type of which murderers are made."

"Are you?" asked the Apothecary. It was monstrously rude to be so blunt with the wife of a peer of the realm but the words came out before giving them his consideration.

"I have thought about it, yes."

"When?"

"When my beautiful sister's looks were ruined by someone throwing acid in her face. I could have killed whoever did that."

"You do not know their identity?"

"No, thank God. Or I would have taken a gun and put them down."

"I don't blame you. I should probably have done the same."

The viscountess began to silently cry, great tears welling out of those beautiful eyes and running down her cheeks. "It was the most wicked act I have ever heard of. All her beauty—both physical and spiritual—ruined in one evil moment."

"Did she not see who attacked her?"

"No, it was done at night. She was coming home from a theatre with a servant for escort. He—the servant—was knocked unconscious and my sister was brutally wounded. It was the most horrible thing I have ever witnessed. When she crawled up to our door I did not even recognise her."

John stood silently, thinking of another terrible night when he had seen a parody of a human face looking at him from outside the huge window in the Jacobean house. Now it made sense. That poor creature, once a great beauty, now made hideous by a vicious attack, had been checking to see who was within before she slipped inside the house and away from prying eyes. And he had thought that it was a ghost—or worse. The Apothecary felt riven with shame.

The viscountess was staring at him curiously. "I see that my story has upset you."

"Yes, it has. And to this day you have no idea who did it?"

"Not to be sure, no. She had many suitors and it seemed that the power of her beauty was sufficient to make some of them behave in an unhinged manner. But the wretched girl paid the highest price of all. My poor sweet sister was turned into something that people turn their heads away from. God forgive them. As for his identity, my sister did not see who attacked her and the servant was knocked senseless. Otherwise I would have gone to the Public Office and watched him hanged at Tyburn—and cheered as he choked to death."

"If I promise to try to track him down will that ease your suffering?"

She laughed without amusement. "It would help I suppose."

But the Apothecary could say nothing further. Miranda forced a smile which turned into a look of genuine affection as the viscount approached. John shook his head from side to side in disbelief. The way the man touched her, patted her hands, kissed her on the cheek. That magic pump had done the trick all right. They were genuinely in love.

He hardly slept at all that night, thinking. Thinking of the wretched woman whose face he had glimpsed and of his cowardly act of fear in turning away. Yet who could blame him? The man who had attacked her in so brutal a fashion had not only ruined her life but also that of several other people as well. Both her younger sisters had been drawn into the web of despair and as for her poor old father—Winterlight the artist—he must have been driven to an early grave by seeing what once had been one of the most beautiful creatures on earth turned into a hobgoblin.

Next day's early breakfast was a miserable occasion. There was a deal of luggage in the front hall and John realised with sadness that

213

today his boys were leaving for their last term at school. They would go by water to Whitehall stairs and from there take a hackney, first to Nassau Street to deposit their sister—who was itching to get back to London—then onwards to catch the Worcester stagecoach due to arrive at their destination at three forty-five in the pitch dark of morning. John, of course, very much the proud father, was determined to see the twins aboard their conveyance and wave them a fond farewell.

They arrived at Whitehall Stairs and there piled themselves and their baggage into one of several chairs plying for trade. As they were passing The Golden Cross the boys left their bags at the inn then continued on to their London home to see Rose safely ensconced, as well as warning her—with a great deal of winking—against going too often to the theatre, to which jibes she smiled good-naturedly, all this in view of the fact that Robert Rotmuller had returned to town and to the Drury Lane playhouse. Then they went back accompanied by John to await the coach.

It arrived with the usual excitement shortly after 8 p.m. The great wheels scraping over the cobbles, the horses nervously moving their heads as if they anticipated the hours of darkness through which they must rush, the small cheer given by the assorted passengers as they clambered aboard, the jingling and jangling of the harness as the coachman hauled himself up onto his box and grabbed his whip. John held both boys tightly, not being of the school of thought that fathers should be undemonstrative.

"Take care of each other, my dears."

"Don't worry, we will Papa."

"Thank you for all the help you have given me."

"Think nothing of it, sir."

"I hope you catch the miscreant soon." This from Jasper.

"I shall do my best. Be good—and be careful."

James, climbing to the top, called out, "Look after Miss Hyacinth for me."

"And me," echoed Jasper, joining him.

John stood silently watching as the passengers settled themselves, the driver was joined by the guard, there was a last wave of hands and then they had headed off into the shadowy evening. He stood on the same spot, looking where once they had been, and then eventually strolled away into the growing darkness. More by chance than design his wanderings took him across The Strand and into the maze that surrounded Half Moon Street. There he found a drinking establishment called The Lamb and Flag and was standing outside, thinking of entering, when he heard a voice that was vaguely familiar. It was purporting to be French and yet something in the man's delivery made John guess that it was assumed. For no reason at all that he could imagine he felt himself grow tense. The speaker was holding forth and showing off to a crowd of rough trade, gathered together at the far end of the bar, who stood listening with half an ear.

"… I invite you all—I really mean this—to come and dine with me at my chateau in the Loire Valley."

The crowd mumbled and somebody cheered sarcastically.

"I hear a note of doubt. Gentlemen, I assure you, that I do dwell in such an establishment. And I ask any of you capable of making your way there to come and stay with me."

"Oh yeah?" said someone, and the gang simultaneously lost interest and moved away.

The Comte d'Etoile pulled a face and looked round to see who else he could impress and his gaze fell upon John Rawlings, who gave him an acid smile.

"Do I know you?" he asked rudely.

"Yes, I believe we met at the Baron Rotmuller's ball."

215

"Forgive me. I meet so many people. Your name, monsieur?"

"Rawlings. John Rawlings."

The Comte, growing more French by the minute, said, "Excuse me, if you please. I have the memory so bad. People flit in and out like butterflies."

"How very disconcerting. Let me remind you. You came with two of the Redwood family, the brothers Roderick and Percival to be precise. The evening ended with a murder—but perhaps you don't recall that."

D'Etoile opened his mouth to reply but at that moment the door of the hostelry opened again and two men came in. The Apothecary glanced at them briefly and thought how very soberly they were dressed. In fact their clothes were almost identical, plain cut and water rat grey. They looked like people who did not visit the capital often and stood, shuffling slightly, in the doorway. And then something quite extraordinary happened. The younger of the two looked round the room and cast his eyes on the back of d'Etoile, then nodded to the older and drew his attention to the so-called Frenchman with a small gesture of his hand. Then they looked at each other and the older man stepped forward.

"Excuse me, sir, but would you happen to be the Comte d'Etoile?" he said.

The Frenchman turned, ran his eyes over the pair of newcomers and said drawlingly, "Who asks?"

"I do, you lousy stinking bastard. Call yourself a Frenchie name when all the time you are Greville Faulkener. I'll give you one just for that." And he punched the Comte so hard in the stomach that his knees buckled beneath him.

"And here's one from me," said the younger of the two, adding another stinging blow.

The Apothecary stepped forward. "Steady on, fellows."

"You keep out of it," he was warned. "Bugger off."

John thought rapidly. To pitch in and save the horrid man from a beating would have been the honourable thing to do but the two strangers—so very meekly dressed—were obviously street fighters of a superior class. It was not, he thought, as if the Comte was anybody he respected. The next thing that was said made up his mind for him completely.

"Promoted to a French Count?" said one. "I know exactly who you are. You're that nasty piece of work who used to live in Gunnersbury Manor and had it away with your sister. Drove her to her death. Made her jump from the roof she was so frightened and scared. Well, this is from her, and this, and this."

He rained blows at Faulkener's stomach and had his arm raised for another hit when the landlord, a great lummox of a man, came up and shouted, "Out, the lot of you. We won't have any brawling in my establishment."

And the Apothecary, somewhat to his chagrin, felt himself picked up off his feet and thrown out of the door onto the cobbles beyond. He looked over at Faulkener, who now lay semi-conscious on the ground, blood streaming from a great cut on his head, and made a reluctant move towards him.

"I ought to attend to the wretch."

"If you do, my friend, you'll end up lying beside him. Any friend of his is an enemy of ours."

"May I ask how you know him?"

The older man answered. "I was chief gardener at Gunnersbury Manor, watched him grow from a horrible child into a total lout—him and his hideous friends the Redwood boys. I loved that little girl who killed herself. She was a good girl, a sweet girl, and then that bastard of a brother raped her and ruined her. She took her own life at the age of eighteen. There was such an outcry that he had to make a run for it, leave the country and go overseas. But I knew he would come back one of these days—and we've been lying in wait for him ever since."

The younger man gave a wolf's grin. "Aye, that's the truth."

"And now, sir, we'll bid you a final good night."

And with that he took the Apothecary by the collar of his greatcoat and turning him in the direction of The Strand gave him a hearty shove in the back which temporarily winded him.

An hour later, he limped through the door of number two Nassau Street, struggled to the decanter and poured himself a stiff brandy, then slumped into a chair and stared at the dying fire. So the Comte d'Etoile had been unmasked and given a severe beating which he had thoroughly deserved. Ethically, as a trained apothecary, he should have gone to his assistance but the attackers had been formidable and hardly in the mood for a chat, besides if anybody had ever asked for a thrashing it was Greville Faulkener. John closed his eyes and a second or two afterwards was asleep.

He was woken sometime later by the sound of someone creeping across the hall. He looked up and saw Rose making her way to the staircase. Glancing at the old clock which had been his father's pride and joy because it played The British Grenadiers on the hour, he saw that it was one o'clock in the morning.

"Rose," he called out, "come and talk to me."

She jumped with fright but peering into the study saw her father and with a fine show of dignity walked in and sat down opposite him.

"It's very late," he said mildly.

"I know," she answered. "I went to see Robert at the Theatre Royal. Serafina was in the audience and has invited us to dine at her house."

"Did she give you a date?"

"Yes. Next Thursday. I said I would ask you." She paused and a pink peony blossomed in her cheeks. "I am glad you are not cross with me for being late. Robert has seen me to the door."

"How was his acting?"

Rose looked at him and there was a sudden twinkle in her eye. "I don't think he will ever play Hamlet."

"Poor boy. But he's young yet. By the way, what is his age?"

"Twenty-five. And I am twenty-two and mature enough to elope."

John shook his head and said with assumed amazement, "Are you really? Why does everyone get so old so suddenly?"

"Oh, Papa. You are the greatest child of all of us. Now, where have you been all the evening? I'll warrant you stayed up in the town after the boys got aboard their coach."

"Yes, and very exciting it was too."

And he proceeded to give Rose a blow-by-blow account of all that had transpired, adding "I know I should have aided the man but quite honestly I was nervous."

"I didn't like him at all," his daughter said firmly. "I met him at the baron's ball and did not care for his manner."

"I wonder if he is still alive. I think those two would have stopped short of actual murder, but one can never tell."

"They probably ran off and left him there. It would depend very much on who found him as to whether he was saved."

"You're right, my sweet girl. As always. Pour your old father a drink and we can talk for a while."

She did so, very prettily, and John stared into the embers and thought to himself what a wonderful family he had been lucky enough to get. It had not occurred to him until that moment that Rose was already of age and able to please herself who she married.

"Has Robert been invited to Serafina's supper party?" he asked casually.

"Yes. He was delighted."

"I thought he might be," John answered, and smiled in the dying firelight.

As always with any gathering organised by Serafina, the accent was on stylish charm. Because it was a summer party a light meal was chosen consisting of oysters and other delights from Neptune's kingdom, together with chicken, rabbit and their livelier cousins, the hare. All these presented without heavy casings or suety accompaniment but frothily decorated and enough to whet the appetite of even those who enjoyed sitting down to a groaning board.

The Apothecary entered alone—Rose having gone to Drury Lane to support Robert who was playing the part of Charles Surface in *The School for Scandal*—and was greeted by Louis de Vignolles, Serafina's French husband.

"My dear John, how are you? What a pleasure to see you again. How is life by the river?"

"Actually it is wonderful, always something new and fascinating to look at. Please, please, bring Serafina to see me soon. And to meet my fascinating neighbour, the painter Zoffany."

"He goes from strength to strength I understand. I hear he is a great favourite of the Queen."

"I believe so."

But their conversation was interrupted by the arrival of the viscount and Miranda, one of the happiest pairs in London, the Apothecary was glad to see. She was looking as delectable as always but the woman who followed her—her sister, the Duchess of Derwent—appeared careworn and ill at ease. John made his bow before them.

"Your Grace, Your Lordship, Your Ladyship, I am as always your humble servant."

"Good heavens," said the viscount, "such formality."

He raised his quizzer and winked at the Apothecary through it. His eye, that blue smoky orb, was crinkled at the corners. John knew for sure that the nasty young man had gone for good and that the real Michael was here to stay. He gave a small sigh of pure satisfaction.

Serafina flew into the room. "Goodness me—and I am not here to meet my important guests." She swept beautiful curtsies at the trio of titled people and gave John a secret smile. As always in her presence he felt a tug at his heartstrings. She had attracted him when first they met, all those years ago in Vaux Hall Pleasure Gardens, and he had never quite recovered from it. Part of the fascination of Serafina had been her uncanny ability not only to socialise but also to gamble. It was almost as if she had communication with some naughty sprite who told her just how to lay the cards or shake the dice pot in order to win and win again. It was even whispered that she was in touch with Old Nick himself. Yet outwardly she had all the charm and style of an elegant thoroughbred, brought up in the top racing stables of the kingdom.

It was just as John was regarding her that a lazy laugh drew his attention once more to the viscount and as he looked across at him an idea came hurtling into his mind. The only thing he could ask himself was why it hadn't occurred to him before—it was such a splendid plan. But if it were to succeed he must see if the rooms were laid out as he suspected. Bowing, he made his way out.

The dining room table had little name cards at the top of each place and there was one marked 'The Baron Rotmuller'. John was delighted. He had been fairly certain that the German financier would be on the guest list and now it was confirmed. He moved into the salon, a beautiful room tricked out in salmon pink and fresh mint green. Two chandeliers glittering with a thousand candles lit the space and threw intriguing shadows over the small tables set for cards after the delicacies had been consumed. Serafina had thought of everything that a good hostess should. John smiled secretly and went back to where the other guests were gathered, chattering and laughing. It was a happy occasion and the Apothecary had no trouble in drawing his hostess to one side for a moment.

"My dear, what a wonderful atmosphere. You really do have the *crème de le crème* as your guests."

She gave him a suspicious glance. "John Rawlings, I know by the very gleam in your eye that you are up to something. Now tell me what it is immediately."

"First of all, you tell me your impression of the Baron Rotmuller."

"Why do you want to know?"

"Because my daughter Rose has received a proposal of marriage from one of his brothers."

"I think she should accept. The Rotmullers and others of similar ilk are the coming people. They are making inroads all over Europe and they are going to become future members of our aristocracy, which could do with some bolstering up in my opinion."

"I love you even more when you talk wisely."

"Oh get along, you old flirt. What is it you want?"

"I want you to play the Herr Baron at dice and win."

"And why, may I ask?"

"Because the young Viscount Lovell is heavily in debt to him and it is the one thing that happens to be standing between that young man and his complete happiness."

"You're certain of this?"

"Positive."

And then the Apothecary, because he knew that she would keep his secret always, proceeded to tell her the incident of the pump

222

and how it had changed young Michael's life. Serafina laughed, a deep endearing chuckle.

"Do you know, you and I are not fit to be grandparents."

"I'm not one—yet."

"I am. My daughter gave birth to a little girl t'other day. Her name is Jacinta. Do you like it?"

"I do indeed. I would raise my glass to her if I had one."

"A mistake that must be rectified immediately. Come on, my friend. I have a feeling that I should give the dice a rattle tonight. Let's toast the next generation."

And they did—several times.

Supper was served and was a great success, Comte Louis saying much in favour of his new French chef. Mackerel, with fennel and mint, a glistening side of beef, pies and hefty tarts with intriguing centres, were finally cleared away. Now the chef showed his greatest talents as confectionaries of every sort graced the table and the guests bestowed their favour by eating prodigiously. John guessed that many of them had only had a bowl of soup that day in expectant preparation. He, too, had eaten little, knowing that the Comtesse de Vignolles's supper parties were talked of with reverence in London society. But now finally everyone was replete, port was being consumed, and people were repairing to the water closet which Serafina had recently requested workmen put in, much to the delight of guests. Far superior, in John's opinion, to the close stools that could still be found in some establishments. Having availed himself of its flushing delights and rinsed his hands in a bowl of water, he wandered into the salon and saw that people were already sitting down to cards. He shot a look at Serafina and she gave him a brief nod to show that she understood. The baron entered the room, smiling genially around and, seeing the Apothecary, made a bee line straight for him.

"Ah, my dear friend, do I find you well?"

"You do indeed, Herr Baron. Tell me, has anything further been revealed about that terrible murder which took place at your ball?"

"No, but one of the guests present on that occasion was beaten up and left for dead in London recently."

John's stomach tightened. "Really? How shocking! May I ask who it was?"

"You may indeed. It was the Comte d'Etoile—a rather shifty character in my opinion."

"And in mine also. I have reason to believe he was involved in a sordid scandal some years ago and told to leave the country, which he did, setting himself up as a French man of title."

"I thought as much. I thought he was too French to be true." The baron paused and suddenly put on a serious face. "It is not so with the Rotmullers. We come from an ancient lineage. We are a very well-established family."

"Indeed you are. But tell me something, Baron, in confidence of course …" The Apothecary had raised his voice so that half the room was cocking its ear, "… is it true that you won your property on the turn of a dice and that the original owner went out and shot himself?"

The baron's face became as glum as a suet pudding without sweet sauce. "Alas, it is a fact. I had but recently arrived in England. I was looking round to buy a property at the time, however I happened to be playing at White's one night and the angel of fortune must have been hovering at my side."

"More than hovering, sitting on your lap more like," called out one of the other guests.

It was Serafina's cue and she rose to it as only a true gamester would.

"Want to try your luck again, Herr Baron?"

"Well, thank you dear madam, but the answer must be no. Good fortune called on me but the once I fear."

"Nonsense. If you are born fortunate then so you will for ever remain. Believe me, I have seen the same man win riches in a night and end by throwing the winning dice. Show us how you play, sir."

"Go on, old boy," somebody shouted. "Be a British sport."

"Very well," the baron answered in a clipped voice, suddenly very foreign and correct. "But I realise that you have something of a reputation yourself, madam."

"Years ago, sir. Nowadays I am just a respectable married woman— and a grandmother. I used to roll the dice occasionally. But compared with you I am a mere amateur."

Across the room Louis caught the Apothecary's eye and raised his brows. John smiled at him reassuringly. Serafina picked up her wine cup and raised it to her opponent.

"To a true sportsman," she said. "I'll wager you a thousand pounds, sir."

"That is a very large sum of money, madam. Are you certain?"

She nodded and threw the dice from a leather cup brought by a standing footman, and though she threw three times, as the rules allowed, had nothing but a paltry score. Nonetheless, she sat calmly, and when the baron threw a full house with kings high wrote an I.O.U. with equal sangfroid. They played on, the baron collecting a pile of I.O.U.s, Serafina drinking wine steadily. By now everyone else had stopped whatever game they had been pursuing and were watching the pair in a tremendous growing silence.

"I think, my dear baron, that we must come to the conclusion," said Serafina, softly but distinctly. "One last throw. If I win I will offer all my debtors a free pardon. Thus, they can win with me."

The baron said, "Then I must do the same. All those who owe me money shall be free of that debt if I lose."

"So be it," said Serafina solemnly.

She threw. It was a full house with aces high and kings below— an unbeatable score. There was no point in throwing further. The comtesse was an outright winner. She raised her glass to the baron who had gone somewhat pale.

"Accepted like a true sportsman, Herr Baron."

"You have the devil's own luck, madam. But I know when I meet a true rival."

"And your debtors, sir?"

"They are free," Rotmuller answered—and as the Apothecary turned his head to look at the viscount, he winked his eye and grinned.

Chapter Twenty

It was, thought Miss Phoebe Feathering, a wretched life indeed. She had given up her room in her house in London and her role as a maid-of-all-work to an elderly lady, who had gnashed her gums at her in anger. Also her visits to the theatre, her outings to Kew and other beauty spots, all to be nearer her very dear Robert Miller, who had turned out to not be Miller at all but Rotmuller and a German into the bargain. Furthermore, her beloved monoculars had been stolen in the most embarrassing circumstances and she had prized them very highly. And to crown all her other sorrows she had sacrificed everything she enjoyed about London life in order to be a companion to Cecily Redwood, who had promptly gone and got herself murdered at Robert's brother's ball. It really was too much and too bad. A small tear trickled down the side of Phoebe's nose at which she dabbed with a lace trimmed handkerchief.

Following Cecily's death her role as companion had been taken over by all three of Mrs. Redwood's daughters, which Miss Feathering was finding a strain to say the least of it. The trouble was that as well as being very different in size the three sisters were equally at odds in temperament. And it was not pleasant.

While one was snappish and bossy, another was whispering and snide, while the third lay on a day bed and listened to the sounds of nature, looking wistful and plucking the threads of a piece of embroidery. It was all very unnerving and one day, quite suddenly, Miss Feathering had had enough. The end was brought about when she was ordered to clear up a heap of dog droppings deposited by Maud's unpleasant hound Boysie, who strongly resisted the idea of house training.

Never being a person who enjoyed confrontation, she had written a note explaining that the call of London was too strong, crammed as much as she could into a piece of hand luggage, and crept out to catch the town bound stagecoach, sitting on the roof and shivering with biting cold. She was deposited as the shadows of dusk shot greying fingers through the late afternoon sky at The Saracens Head, Snow Hill, Holbourn. Where, had she had the money, she would have booked a room for the night, but her dwindling finances could not allow such a wayward display. Instead Miss Feathering crept into a snug reserved for members of the gentle sex and there ordered a cup of tea and a scone. Meanwhile her tired mind wondered whose help she could seek in the crowded capital city.

The trouble was that she had been living on a very small bequest left to her by her father, a pittance which did not allow her to entertain at all. Her income was sufficient to obtain a grim little room off a remote cousin in which to exist and to act as her slave as part of the bargain, buy very cheap seats for the theatre—her only pleasure—and take an occasional summertime outing to the horticultural gardens. These had been the sum total of her life until the first glimpse of Robert Rotmuller, when her passions had at long last been aroused. And now it had all gone to dust. She bit into her scone and thought it tasted very much like chewing sawdust.

Where, she wondered desperately, could a respectable female spend a night alone in London? Even now, though it was barely dusk, she could see a woman crossing the road with purposeful tread, her goal The Saracen's Head. The hat at a risqué angle, the vivid carmined lips, revealed that she was seeking some male traveller for an hour's seedy fumbling in his hopefully unshared room, to earn enough to buy a hot meal for herself later that night. But at least, thought Miss Feathering sadly, she has a profession of sorts which is more than I do.

And then an idea came, quite unsettling in a way but also extremely sensible. Sir Humphrey Warburton had a large house in London and Cecily—who had died such a horrid death—had been a Miss Warburton before her marriage into that strange Redwood family. Surely he would, out of both pity and kindness, offer her a night's accommodation. Miss Feathering knew that she had just enough money on her to hire a hackney carriage to his house and, feeling a great deal strengthened, poured another cup of tea and felt worry lift from her shoulders.

Sir Humphrey was in the throes of decision, wondering whether he should have a small glass of canary before this evening's excursion—an event to which he was looking forward a great deal—when he heard the tolling of his front doorbell. Mildly mannered at the best of times, he nonetheless felt somewhat irritated. That a caller should have had the nerve to arrive unannounced at this hour of the day when all people were thinking of the evening ahead, be it one of merriment or quiet contemplation, was thoughtless to say the least of it. He gulped down the wine rather than taking his usual delicate sips. Whoever had called was admitted and then Phoebe Feathering stood in the room's entrance, cringing with embarrassment. Sir Humphrey rose to his feet, his false leg swinging out gamely.

"My dear lady," he managed, "what a surprise."

"Oh dear Sir Humphrey, please forgive me. A terrible intrusion on your privacy I know but I just couldn't go on any more with their vagaries and whims. I believe you will think it shallow of me but I was in such a bother all of the time. And I just couldn't take to Boysie, however hard I tried. I felt I had to escape."

Her host was at a loss to know what the poor woman was talking about but nonetheless out of politeness he stepped forward and ushered her into the room, noticing as he did so that she was carrying a small portmanteau.

"You seem out of sorts, my dear Miss Feathering. Come and sit down. Would you like a glass of canary?"

"Oh, I don't think I dare. Alcohol flies straight to my head. But on this occasion, I could perhaps …"

"I am sure a small glass would only be beneficial. Now take a seat, do, and tell me exactly what has happened."

A quarter of an hour later and Miss Feathering had unburdened herself and was delicately sipping a second glass. Sir Humphrey, who had not been particularly fond of his late sister and liked his three nieces even less, had nodded his approval throughout her story.

"I think you did completely the right thing, Miss Phoebe—I may call you that?" She nodded. "As far as I can see that trio of females were treating you as a slave. You did the correct thing in walking out and leaving them to stew in their own juice."

He gave a loud laugh and poured himself another glass of canary wine which he proceeded to down with much joviality. A thrill of relief ran through Miss Feathering's frame and she too sipped from her glass with a certain sense of calmness returning to her world.

"Thank you so much for receiving me," she said. "I must admit to a certain amount of dread about coming here."

"That was very foolish of you, dear lady. Am I such an ogre?"

"Oh no, no," Phoebe fluttered. "Not at all. It is just that it is rather late in the day for a single lady to call."

"Be blowed to that," Sir Humphrey replied forcefully. "Those rules are for acquaintances, not friends."

He was rather enjoying his role as amiable host and also watching the way in which Miss Feathering was looking at him as if he were quite the cleverest man in town.

"Now, what were you planning on doing this evening?" he asked genially.

"Well, nothing really. Just hoping that you would let me be your guest and then tomorrow finding somewhere to lodge."

"Piffle," said Sir Humphrey loudly, downing his fourth canary. "I'll not hear of such a thing. You were a great friend to my poor late sister and will be treated as my guest until you make other arrangements. Now, we were discussing this evening. Are you free for a little diversion?"

"I have no plans, Sir Humphrey. What did you have in mind?"

"Do you know Sir John Fielding by any chance?" Phoebe shook her head, her face puzzled. "I see that you do not. He is the Principal Magistrate of this lawless capital of ours, a fine fellow indeed. His brother Henry wrote *Tom Jones* you know."

Miss Feathering—who had not read it—smiled and nodded. She was beginning to feel very slightly light-headed.

"Well, I had arranged to meet him later this evening. I want to discuss Cecily's unfortunate death amongst other things. I am sure he would be delighted if you accompanied me, dear lady."

Phoebe paused on the brink of saying no and then thought that she had had such an exhausting day—and yet in its own way exciting—that she would be foolish to say anything other than yes.

"If that would be agreeable, Sir Humphrey, I should be delighted."

"Then I suggest, Miss Feathering, that we set off in half an hour."

They did so. Phoebe, feeling very grand, peeped out of the window of Sir Humphrey's coach and let out a little gasp of amazement when they stopped in front of the tall house in Bow Street, which reared against the night sky with a certain air of menace. Sir Humphrey patted her hand.

"Don't be nervous, my dear. Within all will be congenial, I promise. Sir John enjoys entertaining let me tell you."

But it was not quite as he remembered it. They were met on the stairs by a flustered woman, not used to a crowd of people it would seem, who curtseyed and said in a small voice, "Sir John has several guests already. I thought the large parlour at the back might be best. His favourite punch will be coming shortly."

Sir Humphrey replied heartily, "Thank you, my good woman. Would you lead the way?"

She bobbed again and holding a candle tree high took them up a small flight leading to a room from which there came a sudden burst of laughter.

"He's in there," she whispered, and disappeared rapidly back down the stairs.

"Who was that?" whispered Miss Feathering.

"I have no idea," Sir Humphrey murmured back.

He opened the door. The cheerful sound continued, echoed by the light thrown by many candles and the glow coming from a fire, in front of which slept a large black cat regardless of the happy tumult. Sir John looked up on hearing it and Miss Feathering trembled a little as his sightless gaze seemed to rest on her. She had never seen the Principal Magistrate before and his great height and hefty shoulders seemed to her to be terribly masculine. He gestured to his guests to be silent and listened carefully as Sir Humphrey made his way in.

"Ha," he exclaimed, "come and join us, sir, do. We were chatting informally. But I believe that you are not alone. Bring your companion in as well."

Miss Feathering shook more than ever as every eye turned in her direction. She saw dear Mr. Rawlings, who had saved her life on that horrible night in Drury Lane theatre. And, though she had never been formally introduced, a man who could be none other than the Baron Rotmuller, whom she had glimpsed on the night of the murder of Mrs. Redwood. There were two other men present at the table. A man with striking red hair above a craggy face and a little dark bird of a fellow, quick and intense, his every move avine.

"Let me introduce the company. Baron Rotmuller, who of course you know. Mr. John Rawlings, apothecary, Joe Jago, one of my assistants, and Mr. Palmer, who is a professional constable in Surrey, but whom I have invited to become one of my Special Fellows."

"Good evening, gentlemen," Sir Humphrey replied. "Hope you don't mind, Sir John, but we now have a lady present. Miss Phoebe Feathering, my guest. I am sure, my good sirs, that you will kindly moderate your tone when conversing."

John chuckled to himself. A meeting held by the Blind Beak demanded rapt attention from everyone present and was hardly likely to encourage raunchy language. However, the great man was speaking.

"Delighted as I am to make your acquaintance, madam, I must point out that this gathering has been called to discuss matters private only to those present. I would suggest therefore that you join my wife for some wine and conversation if that would be agreeable to you."

Miss Feathering—who by this time was feeling that she had entered another world entirely—nodded her head and whispered, "By all means," at which Sir John picked up a small hand bell and rang it determinedly.

A few seconds later came a timid knock at the door which opened a crack to reveal the woman who Sir Humphrey had disregarded.

"Yes, Sir John?" she asked.

"Ah, Mary my dear, would you be so kind as to take Miss Feathering to your parlour below and there talk about matters of the day. Our meeting is strictly private I fear."

Lady Fielding bobbed a respectful curtsey. "Of course, Sir John. Miss Feathering if you would be kind enough to step below I should be obliged."

Poor Phoebe rose and left the room with not so much as a backward glance, thoroughly worn out with the strains of the day. John said nothing, imagining the cool response of Serafina who had beaten more men in the gambling houses than she had received proposals of marriage. But this was not his meeting, having received a summons to it only this morning via a call from that ginger fox, Joe Jago, who had journeyed upriver with an early rising waterman. And now, after a harrumphing of his throat, the Blind Beak was speaking.

"Gentlemen, I have asked you all here to decide what is to be done about these unpleasant attacks and, indeed, cold-blooded murder which are being carried out against anyone connected in any way with the Redwood family. For that is what they are. Flimsy though the contact may be there is not one of these victims who has not in some way been associated with them. That wretched child for one. Pushed into the River Thames, then abducted by the village idiot, because she might be a by-blow of one of the boys."

John, listening intently, marvelled for the thousandth time at the man's remarkable memory. Joe Jago had related the story to the Magistrate with all the latest details and the man had taken each fact and filed it away in his simply amazing mind. But he was speaking once more.

"Not content with causing a riding accident which cost Sir Humphrey his leg and swinging Miss Feathering, naked and ashamed, above the heads of the crowd in the Theatre Royal, Drury Lane, he then goes on to cut the throat of Mrs. Redwood at a grand ball given by the German banker, Baron Rotmuller. It is obvious that the perpetrator of these evil crimes is quite insane."

John asked a question. "But how, sir, do we stop him—or her?"

"Ah, that is where I have a plan which might—I use that word advisedly—just work."

"And that is?" asked Sir Humphrey.

"To promote Gilbert Palmer, the Constable of Berkhamsted, to organise the younger of you into watch parties."

"Will I not be included?" asked Sir Humphrey in pathetic tones.

Gilbert spoke for the first time, looking incredibly birdlike as he turned his head on one side to look at the speaker.

"Perhaps in a more administrative role, sir."

"Well, I'm not as young as I once was," Sir Humphrey agreed reluctantly.

"But the rest of you," the constable continued, "I would ask most heartily to join me. I think there will be five different places to watch and if we can enlist one extra man that will initially be all that we require."

John put his hand up. "May I suggest a worthy fellow?"

It was the Blind Beak who answered. "Yes?"

"A young cordwainer who helped me out with Miss Feathering on the night of the terrible reveal. He helped me cut her down and accompanied myself and my daughter to the hospital. His name is Jem Clements and he is as far as I can see a thoroughly reliable man."

"Then if he agrees to such a delicate mission we are complete."

There was a momentary silence then Joe Jago asked, "What exactly do you have planned, Beak?"

John thought that he would not have dared address the magistrate in such familiar terms, but then Sir John and Jago had worked together for an age and were deep companions.

"My design is that from now on all five of the following places and all that happen therein as soon as darkness falls shall be watched by one of you. After your one-night stint you are to hand over to the next man et cetera. In this way a fresh pair of eyes will keep watch each time. You are to report back to me at two of the afternoon each day."

Baron Rotmuller gave a deep chuckle that John believed could not have been produced by anyone other than a German. "This will be good sport I think."

John said, "May I bring Jem Clements round to see you, Sir John? That is if he is willing to take the challenge on?"

"Yes, providing that the appointment is sharply kept for time. I have much to do."

"And what five properties do you want us to observe, sir?" asked Gilbert, very alert.

"The dwelling places of Lord and Lady Derwent and her sister the viscountess, which means the Redwood family home together with that of the Jacquards. And also the dwelling place of the eminent Baron Rotmuller," he chuckled. "A murderer often returns to the scene of their crime, Herr Baron. Nothing personal I assure you."

"What will they be looking for exactly?" This from Sir Humphrey who seemed fractionally disappointed that his role was less exciting than that of the others.

The Blind Beak rumbled a laugh. "Everything and nothing. How many of them go out, who they receive, their general behaviour."

"But why the Jacquards?" John asked.

"The brother who is very short of sight intrigues me. I think he sounds interesting. Did you not see him creeping off in a strange manner with a person wrapped up like a bundle, Mr. Rawlings?"

"Yes, but that does not point to him being a killer."

After he had said that John wondered why he was defending the man. Then knew that it was a lingering thought of Hyacinth's sweet charm that had turned him away from the idea that her brother could be a murderer. But the Magistrate was speaking once more.

"Gentlemen you have your instructions. Remember to change shifts nightly. Bring Jem Clements for me to meet tomorrow, the earlier the better, Mr. Rawlings. Goodnight to you all."

And tapping his cane before him, the Blind Beak left the room and made his way downstairs.

Jem Clements did not jump at the chance to become involved in a spell of spying for the Principal Magistrate—he positively leapt at it.

"How soon can we start, Mr. Rawlings?"

"As soon as he has spoken to you, I imagine."

"And when will that be?"

"Now."

Fortunately the meeting—though brief—went well, and so it was that as the evening shadows began to fall over the streets and squares of London, Jem found himself behind a clump of trees, spending an evening with the Apothecary, learning the tricks of the trade as it were, staring at the elegant outlines of the Duke of Derwent's town house. Beside him Mr. Rawlings, hands in pockets of a sweeping great coat, a close-fitting hat upon his head, stood in silence.

"What are we looking for, sir? Do you know?" Jem asked eventually.

"Any movements of anybody, in or out. As he told you earlier, the Blind Beak believes that all those people who were attacked in some way or other—including the unfortunate Phoebe Feathering whose life you helped to save—are linked by a common foe. And one of them might reside in this house."

"It's a beautiful place. In fact its elegance is quite outstanding. I may be nothing but a common shoemaker, but I can appreciate beauty when I see it."

John nodded then froze, motioning Jem to do likewise. From where they stood in the public garden situated in the middle of the square opposite, they had a clear view of the house. The front door was being thrown open and a woman—either the Duchess of Derwent or her sister—was climbing into a carriage which came hurtling round from the nearby stables.

"Who was that?" whispered Jem.

"Either Lady Derwent or her sibling. They are identical twins which can be very confusing."

"Very useful in a murder enquiry."

"Not for much longer. The viscountess is expecting a child and it is just beginning to show."

Jem laughed quietly. "So which one went out just now?"

"Hard to tell. But hold hard. Here goes somebody else."

A small gig driven by a servant was the next to rapidly appear. The driver jumped down and a young man rushed out of the main entrance, climbed aboard and hastened off as if the Hounds of Hell were at his heels.

"Rapid turnover," Jem commented drily, and John chuckled.

They stayed at their post but after these two quick exits nothing happened until after midnight when a man—on foot and alone—appeared outside and stood staring at the house for a good ten minutes before sauntering off into the night. Shortly after this John and Jem went their separate ways, very much puzzled.

The next day they made their way to Bow Street at two o'clock in the afternoon. John, who had decided to stay at Nassau Street while these observational duties were ongoing, saw that all but Palmer had a somewhat crestfallen air, particularly the baron whose very moustache seemed to hang with a pendulous air of sadness.

"Well, gentlemen, what have you to report to me?" asked Sir John.

Jago and the baron both stated that all had been quiet but Palmer, looking smart as paint in a dark uniform with gleaming buttons, told rather a different tale.

"I was on duty, Magistrate, outside the home of the Viscount and Viscountess Lovell. They were entertaining a few friends, one of which I noted particularly."

"Why was that?"

"She travelled alone in a hired hackney and was heavily cloaked and masked. She entered the house at eight of the clock and then came out again ten minutes later and was picked up by another hackney and vanished. Then a few minutes later the Duchess of Derwent appeared in a magnificent equipage and went inside the building. Thirty minutes after that she came out again and this time abandoned the coach and left in another hired hackney. After that there was no further activity until midnight when a small stream of guests departed in various forms of transport. Then to crown it all a servant drove the duchess's coach away with nobody aboard it except the staff. It was very strange."

The magistrate sat motionless for a while, then said, "Any ideas, Joe?"

"No, Sir John, nothing occurs immediately."

"Well, if something does, contact me. Tonight, I want two of you to watch the viscount's house. Palmer and Mr. Rawlings. Between you, you ought to spot something of further interest."

As it so happened this plan was not to materialise. John had arrived back at Nassau Street to find a letter awaiting him. It was from Miranda Lovell, the viscountess. It seemed that that very night she was giving a small party and was inviting him to join them. But it was a most unfortunate clash of dates. John had immediately taken a chair to where the constable had booked lodging at The White Hart, Drury Lane, and who—at the precise moment the Apothecary entered—was consuming a pint of frothing liquid. Gilbert Palmer looked up.

"Mr. Rawlings, good to see you. You've obviously come searching for me."

"I have indeed. There has been a collision of engagements. I have received an invitation from the viscountess to dine this very day."

Gilbert's face fell. "And I was looking forward to keeping watch with you. I feel we have much to teach each other."

"I hope so indeed. Tell me, how do you know the Beak? I would have thought Berkhamsted to be rather remote for the pair of you to have crossed paths."

"You're right. It was entirely through the good offices of Baron Rotmuller."

"Really? I'm surprised."

"He appears to be very much the European aristocrat but underneath all that he is a very perceptive and kindly fellow. He liked the way I handled the enquiry into the death of Mrs. Redwood and spoke of me highly to Sir John who he met through some London acquaintances."

"They are an interesting family," John answered with feeling, a picture of his daughter dancing the forbidden waltz and smiling so prettily at Robert Rotmuller coming into his brain. "Now, about

240

today. I shall slip outside occasionally to see how you are getting on and who, if anyone, you want me to watch. If the Viscount's family are going to be present they are a pretty rum bunch I can tell you."

"I know that, sir. I interviewed them after the murder. That is, those of them that I could find."

"Bad luck. So you know the worst. Now, let me buy you a drink."

"That would be very kind. By the way, sir, Sir John has asked me to keep it quiet for the moment that I am to join his Special Men."

Hand-picked, the Special Men—there were about six of them in all—dressed in their own clothes and went to the gaming houses, the public dances, the theatres, the pleasure gardens. At these locations they mingled with the general public and brought back to the Public Office much interesting information, to say nothing of catching pickpockets in the very act of stealing a watch or a wallet and stopping little incidents growing out of hand. They were also extremely friendly with the higher class of criminal who duly respected them and also avoided them whenever possible. The other people who the Blind Beak employed were a set of Brave Fellows, ready to go anywhere in the kingdom at short notice to sort out a problem. They had once pursued a man to Portsmouth and taken a boat in order to arrest him. He had been guilty of stealing tankards out of public houses. And John recalled with a smile how they had also removed a body from the Romney Marsh which had been disguised as a scarecrow but turned out to be an agent of France. Interesting days.

He spent an hour in Gilbert's company then called a chair and returned to Nassau Street to prepare himself for the night's activities. Beautifully attired, he emerged some while later and took his coach to Chiswick. He had left the conveyance behind when he had sailed for the Colonies and stabled it—growing older—in the yard close to Nassau Street. Upon his return it had emerged, looking its age. But John had willingly laid out the money for restoration and had a thought that when Fred—the boy who had attached himself to the Apothecary's shop in Shug Lane—would grow up a little more—he might be invited to be John's coachman. Tonight, though, the reins were being taken by a footman who loved sitting up on the box, dressed in a driver's gear, and flicking his whip in the air.

The Apothecary arrived in Chiswick sometime later, where he found the company already assembled. The entire Redwood family was present, including Roderick and Percival, the viscount's nasty brothers, and his three ugly sisters. Never fully at ease in their company, John mingled amongst the rest of the guests and made small talk. He once popped his head out of doors, looking for any sign of Gilbert. The man was nowhere to be seen but a certain rustling in the trees told him that he was not alone. Eventually they were called in to dine and it was then that Roderick bowed effusively over his sister-in-law's hand and begged permission to be excused.

"So sorry, my dear lady, Percival and I have another engagement. I knew you wouldn't mind, being such a damn good sport and all, if we make a quiet exit."

"A damnable good sport, damme," Percival added brainlessly.

John quivered, on the horns of a dilemma. Did he also make some lame excuse and follow them? Or should he find out where they were going and then follow? Furthermore, how could he signal to Gilbert that the two fellows about to leave were people that should be pursued? Noticing John standing, Percival turned and stared at him coldly.

"Have we met before?"

"Yes, indeed," the Apothecary answered, instantly assuming the air of an amiable onlooker. "T'was at the baron's ball. The night your mother was murdered. You were there with that phoney Frenchman."

"Phoney?" queried Roderick.

John bellowed an idiotic laugh. "I should say so. I was in a hostelry in town, don't you know, and saw him beaten into a pulp. Left for dead actually. I don't know whether he was—I just hurried away. Not much one for a mill, dear boy."

He could feel Miranda looking at him strangely and he contrived to give her a slight nod. Whether she had understood or not he did not know. And it was at that fraught moment that the viscount walked in. He stared, first at his brothers then at the Apothecary.

"Leaving so soon?" he asked Roderick.

"Sorry, old chap. Percy and I have another engagement."

He winked. The viscount did not respond, turning instead to the younger man.

"Where do you intend going?"

Percival hesitated. "To see some people we met recently."

"And who might they be?"

Roderick interrupted. "Lord Leadore and his brothers. Good stock. They've bought a place at Gunnersbury."

John watched as Michael suddenly went molten. "How dare you be so rude to my wife who has organised this party. You are a pair of beastly little jackanapes. Well, you can get out and stay away, the two of you. And don't come here, wimping and whining, when you run out of money."

And with that he sprinted past the footman and opened the front door himself. John stood aghast, then collected himself and decided to make the most of the situation.

"If you'll excuse me, my dear sir, I think I should leave as well."

The viscount looked frankly astonished and Miranda, who had been standing staring at her brothers-in-law with a certain amount of contempt, now hurried forward.

"My dear Mr. Rawlings do you have to go?"

For answer John rolled his eyes in the direction of the two young men and mouthed the words, 'follow them'. A light appeared in the viscount's look and he murmured, "It isn't worth it, you know." John shook his head as if he did not understand, seized his cloak and hat, and followed the unlovely pair out of the front door.

Once outside they gave him a bow which lacked any respect whatsoever and without further ado hurried round to the stables. The Apothecary dived into the bushes so that when they came back, seated in an antiquated gig, he had vanished.

"Where's the bastard gone?" one asked.

"Don't know and care less," the other replied, and they hurried off into the night.

John emerged and called Gilbert in a quiet but penetrating whisper. Much to his surprise the constable's head appeared from behind a tree.

"I saw all that. Shall we follow them?"

"Yes. I've got my coach here but it is very obvious."

"I actually came in an old cart. It is extremely primitive but the horse is tethered nearby. Shall we?"

"We shall indeed," the Apothecary answered, and sprinted faster than he had done in living memory.

Somehow with a little gentle persuasion Gilbert managed to convince the resolute nag pulling them that there was a certain urgency in their mission so that the five-minute start gained by the Redwood brothers shrank a little. As they rounded a bend in the road leading out of Chiswick they glimpsed the back of the gig and heard a loud and somehow unpleasant laugh ring out.

John, seated behind on a piece of wooden planking, called softly, "Slow down. I think they're going to stop."

He was right. As the gig approached Chiswick Mall Roderick pulled the reins tightly and the horse let out a protesting neigh and finally ground to a halt before a large and imposing house built on the left-hand side. The area had been greatly developed in the last twenty years, so John believed, and thought it very much a rich man's enclave. He watched as Roderick got out and ran up the imposing steps, pulling the doorbell with a flourish. A servant answered and took his card within. A few minutes later a young woman appeared and stood in the entrance. Roderick bowed elegantly and took a step closer and then something happened that made John gasp for breath. The visitor seized the girl round the waist and carried her down the steps to the waiting gig. The servant rushed to stop him but it was too late. Percival gave an hysterical and loud laugh and the gig took off at speed. The girl's faint screams echoed behind them.

Chapter Twenty-One

The night was filled with the sounds of the girl's cries, growing ever fainter.

"My God," exclaimed Gilbert. "The bastard's kidnapped her."

"I think it is his idea of having a jolly jape. But I wouldn't trust either of those two as far as I can throw them. Follow them, my friend." He added, "Are you armed?"

Gilbert gave a raven's grin. "Is the king named George?"

"Good. But no firing at this stage. And no racing. Drive gently. It just so happens that we are strolling along behind him if he bothers to turn his head."

The snatched girl was putting up a good fight, hitting Roderick as best she could, a fact not helped by the reason that he was considerably taller than she and most of her blows seemed to land harmlessly on his chest. But as they watched it the gig suddenly veered off to the right, disappearing into a small dark lane.

"I think they are heading for the river," said John.

At breakneck speed the carriage they were pursuing suddenly turned right yet again and vanished into the inky darkness of nothing more than a large track.

"Damnation!" John cried. "Try and hang on to them if you can."

But it was a hellish ride. The track twisted and turned like a serpent and Percy—aware that someone was close behind him—whipped the poor horse without mercy. The girl had been thrown into Roderick's arms and he had made the most of it and held her in a vice-like grip. John, who was usually good about direction, had totally lost his bearings and could only cling to the side of the vehicle and pray that he would remain there when the nightmare chase was over. Eventually they approached civilisation in the form of narrow streets and small decrepit buildings. But the smell of the river was everywhere and tonight—even though it was flowing peacefully—the Apothecary could hear its little sucking murmurs as it pulled against the bank, disturbed by some large craft that had gone upriver earlier. Yet they were not at Strand-on-the-Green, infinitesimally the little noises were different.

"Where are we?" asked Gilbert, pulling to a halt and dismounting. "And, more importantly, where are they?"

But John had spotted a little alleyway leading off beside the building outside which they were standing. In it was parked the shattered gig, one wheel hanging on by a thread, the horse only upright because it was still in the traces. He motioned to Gilbert to follow him, putting his finger to his lips to remain silent. But when they got to the front the Apothecary let out a cry of surprise as he read the words The Dove painted on a hanging sign. They were in the riverside part of the suburban district of Hammersmith, which lay in the hundred of Osselstone in the county of Middlesex, and were currently outside a small hostelry of which John had heard, though never visited.

"They've gone inside," said Gilbert, stating the obvious.

"I've a feeling that the situation might get a trifle rough," John answered.

The constable's dark eyes shone. "I was brought up in a hard school, Mr. Rawlings."

"That's as well."

The door swung open as soon as it was pushed and they had a glimpse of the room beyond. It was small and heavily beamed with a miserable fire in front of which—looking thoroughly worn-out and trembling slightly—stood Percival.

"Good evening," said John in a pleasant voice.

Just for a second he felt sorry for the young man, who seemed like a whipped pup, and then the viscount's brother snarled and showed his teeth.

"You bastards," he shouted. "What gives you the right to follow us here? Who do you damned well think you are? Out for a pleasant drive and then set upon by a pair of upstart Runners. God damn you." And from his pocket he produced a pistol and pointed it straight at them. After that there was a moment of intense silence and then two shots rang out almost simultaneously. John stood flabbergasted. The air was full of gun smoke and the landlord, who had ducked down behind the counter, was slowly peeping above it. And Percival was falling to the floor, dark hair streaming round him, and a trickle of blood oozing slowly from a small wound in his forehead. All the old instincts set in and the Apothecary rushed to gather him up, to tend him, but it was too late. Percival gave a violent tremor and died in his arms.

A wooden door was flung open and Roderick appeared in a dishevelled state of dress. "What's going on?" he said, then he saw Percival, John still carrying him. "What have you done?" he bellowed. "By God, you've shot my brother!" He lunged forward, fists flying, but there was a terrible thump as he too hit the wooden floor. Gilbert stood above him, his arms still outstretched and just for a moment John saw that the bird had become a raven.

"I killed a man who would have killed me, had I let him. And now, Mr. Redwood, I must arrest you on the charge of stealing a young woman from her lawful abode and dragging her off against her wishes."

"You beastly little runt. You awful little man."

With an agility that surprised the Apothecary Roderick rose swiftly to his feet and grabbed Gilbert by the throat. The constable, obviously trained by a master in self-defence, used his hands and swung a tremendous blow in the direction of Roderick's groin. He doubled with pain and abruptly let go of his victim. Gilbert once more produced his gun and said with a great deal of controlled satisfaction, "You are under arrest, Mr. Redwood, and I would advise you to come quietly or risk even longer imprisonment."

The landlord, finally finding his voice, said, "I've got two stout lads out the back who can help you, constable."

And John, gently lowering Percival to the floor, thought what a marvellous thing it was to wear a uniform.

In the end the evening ended on a much happier note than that with which it had started. Roderick was escorted to a safe lock-up at the back of The Dove—obviously used when customers got rowdy and out of hand. The young woman was rescued from upstairs where John had found her trembling and trying to hide beneath a chaise-longue. She had met Roderick at a ball where he had introduced himself as the Duke of Hastings, she had told him.

"Did you believe him?"

"No, of course I didn't. Dukes are of big counties not piddling little places like Hastings."

John had laughed aloud and reckoned her to be a girl of spirit. Later on, when she had cleaned herself up a bit and Percival's body had been removed, she came downstairs and assured the constable in a quiet voice that Roderick had not molested her.

249

"Though not for want of trying."

"I am so glad to hear that."

"I think my brothers used to call it Brewers Droop."

There had been much supressed hilarity.

John escorted her home, hiring a hackney that was plying for late-night hire, and had then returned in the same vehicle to The Dove. By this time Gilbert Palmer was being feted as a hero and nobody talked of Percival Redwood at all. But the Apothecary, going into the quiet room where the young man's body was lying on a bed, felt that it was all such a waste of what could have been a fine person, gone to the dogs at an early age. And then he remembered how he had held Percival's brother the viscount under a pump and wondered—just a little bit—if there had been perhaps some magic in that cascading water.

Chapter Twenty-Two

"He did what?" roared the Magistrate.

"He escaped, sir. The landlord assured me that the place was absolutely impenetrable, that nobody had got out of it ever, but the fact remains that when we went to fetch him, he had gone. I'm so sorry." Gilbert Palmer hung his head.

John Rawlings spoke up. "It was not the constable's fault, Sir John. I assisted when we locked Roderick Redwood up. It was a hellhole, just big enough for a man to sit down, but the fact remains that he got out somehow. I reckon he had an accomplice somewhere or other."

"Someone who worked there, you mean?"

"That is the only feasible explanation."

The magistrate relapsed into his customary silence and Gilbert cast a nervous glance in John's direction. For reassurance the Apothecary winked and put his finger to his lips. Finally Fielding spoke.

"As I told you earlier the watches on the various houses have not proved particularly fruitful. In fact I am calling off those on the Baron Rotmuller's abode."

"All quiet?" asked John.

"Relatively, yes." Sir John added, more thoughtfully, "You know I have a feeling that the answer to this enigma may be just under our noses yet hidden in some way. But first we must find the runaway. Your thoughts, Palmer?"

"I don't think we need look much further than his home, sir. His clothes were torn and stained, his wig was lost, his chin unkempt. He would have to have headed there to get himself together."

"But didn't stay long, I'll warrant. The fellow's gone on the run, I'm certain of it."

"Yet what for, sir? He has killed no-one—at least that we know of—and as for the abduction of the girl t'other night he can simply say that she accepted his invitation. And it will be his word against hers."

Sir John's face, usually impassive, sank into even deeper lines, making him suddenly gain age.

"Perhaps he fears retribution from some other source, Mr. Rawlings. If he generally acts in that cavalier manner to the female sex he is bound to have made several enemies by now."

Gilbert spoke once more. "Very true, sir. So do you want me to guard the Redwood place again?"

"No, I'd rather you did not. I might perhaps ask Jago to keep a watchful eye on the outside premises. You never know who could turn up."

Although the Magistrate was blind Gilbert gave a smart salute. "So where do you wish me to go, sir?"

"To the Jacquard establishment. I particularly want you to watch out for Giles, the short-sighted brother. Now I have over run my time. That will be all. Thank you, gentlemen."

And he was gone, his cane tapping on the wooden stairs as he made his way downwards. Despite their years of friendship John felt slightly annoyed.

"And what about me? What am I supposed to do?"

"Perhaps Sir John intends you to have a night to yourself."

"You're probably right. Good luck, Gilbert. Don't shoot anyone if you can possibly avoid it."

"I won't, I promise."

And with that they parted company and John, still irritated, swung down Bow Street, thinking seriously. By the time he had reached Nassau Street his mind was made up. He would write a polite note to Michael, Viscount Lovell, and ask him if he might call on him that day. To the Apothecary the entire mystery had gone on long enough. He needed to discuss it with someone on the inside who might be able to shed some much-needed light on the whole wretched affair. Yet he knew he was taking a risk. Blood was thicker than any magic water!

Nonetheless as soon as the Apothecary had arrived at his London house he sat down at the desk and wrote to the Viscount and sent it of in his coach—which had returned with a tired and displeased coachman during the night. Within two hundred minutes it returned. There was a charming note saying how he, too, was tired of the investigation and would very much like to see John that evening. He, the viscount, would send a coach for him at six of the clock if that would be convenient. John agreed that arrangement would be perfectly in order and decided, there and then, to have a bath and freshen himself up after all the struggles of the last twenty-four hours.

He was dressed to the hilt when the coach pulled up at 2 Nassau Street and felt momentarily that all the little ghosts of his past were assembling to wave him goodbye and admire his clothes. In a highly eccentric manner he waved back at them and then wished that the most beautiful, most elusive, most captivating women he had ever known—Elizabeth di Lorenzi—could return and sit beside him at least for the duration of the journey. But she did not and so he sat alone as he entered the woody splendour of Chiswick Park and put his past firmly to one side as he prepared for the all-important meeting with the viscount.

Michael was sitting in the great room of the Jacobean mansion, reading a newspaper. He looked up with a fleeting smile but his smoky eyes were shadowed and anxious.

"Ah, my dear friend, how nice to see you. Tell me, has my ruffian brother been up to something terrible?"

"I'm afraid so. But how did you know?"

"Nothing travels faster than bad news."

John nodded and pulled a face. "I am afraid that his addiction to sprightly females got very out of hand. But there was something pretty grim about the death of your youngest brother."

The viscount stood up and crossing to a side table poured out two glasses from a decanter placed on it. His hand shook ever so slightly. "Do you know who shot him?" he asked.

"Yes," the Apothecary answered shortly.

"Well?"

"It was Gilbert Palmer, the Constable of Berkhamsted. It was a case of shoot or be shot. I'm afraid Percival had pulled a pistol on us."

The viscount turned round. "I'm not surprised. He always was a nasty little boy. As a baby he screamed from morning till night. As a child he threw tantrums. As a youth he got into every scrape imaginable. As a young man he copulated with every girl who so much as smiled at him. He also hero-worshipped Roderick, became his unpaid lackey. I am afraid that a wasted life has come to an end. I hope that he meets Mama in heaven and she can spoil him all over again."

The Apothecary did not answer, thinking how true it was that children can be ruined by their parents.

"So let us change the subject. Let me drink to you, my friend, and thank you for all you have done for me."

"I personally don't recall anything in particular. Other than putting you under the pump that day."

The viscount chuckled aloud. "I'm glad you did. I was a total idiot up till then. But as the water cascaded over my head I desperately tried to think of anything good that I had done with my life—which I believed I was on the point of losing—and could only come up with one; that I had made a fine match. And then I realised that Miranda was more than a beauty, that she had a beautiful personality to go with it. From that moment on I began to regard her in a new light."

"I'll respond by drinking to that," John answered and drained his glass, which the viscount promptly refilled.

They sat in silence for a few moments, both heavy with thought. Michael finally spoke.

"So what happens now?"

"You know that Roderick escaped?"

"Yes, I had heard. But let me hasten to assure you that he isn't here and I have seen no sign of him."

"What will you do if he does seek you out?"

The smoky eyes had a gleam of humour in them. "I'd probably give him some money and tell him to go abroad."

"And evade the law?"

"Now you are sounding elderly and grand which I know are two things you will never be."

"I sincerely hope not," the Apothecary replied with a grin.

The rest of the evening passed amicably until at about thirty minutes past ten John Rawlings took his leave, Michael lending him a small, light coach in which to travel back to Nassau Street, the house at Strand-on-the-Green standing currently empty, the servants giving it a good clean out while the master and Miss Rose lodged in London. He was just coming out of the entrance to the drive when another vehicle appeared coming towards him. John's driver slowed but not so the other, instead racing past as if being pursued by the Hounds of Hell. The Apothecary leaned forward to look out of the small window and saw Miranda clad in a scarlet cloak and hood, cowering back as if she did not wish to be observed. Or was it her sister, Lady Derwent? The language of her movements, small as they were, told him that it was the duchess, yet the Apothecary could not be certain. With his head full of strange thoughts, his conveyance sped on into the night.

Despite being well fed and extremely well-watered, John found it almost impossible to sleep. In the end he got up and went to sit in Sir Gabriel's study, poking at the remnants of the dying fire. Closing his eyes for a second while he tried to clear his head, John opened them again to see his father had glided into the room. He was not alarmed, instead he leapt out of his chair and went to embrace the grand old man. His arms thrashed in mid-air—there was nothing there—but still John spoke aloud.

"I thought I saw you, my dear, just for a second. So I am going to ask your advice. There are twin sisters—Lady Lovell and Lady Derwent—who are playing some sort of game, wearing each other's clothes and generally taking one another's place. What should I do about it?"

There was no reply, but the ticking of Sir Gabriel's beloved long case clock suddenly seemed to grow much louder.

John smiled. "You are telling me to be patient. All will be revealed in the fullness of time. Am I right?"

A piece of coal suddenly fell over in the fireplace even though the fire had gone out long since.

"Thank you, my dear Papa. Goodnight."

There was a fluttering of air and John finally closed his eyes, sighed a deep sigh, and went to sleep.

He had fully intended to go to Bow Street next morning but a letter from Joe Jago, delivered by a street urchin, had come even before the Apothecary had tackled his usual hearty breakfast. It had been hastily scrawled—a strange event for Joe whose writing was incredibly neat, totally at odds with his extraordinary character—and informed the Apothecary that he would call at half past nine punctually. In fact he was a little early and John observed him through a window pacing the cobbles and looking at his fob watch. Jago knocked at the door on the dot of the promised time and swept off his hat as he entered.

"Joe, my friend, I take it something of interest is afoot?"

"Yes, indeed, Mr. Rawlings. I have seen that skunk Roderick Redwood just last night. He's in London and looking mighty pleased with himself."

John swore loudly. "Where the hell was he?"

"In the Seven Dials district with some flaunting slut. Couldn't keep his hands off her."

"He needs castrating."

Joe laughed. "I wonder how many times he would have to suffer that fate. Why if all the fathers and husbands descended on him he would have the highest soprano voice in England."

"Did you follow him?"

"Of course. He went into the whorehouse last thing I saw and—but now I come to the strange part …" Joe paused for dramatic effect.

"Yes?"

"As he went within I noticed a woman standing in the shadows—watching."

"Who was she? Did you recognise her?"

"It would have been difficult because she was not only masked but wearing some concealing cloak and hood. Yet she had an air about her."

"What do you mean?"

"Mr. Rawlings, in my job as clerk to Sir John I have observed women of all sorts and classes, all types and tykes, baronesses and bawds, madams and milliners, gentlefolk and guttersnipes, and there is something about the way they carry themselves that reveal their origins. I can tell you that this woman carried herself well."

"Interesting. Have you any ideas?"

"None whatsoever. Anyway, I went to follow but she had vanished. Gone down an alleyway and disappeared. It was an odd night altogether."

John nodded slowly. "I think we should inform Sir John."

Five minutes later they set out, only to find that Gilbert Palmer had already arrived and was in full oratory.

"It was all very quiet at the Jacquard's house and yet I believe that they knew they were being watched."

The Magistrate was clearly being short with words. "Why?" he asked.

"Because every so often one of them would come out into the garden and look round. And I knew that they were searching to see if anybody was spying on them."

"Did they find you?"

Gilbert looked fractionally annoyed. "No, they did not. I pride myself on my observation techniques, Sir John."

John and Joe, who had entered the room quietly, smiled at each other, a fact which Gilbert did not, and Sir John could not, see.

Joe spoke. "It seemed something of a wild night for us all, Magistrate."

And he and the Apothecary told their tales, listened to in complete silence. When they had finished the stillness continued. Sir John was doing his usual trick of sitting absolutely motionless, giving the impression that he might have dropped off for a brief nap. Gilbert on the other hand was alert, his eyes glistening, his head on one side.

"So what do we do, sir?" he asked eventually.

"Nothing," said Sir John, still without moving.

"What do you mean?" asked John.

"We continue to watch and they—whoever they are—will slip up, mark my words. Let them play their little game. The only thing that is imperative is that they do not realise we are on to them. These people will eventually come unstuck."

Outside, walking down Long Acre, John turned to Joe Jago. "Those women can't be the Winterlight twins, can they?"

"Possibly. Though what their motive could be is shrouded in mystery."

"I quite agree. It is clear as day that Miranda loves the viscount and the fact that he returns the compliment is plain to see."

"But the other woman is married to that mighty thug the Duke of Derwent. He has never loved anything in his life—except perhaps his dogs."

The Apothecary laughed. It seemed a ridiculous conversation to be having.

"Well, as Sir John has given me no further instructions, I think I will return to Strand-on-the-Green."

"Don't blame you, sir. Get some river air into your lungs."

As if to emphasise the point a cart loaded with steaming dung rolled past.

"Phew," said John, reaching for his handkerchief, "I quite agree. I'll be off tonight."

Rose was none too pleased. "But, dearest Papa, I don't really want to leave London."

"My darling, I know exactly how you feel. Robert is at Drury Lane and you are having fun. But, sweet girl, you leave me no choice. I have decided to get back to Chiswick and to Chiswick I will go. I will leave you in the care of the servants and hope that your good sense will prevail in my absence."

Rose looked chastened and hung her head a little though John could see the beginning of a smile creep round her lips.

"And don't think that it will be liberty hall once I have gone. I shall leave stern orders with the staff to keep a very strict eye on you indeed."

Afterwards in the boat rowing him up-river to Strand-on-the-Green he thought about what he had said and took himself to task. His Rosebud, his girl, the child he adored, was old enough to be married and he was still treating her like a baby. Why, he considered, was he so open-minded with the twins and so old-maidish with his daughter? It was a grievous fault and one that he should eradicate now. Let her marry who she wanted to.

At that moment John Rawlings made the momentous decision not to worry about it for a second longer and let what will be, be. He would tell his daughter as soon as he returned to town that she had his complete and utter blessing to do whatever she pleased.

As soon as Zoffany spied him coming ashore, he threw open his front door and hurried to greet his friend.

"Oh dear soul, much has been happening I believe. Come in as soon as you can and tell me everything."

John was only too glad to do so, hurrying through into Zoffany's house as soon as he had parked his traps in the hallway. He was somewhat surprised to see a forbidding portrait of Jocasta—Samuel's wife—on the easel.

The painter pointed at it with his brush.

"I took many sketches when I stayed with them. It was your friend's great wish that I should do a painting of her for the family."

"That will please him enormously. He's a dear chap. He and I go back a very long way."

Zoffany nodded, then gave a vast wink. "I know I shouldn't tell you because it is meant to be a total surprise but I am quite hopeless when it comes to keeping secrets."

"Don't tell me he is on his way here?"

"He is indeed. He says he wants to be in at the kill—his expression not mine—when the Blind Beak finally unravels the mystery."

John groaned aloud. "How typical. The Blind Beak indeed! While the rest of us have been putting ourselves in mortal danger to tear the wrappings off who the real killer is."

"Do you know now?"

The Apothecary grinned and spread his hands. "I've only a vague idea and that could easily be proved wrong."

"Are you going to tell me?"

"Quite definitely not. Why with your dubious ability to keep secrets half of London would be in the know. My good friend as far as I am concerned silence will be well and truly golden."

Zoffany let out a great roar of laughter and handed John a wine cup full of claret, which he proceeded to consume with some zest.

Chapter Twenty-Three

No sooner had John unpacked his clothes and told the servants he was back than there came a thunderous knocking at the door. Even without seeing him he knew that Samuel had arrived, busily shouting that he had come to assist with the current puzzle the Apothecary was wrestling with.

"Ah, my great friend, two heads are better than one, what ho." Sam rubbed his hands together. "Felt I couldn't leave you in the lurch a second longer. I've come to stay until the bitter end."

"What do you mean by that exactly?"

"Well until you've caught the villain—or villains as the case may be."

"That's very kind of you indeed, Samuel, but I'm not sure when that will be."

His friend sat down, looking important. "I think you'd better catch me up with all the latest, my chap. I am a little bit confused."

"You're not the only one," John answered, and started to peel off the various layers of the case.

Half an hour later, including Samuel's interruptions, he had told his friend everything that had taken place recently.

"My word, what a puzzler," Sam stated solemnly. "But my money is on Roderick Redwood. He sounds a truly rascally piece of work."

"Yes, but who was the female watching him? Joe Jago insists that she was a woman of bearing."

"Probably one of his many lovers. He is bound to have had dozens."

"I'm not so sure about that. Word must have got round by now that he is nothing but a rakehell. And not even a particularly handsome one at that."

Samuel sighed heavily. "Catching villains is not as much fun as it used to be, is it?"

"Nonsense," John replied cheerily. "It is as satisfying as ever it was. You're getting old, Mr. Swann."

"Yes, you're right. We're neither of us the young blades that once we were."

"Speak for yourself. Personally I feel as sharp witted as I did twenty years ago."

Samuel raised a bushy brow and looked at John with a grin. The Apothecary stared at him, very straight of face, then he gave in and collapsed, laughing.

"Point to you," he said.

Samuel clapped him on the shoulder. "Nonsense," he replied.

Later when they had dined, they went for a stroll by the river. Autumn was laying its sharp hand on the landscape and the water looked dark and cruel. The trees on Oliver's Island were the colour of a topaz, piercing as a glittering tiger's eye, while the shrubbery that grew along the riverbank had turned into an amber medley of leaves which glowed, vivid as a fire's heart. The evening was drawing in, the sky filled with dyed red clouds, like a regiment of soldiers marching towards battle. The river's inky depths were suddenly pierced by the sun's triumphant exit and flowed, red as blood, from a freshly gushing wound. John, sensing the

263

drama of it, stood stock still and gazed all about him, while Samuel sighed deeply and said, "Ye Gods, what a glorious sight."

"It is indeed. Come, my old friend. When you have seen enough let us go and relax in The Bull's Head. It is a newly built place but quite good so Zoffany says. There we can be comfortable together."

And linking his arm through Samuel's the two of them made their way like the good companions that they were and walked into the shadows and out of the dying of the day.

That night John had the strangest of dreams. He stood with his son, James, in the pouring rain and watched Giles Jacquard, a pitiable figure because of his tragically poor sight, meet a person—of which sex it had been impossible to tell because of the number of wrappings the creature wore—and hurry away in the direction of the Duke of Devonshire's worker's cottages. At the time it had had a curiosity value, nothing more, of the kind when one spots a friend out with a stranger to whom one has not been introduced. But in the dream it seemed of paramount importance. As if the key to the whole set of mysterious circumstances were bound together by this event. John woke suddenly, sitting upright, his mouth parched. Convinced that he had the answer—if only he knew what it was. In the darkness he could have sworn that somebody was whispering to him but as he returned to full consciousness he realised that all was tremendously silent. It had been a trick of the mind and yet he felt strongly that somehow the way was being shown to him. He told Samuel of it over breakfast which was, as usual, tremendously hearty.

"How extraordinary. Personally I slept like a log," Samuel answered, with just a note of superiority in his voice that John found somewhat irritating.

"Oh well done. What good news."

Sam gave him a suspicious glance but persisted. "And what are your plans for today, John?"

"I thought we might walk up to Chiswick Park and you could see the mansion in which the viscount lives. And his beautiful wife, one of the former Miss Winterlights, of course."

"I should like that very much."

They took a route that led them up Sutton Lane and the cottage in which Lucinda had stayed with her aunt was duly pointed out.

"And where is the little girl now?"

"In London with her parent I presume. A nice chap by the name of Buffitt. The only fault with the child is that she was fathered by one of the reprobates living locally—but which one I have never been able to work out."

"And what happened to the mad man? The one who slept with his sister and pretended to be a French marquis or something of the sort?"

"I don't know. As I wrote to you, I left him dying—or so I thought—outside a hostelry in Half Moon Street. I can tell you, Sam, that all my training rebelled against leaving him. It was agony for me to break my oath and walk away. But then I thought of his sister's suicide and hardened my heart. But what became of him I couldn't say."

"I wonder if he returned to life and is behind all this?"

John shook his head. "I don't think that would be possible. He must be crippled to say the least."

Samuel rubbed his hands together and said, "Good!" with great emphasis.

The Apothecary laughed. Samuel was so exuberant, so devoid of correct manners, so true in his real feelings, that he would never be accepted by the *beau monde.* Yet he was the most wonderful person to call a friend. John put an arm round Sam's shoulders and gave him an affectionate hug.

They had left Sutton Lane and were heading in the direction of the extensive gardens and woods that surrounded the small villa built by the Earl of Burlington, who had left the Italian part of his Grand Tour obsessed with the Palladian style of architecture. On coming home, the young aristocrat had commissioned a house to be built, created in that exact form, in which he intended to live. But now the Duke of Devonshire, who had inherited the place through marriage, together with his flamboyant wife Georgiana, had decided to enlarge, add rooms, generally bring the building up to date so that they and their various entourages had enough space to hold court therein. So, as usual, signs of workmen were everywhere and lights were on in Old Chiswick House, the Jacobean mansion that John admired greatly.

"I'd like to see inside," said Samuel, a slightly wistful note creeping into his voice.

"I don't think you'll be able to today," said a bush behind them.

Samuel gave a violent jump, rigid with fear, but John laughed gently.

"Mr. Palmer if I'm not mistaken."

Gilbert's head rose slightly from its verdant surroundings looking just like a dark bird sipping the morning dew.

"Good evening, gentlemen. The Beak has sent me here on lookout duties, let me explain."

"And is there anything worth looking at?" asked John.

"Not really. I think the viscountess is entertaining a midday party because several women have been going in and out, while the viscount saddled up early in the day and went for a ride."

Samuel was on the point of asking a question when Gilbert hastily pushed him down into the bush and John followed suit. A grand coach was arriving even as they stood chatting. It bore the Derwent family crest painted on the side. The door was flung open by a servant and a female, huddled in a voluminous blue cloak and hood, got out, followed by another one, equally heavily garbed.

"What is going on?" said John, more to himself than to his companions. "They've been up to this trick for several days now."

"I can't imagine," Gilbert whispered. "It all seems to be about disguising themselves from any onlooker."

"Perhaps they are nervous of over-eager young men."

"Who isn't?" replied Samuel in a solemn voice.

The trio crouched down once more as a horse's hooves thrummed on the midday air and they were still bent double when a voice behind them said, "And who gave you permission to hide in my bushes?"

John rose with a start to see the grinning face of Michael Redwood, Viscount Lovell, descending from a pale grey horse and looking very far from angry.

"Oh, it's you Rawlings. I might have guessed. And is that not Mr. Swann attempting to huddle beside you? Is this yet another new dance mania that is about to sweep our shores? Should I come and crouch beside you in order to learn it?"

"If you wish, my Lord." The Apothecary answered, straight-faced. "It is not very comfortable, particularly as from this position one is supposed to leap upward suddenly and then remain upright, straight and tall like a tree, waving your hands wildly over your head."

The viscount gazed at him in astonishment, then saw the joke.

"Ah, you mean like this."

And with great enthusiasm he jumped up, his feet leaving the ground, whilst flurrying his fingers in the air. Samuel stared at him as if he had taken leave of his senses and Gilbert Palmer looked frankly amazed, wondering if he was about to be reported for conduct unbecoming.

"May I suggest," Michael said a little breathlessly, "that I invite all three of you in to take a small glass of canary with me. Yes, you too, constable. Don't worry. I am not going to report you to the Beak."

"That's very good of you, sir."

"Think nothing of it. My wife is presiding over some Poetry Followers at the moment so I suggest we retreat to my study to escape them."

The grand entrance hall was indeed populated by several members of the delicate sex, all dressed—John noticed—in cloaks of a deep midnight blue. Instantly his pictorial memory flashed an image. The picture of a chair on which Rose had thrown down some samples brought back from a seamstress's shop. There had been swatches of colour—violet, daisy and a strange and disturbing blue. Why it had struck him he could not possibly say but he had asked Rose about the sample and she had answered that it was a new shade that the dyers had discovered by mixing in a sliver of green. Now he wondered whether it had any particular significance or perhaps was regulation dress for Poetry Followers. Yet all seemed very amusing and joyful, and Miranda and her guests were laughing and joking and sipping sweet drinks. So involved were they in chatter that not a head turned as the viscount and his motley crew of guests passed quietly into a room leading off the hall.

Yet the Apothecary was filled with a strange thought as he walked past the chirruping females. To his mind, it was like looking at an excerpt from a play, like something one could see at Drury Lane Theatre, a scene that seemed other worldly. Yet it was real enough. The viscountess was entertaining her friends and for some kind of a poetic lark they had decided to dress identically. But none the less it was odd that they had chosen that particular shade from which to fashion their costumes.

The viscount, however, made no comment on it but merely waited while a servant poured out four shots of Canary, that excellent wine that came from the isle of Madeira and which the Apothecary so much enjoyed. Several glasses later, as he and his two companions walked quietly away, he was delighted to see Miss Phoebe Feathering sitting amongst the throng.

"Why Miss Feathering, how very nice to run into you again. Have you returned to London once more?"

She became rather flustered. "Why yes, yes I have actually. It's rather a strange turn of events. Sir Humphrey has asked me to reside in his house—temporarily of course—as his lady companion. To escort him to places of interest and so on. I felt I should accept. I do hope you don't think it too forward of me."

"Not in the least. A capital idea."

"It is, isn't it? I do hope nobody gets the wrong impression."

"Oh no, I'm certain your reputation will remain intact." John changed the subject. "So how do you come to be in Chiswick, Miss Feathering?"

She fluttered. Her colour changed to peony. "I don't really know. I had the kindest note from the viscountess inviting me. Of course her late mother-in-law was Sir Humphrey's sister. May be that's why."

"That explains it. But tell me about the matching cloaks. Was that the viscountess's idea?"

"Yes. I thought it rather delightful. As every guest arrived she found a blue cloak awaiting her. Such soft material and so beautifully sewn, quite the most charming gift don't you think?"

"I do indeed—but what was the occasion?"

Miss Feathering looked bewildered. "To denote that I am a Poetry Follower I believe."

"Good gracious. I didn't realise you were that interested."

"Neither did I."

Mentally John's eyebrows hit his wig. He bowed to her and parted company. Samuel immediately detached himself from the background. "I say. Do you believe it? Poetry Followers? Don't you think that was rather extraordinary?"

"Damnably odd. There's something afoot, I know it."

Gilbert Palmer, walking a step behind them, said, "I must get back and report the matter to Sir John at once. It might just be a caprice, a little notion of the hostess. But on the other hand it could be something quite complex. Will you gentlemen excuse me."

The Apothecary paused, then asked, "Do you have any transport here?"

The constable shook his head. "Only my little chaise I fear. I rode in it all the way from Berkhampstead."

"Oh no, not again," groaned Samuel.

"Yes again," answered John firmly. "Gilbert, would you be kind enough to give us a lift back to London? I feel I must add my voice to yours and see the Principal Magistrate about the odd affair of the blue cloaks."

"I am at your disposal—and my little conveyance also," came the reply.

"Then we accept a ride with pleasure."

And before he could groan again, John's elbow dug Samuel firmly in the ribs.

It had grown to high afternoon by the time the small conveyance clattered along Bow Street and stopped at the tall house in which lived the Principal Magistrate and his entourage. Joe Jago had already arrived—whether by design or coincidence it was difficult to judge—and climbing up the winding stairs John and company added to the number of those gathered for the informal meeting. Sir John turned towards Jago.

"Anybody missing, Joe?" he asked.

"Young Jem Clements, sir. He is working in his shop. Baron Rotmuller is attending a rout in Piccadilly. Sir Humphrey Warburton is not called upon to attend evening gatherings. The rest have just walked in."

"Report," ordered the Beak.

"Something strange and interesting," said the Apothecary—and there was immediate silence, broken only by the distant noises of everyday life, the maids chattering like calling birds, the distant hum of the Runners and Fellows who policed the downstairs offices, the general intangible excitement of the atmosphere that always filled the home of the Principal Magistrate of the Metropolis.

Sir John raised his head and appeared to stare directly at the Apothecary with his sightless eyes. "Go on."

"It could be nothing, on the other hand it could be important." And John proceeded to describe exactly what had transpired earlier that morning. When he had finished, Samuel said—in a voice quite small for him—"Yes, that is how it was, sir. It could just have been m'lady's whim, mind you."

The Blind Beak said nothing, nodding slowly, his face expressionless. Eventually he spoke.

"I've a feeling about this. Don't ask why because I can give no reason. But there is something damned odd about the whole business. None of it fits together."

"And there's something else," put in John. "She and her sister—at least that is who I think it is—are wearing the same cloaks…." He stopped dead as he realised what he had just said.

The magistrate sniffed the air, like a dog scenting something.

"I want a close watch put on both these women—and on the viscount, too. I know, Mr. Rawlings, before you protest, that he seems to have reformed and that his gambling debts have now been removed—but has his character been cleansed too? I wonder."

"Sir…" the Apothecary began.

The Beak drowned him out in full voice. "Jago, you and Constable Palmer are to watch the Duke of Derwent and his wife like hawks. Mr. Rawlings and Mr. Swann have the task of secretly surveying the Viscount and Viscountess Lovell. These are my orders."

He looked round, his blinded eyes seeking out each person as he mentioned them by name, his face inscrutable. Nobody dared defy him, they were all his people at that moment, such was the power of the man.

"I take it from your silence that you are in agreement with my plan." No-one moved a muscle. "Then, gentlemen, I would advise you all to return to your quarters and get a decent night's sleep. I would like you to start your vigil at six of the clock tomorrow evening. A spare coach can be loaned to you by my Brave Fellows."

"Who will watch in the daylight hours?" asked Jago matter-of-factly.

"Four of my best men, Joe. But it is my belief that we shan't see trouble until the evening. Which reminds me—have you all got a pistol? If not, can you make arrangements to carry one tomorrow night?"

"Gracious," Samuel muttered, "he really means business."

"Yes," John whispered, "I think he's right. I believe we are coming to the conclusion at last."

Chapter Twenty-Four

Outside the public office John caught Joe Jago by the arm.

"Joe, are we in for trouble?"

"Assuredly, yes. If we are seeking out whoever caused this terrible train of events then we are dealing with an individual who will stop at nothing to achieve his aims."

"And that is the sort of person we are looking for?"

"The Beak thinks so and I have never known him wrong when he sniffs someone out. Have you?"

The Apothecary shook his head. "No, but he has so little knowledge of the case."

"Ah, now that is where you are wrong. He has been interviewing as many people as he can behind the scenes—Sir Humphrey Warburton and Baron Rotmuller to name but two."

Samuel spoke up. "It is obvious John. He probably sat up all night working it out."

"You're right as usual. Come on lads, let's to a tavern and take a little refreshment before we get some sleep."

An hour later and the front door of 2 Nassau Street was being opened by a servant, who smiled and said, "Miss Rose has company, sir."

And true enough from the small salon came the sound of a piano and a man's voice singing most pleasantly 'Passing By' by Henry Purcell. Sam motioned John to be quiet.

"Anybody who can sing like that has to have a good heart, my friend."

There was a smattering of applause and then the couple changed to 'Where'er You Walk' written by Mr. Handel, which they sang as a duet, their voices as crystal clear as sunshine.

The sound of the piano suddenly stopped abruptly and Rose raced into the hall followed by Robert, looking somewhat apprehensive.

"Papa, you've come home and brought dear Mr. Swann. Robert has called round."

The young man gave a stiff and formal bow, rather Germanic in a certain way. John responded, then took him by the hand and shook it enthusiastically.

"Nice of you to call again, my boy."

Robert looked astonished and Samuel gave a jovial laugh.

"Happy times, what ho. I expect you're amazed to see us, my dear little Rosebud, but your father and I are on an important mission for Sir John Fielding. We shall be off early tomorrow morning. I can't tell you what, dear people, even though you might beg me to do so."

Rose and Robert exchanged a glance and John nodded solemnly before chuckling uncontrollably at his voluble friend. But nobody begged Samuel for information—possibly to his slight disappointment—and the rest of the evening passed convivially enough with a cold collation, further renditions on the piano, much singing, the conclusion being provided by John and Samuel duetting together 'The Lady's Birthday', which was extremely rude and had the audience in stitches when a rendition was given by Mr. Platt at Sadler's Wells.

The next day, almost as soon as it was light, they went to the Stairs and were picked up by a waterman who rowed them upstream to

Strand-on-the-Green. Here they changed into dark inconspicuous clothes and eventually set out on foot for Chiswick Park. While still in London they had been assured by Joe Jago that a carriage driven by one of the Brave Fellows would await them near the gates and, sure enough, as they approached their destination they saw that a coach—extremely well-worn but obviously serviceable—stood waiting for them. The driver raised his whip three times and John saluted in response before setting off up the drive.

It would seem that much was ado in the big house and the Apothecary immediately concluded that the viscount and his entourage were moving out of the Jacobean mansion which, after all, had only been loaned to him by the extraordinary Duke of Devonshire while he sought another home for himself and his growing family. Carriages and coaches were thundering up and down the way carrying bits of furniture and various people, many of whom were wearing blue. A very large dog which had ambled up the entryway after them growled and bared its teeth in an extremely menacing manner. John, who had experienced members of the canine fraternity before, gave it a dark look, to which it responded by curling its lip even higher. Fortunately at that moment a luxurious coach, in which sat a woman, heavily masked, with a blue cloaked hood drawn tightly round her head, passed close by and the dog was forced out of the way.

"What's happening?" asked Samuel, *sotto voce*.

"I presume that the viscount is moving," John whispered back.

"But who are all these people?"

"I have no idea. Unless he has called in a few relations to help."

But further conversation was made impossible by a smaller coach, hard on the heels of the other one, careering past them towards the house. The curtains of this conveyance were drawn but as it swerved in order to avoid hitting the two men the cover fell back slightly and John glimpsed Miranda sitting bolt upright and looking tight-lipped.

"Good heavens!" he exclaimed.

"What?"

"That was the viscountess."

"What's so odd about that?"

"I don't know," John answered. "There was just something strange about her manner."

By this time they had reached the Jacobean mansion and were just standing, looking around and wondering what action to take, when the viscount appeared, dressed in his shirtsleeves and breeches and minus a wig. He glanced at them distractedly and then rallied as he recognised who they were.

"John, Samuel," he called. "Come in, do."

His smoky blue eyes were tired and he looked worn to a shadow the Apothecary thought as he made his way into the house, Samuel bustling behind him.

"We are moving today," Michael explained. "Georgiana only told us last night. Not that I hold that against her for a moment. She came here unannounced and said that this house was due for demolition and we must vacate it forthwith."

"How was the lady looking?" asked Samuel, much interested.

"Very scarred about one eye," the viscount answered.

But further conversation was interrupted by the arrival of Miranda, whose coach had overtaken them in the drive. John, glancing at her, thought for a moment that she had changed somehow but realised after a second that his eyes were deceiving him. It was her undoubtedly, pregnancy and all, and yet … She was speaking.

"Greetings my friends. I wish I could spend some time with you but as you have no doubt noticed we are to be gone by nightfall.

276

Fortunately I had arranged a meeting of my Ladies Poetry Following for today and now, poor creatures, they are rushing hither and thither to Berkeley Square carrying items of furniture, to say nothing of china and accoutrements."

"Would they be the ladies wearing the blue cloaks?" John asked.

There was a fraction of a second's pause, then, "That is right. A little whimsy of mine. Too foolish."

John decided that it must be the strain of the move but Miranda was certainly behaving in a very odd manner.

"Berkeley Square? Is that where your new home is?" asked Samuel.

"Yes." The viscount spoke for the first time. "My gambling debts—which were fortunately removed by some very sharp play from that wonderful woman Serafina de Vignolles—precluded me from buying anywhere but now I have enough money to get a house there."

Samuel was already to ask another question but the party was broken up by Miranda saying, "Come, Michael, we have a great deal to do. We mustn't keep these good people a moment longer."

It was bordering on rudeness, the Apothecary thought, considering the fact that the viscount had invited them in, but John stood up immediately.

"Madam," he said, and seizing the viscountess's hand, kissed it. Then he knew the answer—or thought he did. Turning to the viscount he said, "Sir, I wish you the happiest of new abodes." And he had bowed his way out before his friend had had time to draw breath.

"I say," Sam protested, "that was a bit sudden. Did we do wrong in accepting Michael's invitation?"

"No, my friend, rather it was the arrival of the lady that was the fly in the ointment."

"Oh, I see," he answered, but clearly did not understand a word.

* * *

They spent the next hour lying low. The driver of their coach got down and introduced himself as Charles Jealous, a name to be reckoned with indeed. They watched as several conveyances went in and out of the fast-emptying house—women in blue cloaks occupying the majority of them—until finally the viscountess appeared, with curtains drawn but the monogram blazing on the coach's side.

"Is that her?" asked Samuel.

"Yes, definitely."

"Then we must follow discreetly."

Charles Jealous—both by name and by nature it would seem—with a hat tipped over one eye, set off at a leisurely pace in pursuit. But he soon gathered speed when, on rounding a bend, he saw the viscountess's conveyance drawing ahead fast as they entered the confines of outer London. He whipped the two great beasts pulling them to further effort but soon lost Miranda's coach in the press of traffic in The Strand. John knocked on the ceiling with his stick and the Brave Fellow slowed to a stop.

"What do we do?" asked Samuel.

"We'll try the Duchess of Derwent's house. I should think it highly probable that is where the lady has gone."

Having imparted this information to Charles Jealous, the Apothecary watched in amazement as the man hastened up Woodstock Street and then in full flight joined the beginning of St. Martins Lane. After that, having turned the coach successfully, he went like all the devils in hell were in pursuit of them up Cockspur Street and into Pall Mall.

"The Duchess of Devonshire will get out, not the viscountess. Mark my words," said John importantly.

"How do you know that?" asked Samuel.

"Because the duchess has no scar on her right hand. Miranda has a small mark there. For some reason they have changed places."

But he was wrong. As the coach they were pursuing drew to a halt by the gardens opposite the elegant house in St. James's Square, two women—dressed identically in the blue cloak of the Ladies Poetry Following—got out. At this at least half a dozen women, all wearing the same rig, emerged from the gardens and clustered round them.

"What the hell's this all about?" John called up to Charles, who was sitting, gazing, his mouth slightly ajar.

"I've no idea, Mr. Rawlings. Looks like some sort of meeting to me."

The Apothecary turned to Samuel, a furious expression on his face. "Don't say I have been wrong all the time."

But further conversation was impossible. There was a collective 'Ooh' from the ladies and two coaches appeared from the stable yard behind the fashionable dwelling. They piled in, six in each, and set off. Without being told Charles Jealous went in pursuit. Praying that their tired horse would not die of exhaustion, the Apothecary sat back, wondering yet again whether he had made an error of judgement.

A further frantic chase to the Covent Garden area ensued. The flagging horses pulled them—straining every muscle as they did so—up Pall Mall to the monumental cross at Charing—the place name of which, John had always thought, had grown out of the French 'chere reine'—dear queen. For it was a fact that King Edward I had erected twelve crosses at every place his wife—Eleanor of Castile's—body had lain overnight on its final journey to burial in Westminster Abbey. He had loved her with all his heart and they had been married for years, only to be torn apart when she had died suddenly in the East Midlands in November, 1290. A sad and true story marked to this very day by a great stone cross.

Just as the Apothecary was thinking this the two coaches they were following suddenly turned off The Strand and went up Southampton Street to the Covent Garden market area itself.

279

"Good God," Samuel exclaimed. "These ladies are taking their lives into their hands."

"I think," John answered with a laugh, "that they are probably going to the theatre. Drury Lane is not far away. They are most likely walking through the market to see the ladies of the night."

And there were plenty of them on view. Aged between nine and ninety years old they had forgathered round the outskirts of St. Paul's Church. John, regarding them with feelings mixed between horror and hysteria, thought of what the Blind Beak had said of them. "One would imagine that all the prostitutes in the kingdom had picked up on that blessed neighbourhood, for here are lewd women enough to fill a mighty colony." An idea to which Samuel added, "My God, there are enough present to keep a man at work for every hour of his life." A simple truth.

The ladies in blue were hurrying along in the direction of the theatre but, John could not help but notice, their formation seemed to have changed. Where they had started out as twelve—including most probably the duchess and the viscountess—now there were not so many of them gathered. Samuel, who was in a state of high excitement after the frantic ride and the sight of so much female voluptuary, did not comment. The Apothecary, wondering if he was getting old or just noticing more, looked round the great crowd of people as best he could. Figures in blue cloaks were dotted here and there but a rapid count still produced only eight. He tugged Samuel's arm.

"Something is going on but I'm not sure what."

"What do you mean?"

"I'm not certain. But we must try to follow them."

Possibly to make it difficult for any pursuers the ladies, laughing and exclaiming in joyful hilarity, were moving in slow groups of three or four, running from one cluster to another, making it impossible to check their numbers. Having circled right round the Market they made their way out by Russell Street, then turned right into Bridges Street where Drury Lane Theatre was situated. They began to enter the building, probably waiting for the holder of the tickets to arrive. She did, a few moments later. It was not anybody that the Apothecary recognised.

"I do believe that the viscountess has gone into The Rose," he whispered to Samuel.

"No, she can't have done. I mean it is no place for a lady of any station in life."

"I know."

John stood rigid, looking this way and that, his body twisting in every direction, his heart pounding with fear, yet for no visible reason. And then he saw them. Right at the end of Bridges Street, where it conjoined with Catherine Street, two figures in blue cloaks and matching hoods, turning right into Exeter Street.

"Oh, sweet Jesus, they're going to Tom King's," he gasped.

"They can't be," answered Samuel, thoroughly shocked.

John did not waste time arguing, he simply shouted, "Come on," and set off at a run.

Years ago, when Tom King and Moll Adkins—he apparently a public-school boy, she the daughter of low-life parents—had opened the place as a Coffee House, it had been in a shack. But what a shack. Filled with doxies of every age and circumstance it had been ripe for courting but not for consummation. Tom and Moll had not provided a bed in the place, instead suggesting that a needy couple should go to the brothel close by. In this way they had avoided being prosecuted for running such an establishment as a bawdy house.

Gentlemen of the highest rank would come straight from court in full dress, rich silk brocaded coats, with swords and bags, to meet the prettiest prostitutes, so that kissing and cuddling would begin immediately. Breast fondling was encouraged but let his hand slip downwards and Moll would call a servant to light the couple the way to the nearest bagnio.

"I believe they sell sheaths to protect their clients from the pox," murmured John with a kind of admiration.

"A splendid notion," answered Samuel, not without a certain sarcasm.

"But what are our two respectable ladies going in there for?"

"I tremble to think," came the reply, said heavily.

They made their way inside. Their targets were immediately visible, still wearing the floor-sweeping blue cloaks, their hoods thrown back to reveal faces fully covered with silver masks, obviously made for a Venetian carnival. They stood aloofly to one side, silently ordering coffee from Betty, a pretty black girl who was gazing at them, open-mouthed. Neither of them uttered a syllable. A gentleman in glittering court dress approached. He made an elegant bow.

"Ladies, you enchant me. It is an age since I saw two such bewitching creatures. I would like to have the company of you both. Now and later."

The two silver masks remained motionless. The gentleman continued.

"May I pay my attentions?" He patted himself suggestively. "Or is it your custom to tease a chap by not speaking?"

They turned their backs on him, moving together like marionettes.

"Are you always this rude?" the man asked "'Cos if so, be damned to you."

"That's no way to speak to two such delectable whores," drawled a voice from the back of the establishment and Roderick Redwood strutted forward, his hand fingering the ebony knob of his walking cane, his eyes blue as bluebags in the candlelight.

John's heart sank and he went to move, to intervene somehow, but found that his legs were like lead, he was quite literally rooted to the spot. Samuel turned a stricken glance on him and rolled his eyes but also seemed incapable of uttering. The older gentleman spoke.

282

"And who gave you permission, young man, to intrude upon another's arrangements."

"I need none, sir," came the mannerless reply. "And especially from an elderly fart like yourself."

The older man, still carrying all the accoutrements of court, drew his sword and waved it in front of him. The two silent women turned to stare at one another, though all they could see beneath the expressionless masks from Venice would be the glint of the eyes of the other. As if a silent signal had been exchanged between them they grasped hands and glided out of the shack, not hurrying, not running, but merely walking in harmonious step. Roderick, regardless of the waving sword, punched the older fellow squarely on the jaw and watched him fall heavily to the ground. Then he walked out, his steps mimicking that of the two ladies. John was released from his trance.

"Samuel, come on, quickly. After them."

They hurried out, John turning to look round. Much as he had thought, Roderick had caught the pair up and now stood talking, his face yellowed by the light of an oil lamp suspended between the wrought iron work outside a large building. The couple stood silently regarding him, their silver masks gleaming eerily in the glow of that uncertain illumination.

"Roderick Redwood?" It was a sibilant whisper floating on the night air.

"Yes, that's me. I'm called Lord Prickit by my many lady friends." He gave a drunken giggle.

"Tell me, have you ever courted a girl called Arabella Winterlight?"

"One of the famous sisters? Yes, I fucked her well and truly."

"You ruined her looks when you threw acid in her face because she refused your bedchamber. Is not that true, Roderick Redwood?" The questioning voice still had that high unearthly note.

He was shaken, it showed by his tone getting louder, his attitude more menacing. "I don't know what you're talking about. Who are you anyway? I don't recall seeing you two whores before."

"No. But we have seen you many, many times Roderick. And now it is our turn."

"To do what?"

"This."

They wheeled to face him and then one of them reached within her cloak and produced a bottle from an inner pocket. Roderick stared at her aghast, then turned to run. But too late. She hurled the liquid contents straight into his face. He screamed, the most awful cry that John had ever heard, then fell to the cobbles below, clawing at his skin. The two women merely glanced at him, then picking up the hems of their skirts, they sped off into the darkness, their silver masks glinting eerily as they disappeared into the night.

"Oh dear God," said Samuel, looking with horror at the figure writhing on the ground.

John answered grimly, "It was vitriol. Sulphuric acid. His face is being eaten away and there's nothing I can do to help him. But we must find the two women. After them, Samuel, quick as you can."

Yet even as he said the words the Apothecary knew in his secret heart who the couple were, though which one had actually thrown the acid he had no idea. Then he pulled himself up short as the creature lying on the ground let out a terrible cry.

"Oh help me, I beg you. I am in agony."

All John's old training came out and he temporarily forgot what a ghastly piece of work Roderick had been and tended to him as best he could. People were by now wandering out of the shack to see what was going on, one of them being a pleasant-looking young man who hurried across and knelt down beside them.

"How dee do. I'm Rawlings, an apothecary. This chap has had acid thrown in his face."

"There's a nasty habit for that kind of crime growing. We see more and more of it at St. Thomas's."

"I take it you're a doctor?"

"I am indeed. Yes, we have one of these cases handed in quite regularly. One wonders sometimes what the human condition is coming to."

"There is a factory making the stuff based in Twickenham. The trouble is it is now too readily available."

"We could talk about that for hours. But I must get a hackney and take him off to St. T.'s. I expect you'll want to join us."

John sighed deeply. "What is it that tells me I must go even though I detest the man."

The doctor sighed deeply. "What is it that tells me I must leave a very pretty doxie and go on duty. It's training, my friend, that's what it is. Years and years of it."

In any other circumstances the Apothecary would have nodded agreement but these events were too cruel, too terrible for idle banter. Betty, the good-looking black girl, ran out with a towel which had been dipped in cold water and the three of them carried the barely conscious man into a hackney and went through that terrible night to the hospital.

It was in the small hours of the morning that John literally staggered into his house in Nassau Street. As he went into the little study in which Sir Gabriel had always sat in his high-backed chair, often with a measure of pale sherry in a fine cut glass reflecting the flames of the comforting fire, he thought for a moment that his father was with him once again. But as he narrowed his eyes and stared he realised that it was his old friend Samuel—his wig snatched off and still held in his sleeping hand—who was curled up there and waiting for him. John was immensely touched as he softly called his name.

"Sam, it's me. How are you? Let me get you a sherry and then listen to your adventures. Did you manage to catch up with the two women?"

"No, alas. They had disappeared into the wilds of Covent Garden."

John nodded then sat in silence for a while as they slowly finished their drinks. Then he said, "He died you know."

Sam looked up. "You don't mean …?"

"Yes, I do. Roderick Redwood died. He survived the journey to the hospital but his life ended a short while later."

"John, I believe I know who those two women were."

"Then keep it to yourself I beg you."

"But you do too, don't you?"

"Yes. But I intend to remain silent for the sake of us all."

"I know you must be right so I will agree. Shall we drink to silence?"

"To silence," echoed John and refilled the glasses from the diamond bright decanter.

After that nothing stirred in number 2, Nassau Street. The fire went out and the moon slowly faded as the first fingers of the sun scratched at the shutters. Samuel snored, not loudly but rhythmically. John was quiet, his head full of dreams, of the past and of the present. It was a moment when one felt that time had no meaning at all and that Sir Gabriel's great clock was merely keeping up a pretence in solemnly counting out the final hours of a villain's last day.

Chapter Twenty-Five

It was as if every house in Strand-on-the-Green was brilliantly lit that night. From every window came flashes of splendour which cut razor sharp through the leaves of the trees standing on the embankment, throwing fantastic images onto the rippling surface below. The owners had, of course, all been invited to a soiree given by their neighbour John Rawlings and had agreed, by means of communal chit-chat, to make it a festive occasion and let every house gleam with welcoming illumination. So the charming little riverside hamlet glowed beneath the lights of that early September twilight and looked so welcoming and lovely that those passing in boats exclaimed with delight.

The first to arrive was—naturally enough—Zoffany. Despite the large entourage of ladies who dwelt within his walls—John to this day was not sure who was who—the painter always appeared unaccompanied. In this way, so he had explained, he always had a better time and was never corrected about the amounts he ate or drank. He was greeted with much enthusiasm by John's daughter who was looking delicious, topped with a waving new hairstyle and pink and white make-up, dressed in a sumptuous green ensemble which became her enormously. Various neighbours then appeared and several of the Jacquard family, the star of which was, as usual, the glorious Hyacinth. Next, crimson with pleasure and breathing rather swiftly, was Miss Phoebe Feathering, Sir Humphrey Warburton hobbling magnificently behind on his prosthetic leg.

Neighbours turned up, all cheerful and putting on a good show of enjoyment. Then, somewhat late and fractionally flustered, appeared the Baron Rotmuller and his younger brother, both wearing German naval uniform and looking terribly correct. Rose swept a dramatic curtsey, the green velvet gown swirling to perfection, and Robert went very red and appeared as if he were going to have a seizure. Fortunately Miss Feathering, who once had loved him so earnestly, was absorbed in trivial chatter with Mrs. Meakin—a kindly acquaintance—and did not notice him.

The doorbell tolled again and John was amazed to see young Nathaniel Hall standing there, his apprentice gear abandoned and a sleek silver evening ensemble in its place.

"Good evening, Mr. Rawlings. I am delighted to see you again. Miss Rose told me to be here at eight o'clock but I have only just managed to get away from my master. I do apologise."

And with those affable words the elegant young man walked into the house.

John had just settled into a meaningful conversation with the local vicar—a serious, fresh-faced person with a slight stutter—when the bell rang once more. John looked across at Rose, who was engaging both Robert and Nathaniel in conversation, and raised his eyebrows. She gave him a delightful smile but other than that showed no sign of understanding.

Julian Merrett stood in the doorway looking as he always did, still shocked by the death of his wife but definitely making huge strides back into the world again.

"Good evening, sir. I do apologise for the lateness of my arrival but I had an influx of customers who came in just as I was preparing to lock up."

"Don't tell me—I shall guess. Young rakehells going on the town."

"Correct. But at least they all bought condoms."

"Well that's a blessed relief. Do come in. I'd forgotten…" The Apothecary had been about to say that you were joining us but realised how rude it would sound, "… you were going to be somewhat delayed. Rose will be pleased to see you."

Finally, when the gathering had reached the heights of jollity and everyone present had had a glass too many, the doorbell pealed for the third time. Rose was beside John in an instant.

"Let me," she said.

And there he stood. The young cordwainer from London with a parcel under his arm.

"Jem, I am so glad you could get here."

"Nothing would have kept me away." He bowed deeply. "Pretty shoes for a pretty lady," he said and Rose gave him a beautiful smile as he handed her a package.

The party went on until the morning sun had peered over the horizon. Most of the guests had gone long since. Zoffany was snoring in the parlour, Rose was singing a love song, the brilliant Miss Hyacinth had left accompanied by her large and protective brothers. John stood in the doorway and watched the sun stagger up.

This day it was fighting every inch for supremacy, forcing its way through layers of clinging cloud. With a push it finally made its reluctant entrance and the sudden brilliance lit the Apothecary where he stood. He turned his face up to the welcome light and closed his eyes. It was too late for bed, he decided, so instead he went to wash and change his clothes. But he was restless and despite the fact

289

that it had started to rain he decided to walk. His mood was deeply introspective. Last night's party had been a great success, he had been surrounded by people who were fond of him, everyone—even Miss Feathering—had been happy, particularly when Robert Rotmuller had bowed very formally and presented her with a parcel containing her much loved monoculars.

"But how did you get them, sir?" she had asked breathlessly.

"Whoever stole them from you sold them on to a dealer. I saw the advertisement and went to retrieve them. I hope you forgive me, Miss Feathering. For everything?" he added in an undertone.

"Of course, dear. Of course. I would rather that it is not spoken of again. I am living as Sir Humphrey's lady companion now and I think …"

Robert bowed several times, clearly extremely relieved. "May I kiss your hand, madam?"

She fluttered. "Well I …"

"Go on, Robert, behave as a true Rotmuller would." This came from the baron who had awoken briefly from a snooze.

Now, walking by the river in the drizzling rain, he realised that shortly he would have to go to London and give an explanation as to the death of Roderick Redwood and knowing—even as he thought this—that he would never betray the secret of the two women in the Venetian carnival masks. That their identities must remain for ever concealed.

Even without his conscious awareness his footsteps were leading him towards Chiswick Park. He decided at that moment that he would take one final look at the old house, standing forlorn and empty with Michael and Miranda gone to join the Londoners in Berkeley Square. What was it about deserted buildings that held such an attraction for people. They must pry and poke around and make muffled cries of annoyance at all the ruin and despair that they encounter but still have to look. Strange fascination.

He was nearing the Jacobean mansion and even from this distance it already had an emptiness about it. John slowed his pace. Not for him the curious eyes of the masses and yet deep within he felt a longing to look once more at the place where so much of interest had happened. The thing that pleased him most had been the change in Michael, from languid coxcomb to a man with deep emotions, capable of loving with the whole of his heart. And, similarly Miranda, from a vapid creature of fashion to a woman who allowed love to possess her. The gift of the viscount's debt being washed away—John thought of the pump and grinned at the simile—by his friend Serafina's sleight of hand had been the final triumph.

As he approached the building it grew in desolation. John found himself thinking that Georgiana, Duchess of Devonshire, must be a tough little nut indeed to order its destruction so that she could build wings on to the charming villa built by her husband's ancestor. No good would come of it he felt certain. He drew nearer and realised that somebody had left the magnificent entrance wide open so that the elements could creep in and do their worst on what had been a wonderful dwelling. With fortitude the Apothecary stepped forward to swing it shut. And it was then, with his heart quickening pace, that he realised that Miranda had not left after all because he could see her, sitting in a great oak chair, her back to him. He stepped silently within and cleared his throat deferentially. She spun round and looked at him and the Apothecary nearly died of shock. He had seen that excuse for a face once before. It had been outside the huge window, staring within, and it had frightened him to death. For it was not a face as he knew it but the bones of one with scarred and terrible skin dragged over it. It was like gazing at a living nightmare.

For a long minute the two people stared at one another and then the poor wretched woman turned away and pulled a thick veil down, concealing her features. During that terrible moment the Apothecary wrestled with himself, feeling shabby and ashamed that he should have been so obviously frightened. Then he decided to bluff it out. To act as only he could when put to the test.

"Oh, forgive me Lady Lovell, I thought you had gone to London. I merely came in to pull the great door closed. I was afraid that the rain would enter and soak the precious flooring."

There was a long pause and then the poor creature whispered, "I am not Lady Lovell. She is my sister. She has indeed gone to London."

"Oh, an even worse gaffe. Excuse me please Your Grace."

"No, I am not the Duchess of Derwent either. My name is Arabella Winterlight."

John bowed again, most fulsomely. "Again I beg your pardon, madam. I have not had the pleasure of meeting you. You must be the third of the three great beauties."

"I was," she murmured.

He ignored it. "Allow me to introduce myself, Miss Winterlight. I am John Rawlings, Apothecary, of London and Strand-on-the-Green. How do you do?"

"I am waiting here for a friend of mine," she continued. "He is coming here to take me out."

"Oh yes?" he continued pleasantly.

"His name is Giles Jacquard. He has spoken of you."

"Very favourably," said a voice from the doorway.

And John, turning to see who it was, finally understood everything. It was Hyacinth's poorly sighted brother, who wouldn't give a tuppeny damn if his lady had had acid thrown into her face. For he had long ago ceased to value such paltry things as physical beauty.

As he came forward and took Miss Winterlight into his loving arms, the Apothecary gave them a wonderful bow and slipped quietly out of the front door.

As he hurried home, John Rawlings was not sure whether it was raindrops or tears that were running down his cheeks. Perhaps a combination of the two. For who could see the ruination of such a beautiful creature and at the same time be taught the greatest lesson of all—that in the end nothing mattered but the person who dwelled within the shell. That poor Miss Arabella was greatly adored was obvious. She and Giles would indeed have a wonderful life together regardless.

The note came during the hours of darkness. The first John knew was a tap on his bedroom door and the night porter murmuring something about an urgent message having been delivered. When the Apothecary read it he dressed immediately and went downstairs, then walked along the tow path to a place where small coaches could disgorge or pick up passengers. There he entered a small, dark conveyance that drove him rapidly through the night to London. The lady who awaited him at the other end obviously did not wish to be kept waiting a moment longer than was necessary.

She was dressed in a flowing shift and was nearly at full term. John was flattered that she should think the matter so important that she had asked him to come to her like a thief in the night.

"Do sit down," she said as soon as he was shown into the room in which she awaited.

He did so. "You have something to tell me?"

"She's gone," she answered abruptly.

He was astonished but cautious. "Do you mean …?"

"I refer to the Duchess of Derwent."

"What do you mean, 'she's gone'? Where?"

"To Europe. When her coach pulled away from Covent Garden it was bound for Dover. She had a few things packed with her and she was taking leave of her old life and going abroad for good."

"And you? What did you do? Did you try and stop her?"

"No. I wept. Wept for what she had once been and what she had become. A wicked creature who tormented all those who had any relationship—however slight—with that terrible creature who ruined Arabella's life, may he rot in hell."

"You were one of the two masked women, weren't you?"

"Yes."

"Did you throw the acid?"

"My dear friend—and I consider you as my friend or else I would not have sent for you in this clandestine fashion. I knew that you had seen through our pitiable disguises but nothing could have stopped me in my effort to succeed with what we were doing that night. You see at the time of the acid attack on Arabella he was trying to seduce her in his usual style, but she eluded him. So some days later he waylaid her on her way home and threw acid in her face remarking that henceforth she should be grateful for anything she could get. I am afraid that this sent my twin over the edge and she declared war on all those who had had anything to do with him. The child in the Thames was his little bastard, poor Miss Feathering had imagined herself in love with him before the wretched woman's attentions moved elsewhere, Sir Humphrey Warburton's accident was set up by my sister with the most ghastly consequences, all because he was Roderick's uncle. Have I said enough?"

"Not quite, my lady."

Viscountess Lovell gave a bitter laugh. "The murder of my mother-in-law at Baron Rotmuller's ball? Yes, that too was her handiwork."

"And you cooperated with all these things?"

Arabella got to her feet and John realised how close to her time she was, as deep within her stirred a contraction. "Most certainly not. When Sir Humphrey had his accident I was suspicious but she denied it and I believed her because I wanted to."

"And your mother-in-law?"

Arabella gave a half smile. "She never liked me, not at all. Quite frankly I was glad to see the back of her. But not in such an horrific way as that."

"I see."

The viscountess slumped back upon her chaise. "Forgive me for sending for you in such a cloak-and-dagger way but I know that the duke will be returning from his hunting trip tomorrow and I am sure that the story of the duchess's disappearance will appear in the evening papers."

"You realise that I saw your other sister yesterday?"

"Yes. She sent me a note. One additional and vital thing, Apothecary."

"Yes?"

"I trust that you will keep this absolutely confidential."

He bowed. "I promise you that I shall not speak a word."

"Not even to your friend Samuel?"

"Not even him."

Dawn was breaking over London as the Apothecary climbed into the coach to take him back to his riverside residence. The Thames, wide and beautiful, was catching the first rays of the sun as he did so. John leaned forward to look at it through the window. It had gushed at the feet of the Roman legions and would sparkle on long after he and all his generation had turned to dust. It was there, almighty and uncaring, but magnificent always. The Apothecary sighed and closed his eyes as the great river silently flowed on.

Historical Note

Forty years ago I was asked by Canada Dry, the drinks manufacturers, to research the origins of a firm they had acquired during a takeover. It was H.D. Rawlings Tonic Waters which purported to have been around a very long time. Thank God I did. For from out of the old documents of the Society of Apothecaries, which I looked at during my research, leapt John Rawlings. I could almost see him grinning as he bowed and introduced himself because he has brought me nothing but joy ever since. He was born circa 1731, though his actual parentage is somewhat shrouded in mystery. He became a Yeoman of the Worshipful Society of Apothecaries on 13th March, 1755, giving his address as 2, Nassau Street, Soho. This conclusively linked him with H.D. Rawlings Ltd. who were based at the same address over a hundred years later, and who manufactured sparkling water.

Sir John Fielding, the blind magistrate, was another real-life character who was alive at the same time as John. He was the half-brother of Henry Fielding, also the principal magistrate and a celebrated writer who created the unforgettable character of Tom Jones. John not only succeeded Henry as magistrate but had an interesting life and a remarkable ability to recognise villains by their speaking voices alone.

William Bromfeild (yes that is the correct spelling) was an English surgeon whose brilliance led him to the top of the tree. He actually conducted an amputation, similar to the one I describe, on Samuel Foote, the actor, whose performances gave rise to the word 'drag' from the dragging of his skirt over the stage when he played comic female characters. Bromfeild rose to become one of the most eminent surgeons of his day, his lectures attended by literally dozens of students and doctors. He too was alive at the same time as John Rawlings.

Last but far from least is the great painter Johan Zoffany. His life was very intriguing to say the minimum of it and once as a young child I was invited to tea in his beautiful house in Strand-on-the-Green. I remember it still with awe and immense pleasure. What a huge character he was, rising to become a great favourite of Queen Charlotte, whose portraits he often painted. The house is marked with a Plaque and is well worth a visit if only to gaze at the exterior.